PRAISE FOR UNTIL THE STARS FALL

"Original, creative, and immersive. It feels very human and organic, and you'll be rooting for everyone—side characters as well as the MC and her sexy LI—along the way. This one gets my wholehearted, well-deserved recommendation."
Mindi Briar, author of the Halcyon Universe Series

"UNTIL THE STARS FALL is full of everything I adore: a witty, headstrong protagonist, intricate, witchy magic set in space, and a swoon-worthy romance teeming with flirty banter and spicy tension that jumped right off the page."
Kalla Harris, fantasy author

"One of my favorite reads of the year, UNTIL THE STARS FALL had me laughing out loud and falling in love with Beck before Gemma gave him the time of day. The characters have such great depth that I found myself utterly invested. This is one you should NOT pass up!"
Sarah Bottoms, book reviewer

"Holly Rose cleverly weaves together fantasy and science fiction with whimsical, high stakes action and heartfelt characters. The romance between Gemma and Beck is at once tender, sweet, and steamy, and as soon as they get put together on the page, you can't put the book down. It's the perfect story for anyone looking to bridge the gap between fantasy and science fiction, or vice versa."
Marina Massino, fantasy author

HOLLY ROSE

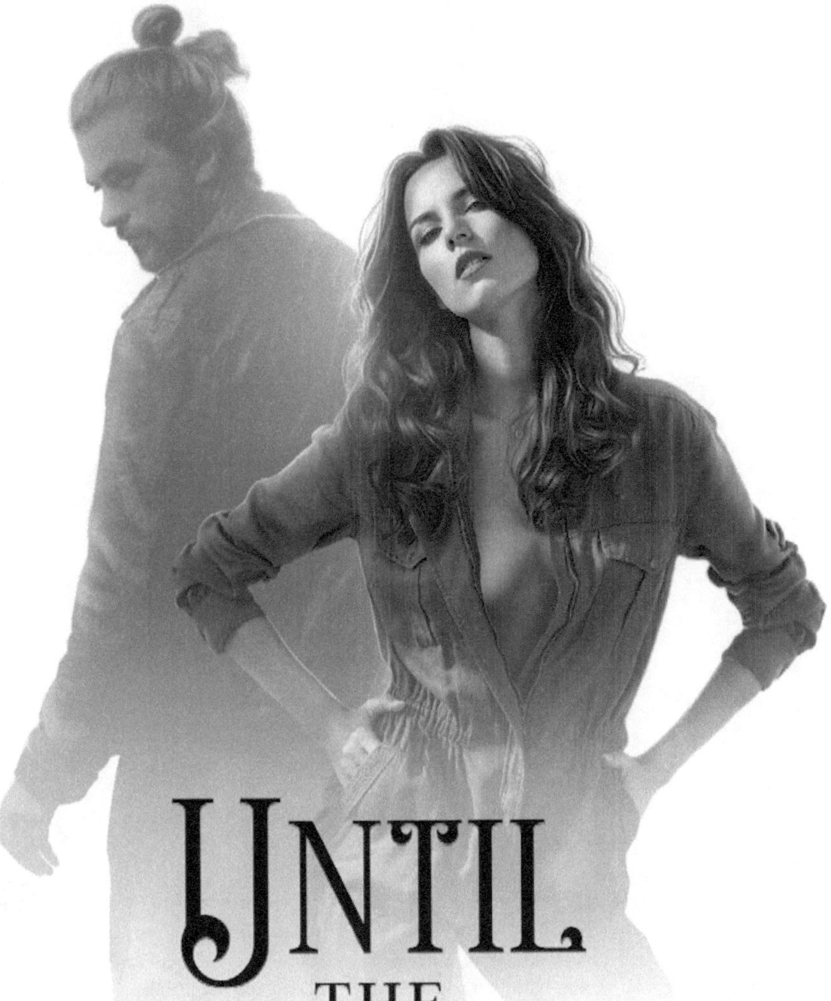

Until the Stars Fall

AN INTERSTELLAR WITCHES BOOK

UNTIL THE STARS FALL
Interstellar Witches, Book 1

Cover design by MiblArt. All stock photos licensed appropriately.
City Owl Press was the original publisher of this book.

Print Edition ISBN: 979-8-990-11460-9
Digital Edition ISBN: 979-8-990-11461-6

Printed in the United States of America

To Schoener Ann, whose unconditional love and encouragement both made me who I am and this book possible. I love you until the stars fall. Now it!

HOLLY ROSE

UNTIL THE STARS FALL

AN INTERSTELLAR WITCHES BOOK

Chapter 1

Crazy Al's Pick-A-Part

If I could change one thing about my life, I wouldn't be a witch. I also wouldn't be driving a rented hovervan containing all my possessions into Crazy Al's Pick-A-Part, although I guess it was a fitting place to say goodbye to this trashy planet.

My stomach churning with station coffee, I drove past a crumbled cinder block wall with a faded, chipped mural of Crazy Al himself. His cartoonish, gap-toothed smile leered at me, a mobile of stars orbiting his head like he'd just been KO'd in a fight.

If I could ask him, I bet even Crazy Al wouldn't believe in magic. Most people thought it was a joke, a collective delusion perpetuated by crazy people on the internet writing love spells under a full moon and thinking the stars held meaning.

Bullshit. Magic was my daily nightmare. It was the fizzy feeling in my marrow that bubbled up, shooting through my veins in a jolting pantomime of adrenaline, itching under the skin of my palms like buzzing bees. And if I hadn't been struggling against years of pent-up power rattling in my bones, maybe I would've had a kiss from a handsome, brilliant man to think about for the two-month journey to Gaia.

Instead, I lost my job and considered myself lucky that the police hadn't been waiting for me when I arrived in New Orleans this morning.

I took a sharp turn into the junkyard proper, agitating the butterflies in my stomach into a mosh pit. The geo-locater on the dash marked me one hundred feet away from my sister Hannah's pin. I couldn't see her ship yet, only piles of bent dilating doors staring like the dead eyes of metal gods, the steel skeletons of stripped hulls, and everywhere, rusted sheets of riveted metal.

I paused and flipped the visor down to check my hair and makeup. I couldn't look a mess meeting all my sister's friends, even if they were all witches. Sure enough, one wayward strand had the audacity to slip out of my careful chignon in this wretched Louisiana humidity. I hadn't missed this place at all, not the memories, not the wild, humid heat. I wiped a stray, faint smear of eyeliner and dove my hand into my bag in a practiced search for my lipstick, trying to ignore my lab coat thrown across the back seat.

Just seeing it stirred up dread in my chest like mud at the bottom of a canal. I held my breath, pushed it all down. I never wanted to use my magic again, much less lose control of it. And yet I did. I did, and I'd lost everything. Again.

After a deep, shaky breath, I pressed the pads of my fingers under my brimming eyes. All crying would do is mess up my makeup. It wouldn't make anything better. The only way to get rid of my magic was to get to Madam Indigo on Gaia. The only way to Gaia was my sister's ship.

Setting the hovervan into motion again, I pinged Hannah's phone to let her know I was here. I turned past more piles of shield doors with fire scarring, an antique Zephyr hover from the 2130's with the rounded decorative fenders like my grandpa used to collect, past the spiderwebbed metal of dented satellites dusted with ash, their guts rusting in the moisture-laden air.

My thoughts drifted ahead to Gaia. I'd be lucky to get another job in the astro-engineering industry. I was probably on some secret blacklist now. But even losing my job hadn't been the worst of it—and I needed money badly—Madam Indigo didn't come cheap. I'd caused so much damage, scared so many nice people.

After another turn, a silver behemoth emerged from the dead oaks and metal trash, and my chest tightened. "Holy Mother of God, is that her ship?" I ducked to get a better look through the windshield.

Al may have been "crazy to sell parts this low," but my sister must've lost her damn mind if she thought this ship would be a good idea.

If it was meticulously restored instead of dented and scarred by the fires of re-entry, I might've called it "vintage." Its sleek, silver exterior, curvy stern, and gratuitous bevies of windows were typical of the golden age, hotel ships put out to pasture when interstellar travel boomed almost fifty years ago. When cruising around the rings of Saturn wasn't fashionable unless it was a sentimental circuit on the way out of this godforsaken system.

Hannah appeared at the top of the ramp by the open cargo doors, her long blonde hair beachy and wild. She jumped and waved as I steered around another pile of disembodied ship parts and up the ramp. When I got closer and saw her sweet face more clearly, my chest hollowed out with relief, so pleased that my little sister looked happy and healthy.

I followed her pantomimed directions into the decrepit maw of the old ship, its cargo bay clogged with baggage. After squeezing down a narrow aisle, I shoehorned my vehicle into a spot beside a battered hovervan sporting a mural of a vampire queen riding a black Pegasus.

The moment I opened my door, Hannah squealed and launched herself into my arms. "Gemma!"

"Hannah!" I cried, squeezing her close. She smelled like lavender and sunshine, and I reveled in her fierce hug, tears stinging behind my eyes. It may've been the first honest affection I'd gotten since I left her five years ago. I didn't want to let her go.

She pulled back and examined me, her blue eyes sparkling in the morning light. "Gem, you're *gorgeous*, so sophisticated as always! Only you could come out of a two-day Tube trip without a hair out of place."

I hugged her again. "I missed you *so much*." She squeezed me in another tight hug and released me too soon. "Did work give you any trouble about the new launch date?"

My whole body went on edge, spooling up the lie I'd rehearsed all the way to New Orleans to cover for the magic Hannah didn't know I still had. "Not exactly," I said, choosing my next words carefully. "When I asked Evander, my boss, if I could have my leave early, he said no. And this was the leave he granted me a couple of months ago."

Her mouth opened in outrage. "Wait, are you talking about *the* Evander Noble? The hot CEO's son who's been flirting with you for months? Why would he tell you no?"

I bit my lip to keep the truth in, that he'd really said *yes, of course.* That we'd flirted some more, and he'd leaned in to kiss me.

"Oh Hannah, I made such a big scene." I hiccupped a sob. I wanted to kiss him, but my magic threw him across his office instead.

"Such a big scene. And he fired me." Technically I ran away before he could fire me. Or have me arrested. He was yelling my name when I ran, so he couldn't have been *too* badly injured. Guilt twisted my insides, laying the blame on an innocent man.

She wrapped her arms around me again. "I'm so sorry. This is all my fault."

"No way. You were surprised by the early slot too." And she wasn't the one who fled in terror, slamming open a glass door so hard it shattered down like a prismatic waterfall.

She released me, her mouth a line. "When we get to Gaia, you'd better hire a lawyer. They can't just fire you like that."

"I'll deal with it when I get to Gaia." I bit my lip on another lie. Would I ever not lie to her?

"It's okay, Gemma. You know what? I think it's a blessing in disguise. You told me you were happy in San Francisco, and I wanted to believe you, but you never looked happy. You can live with me and work at a local firm if you want." She glanced at her watch. "But look, we have to get inside. Let's get your most important stuff unpacked. I've got a cart ready."

I tried to take a deep breath, pulling a suitcase with my toiletries from the passenger seat, but gills would've been more appropriate for breathing in the hot, humid air pouring in from the outside. While San Francisco had vented surface tunnels in the heart of the city to deal with the building planetary heat, we were only able to be outside in New Orleans because it was November. Extreme areas of the planet still got cold weather, but here, all winter meant was the weeds had a chance to grow before the blistering heat of February through October hit, withering everything.

"Do y'all need help?" A young woman near Hannah's age appeared from behind me. I got the impression of a smile and brown and blue curls just before she came in for a hug.

"Summer? Hi!" I returned her hug. "I'm so glad to finally meet you in person!"

"I'm so glad you made it safely! Ooh, I love your blouse," she said to me before rushing to help my sister. "Here! Let me get that." Summer's dark brown eyes tinted warmer in the red morning sunlight, and she looked at Hannah like she was the rising sun, rushing to help her unload my most pressing things.

My heart squeezed watching them work together, so in sync, so in love. I didn't know if I'd ever have anything remotely that good. I wanted love, dreamed of it. But I wouldn't be worthy of it until I burned every trace of magic from my bones.

I wasn't lying to Hannah about my magic just for fun, or because I was embarrassed of its volatility and my lack of control. I lied because it was responsible for the hover crash that killed our parents nine years ago, and I'd been trying to atone for it ever since.

Hannah checked her leather-banded watch again. "You made it just in time. Our launch slot's in a few minutes." She gazed out the ship door wistfully. "I guess it's time to go in."

Something that had been tickling my elbow rose to my full attention: a feeding mosquito. *Gross.* I slapped it against my arm where it left a smudge of bright red blood. *God I hope that's mine.* I dug in my purse for a handkerchief.

Summer looked out too, the humidity frizzing her curls and pinkening her cheeks. "I can't believe we're never coming back here. It's so hard to leave, isn't it?"

"I guess." I rolled my eyes a little. I couldn't get off this planet fast enough. My blouse was already soaked with sweat, and *damn it* the filthy bloodsuckers were biting my legs now too. I slapped at my calf and scratched my ankle, wishing I hadn't worn a skirt.

I was a few weeks away from twenty-seven, but I was still waiting for my life to begin. On the Tube ride in, I decided that Gaia was going to be my promised land, my long-overdue fresh start. As far as I was concerned, I hoped the door didn't slam on Earth's ass as it walked out. Okay maybe that didn't make sense, but I meant it anyway. My magic was a worn-out siren song, and I was tired of stuffing wax in my ears. If my appointment with Madam Indigo went as promised, my magic would be gone, and it would've cost me nearly everything I owned, including the diamond ring my mother left me.

Worth it.

A loudspeaker crackled to life. "T-minus eight minutes," a man's deep voice called. "Time to go!"

"Let's rock and roll." Summer flipped up the kickstand with her foot, and I pushed it behind her and Hannah, trying to match the man's voice to my knowledge of Hannah's friends. Hopefully it wasn't the guy she'd been trying to set me up with. I had no interest in a two-month-long blind date.

The leather handle of my knockoff Pia Casale bag pinched my sweaty arm as I paused to watch my last bit of Earth daylight glinting off a pile of console panels with their wires sticking out. Then the shield doors shut out my home planet with metal finality.

As the elevator doors closed behind us on Summer going up to the bridge, I pushed my luggage cart into the ship-hotel's lobby behind Hannah. "You didn't tell me the elevators were a time machine. Are we back in 2125?"

She laughed. "I thought you liked the art nouveau revival."

"In art and architecture, not when it's original to the ship bringing me across the galaxy." I followed Hannah along the dull walking path on the bamboo floor which led to the paneled check-in desk, the launch room, and a few other doorways. Movement against the retro-stylized flowered wallpaper caught my eye. Smoke? An incense stick smoldered from the open mouth of a green ceramic dragon, right there on the desk. Safety violation number one. I paused to snatch it up and douse it in water from a flower vase.

Hannah was nearly to the launch room. "I can't wait for you to meet the rest of my coven!" she called back.

Coven. The verbal equivalent of walking under a ladder. When I'd let my siblings believe that my grief over our parents stole away my magic,

Hannah had only been fourteen, her magic strong and growing. Our older brother, Noah, took it upon himself to further her training in witchcraft, despite not having an ounce of magic himself. He'd even gotten engaged to a witch with her own coven, which only encouraged Hannah more. If he only knew how magic had torn our family apart.

I nudged my cart against the gravity wall three times before it latched on, securing my things gently against the wall—it probably needed a tune-up seventy years ago—and followed Hannah into the launch room, a large area with funky geometric hotel carpet and theater seating.

Summer's voice boomed like a sky goddess over the intercom. "Five minutes, people. Strap in!"

A beautiful woman with a red scarf around her tightly coiled dark hair stood up in the launch room when we entered—Zola, my brother's fiancée. She rushed forward, straightening her tight black T-shirt that read "Witchy Woman" in a runic sort of font.

"It's so lovely to see you with my own eyes, Gemma," Zola said, reaching out for a gentle hug, "and not over a screen." She pulled back and held my upper arms. "I'm so relieved your work allowed you to accompany us, even with our early slot! We're in dire need of your expertise." Her eyebrows drew together and her dark amber eyes filled with concern, as if she saw something behind the facade of my smile. "Are you doing alright?"

I nodded, tightly shutting the windows to my soul. I couldn't afford the breakdown that normally came the moment someone genuinely asked if I was alright when I really wasn't. Not right now. "I'm great. Just ready to leave this stupid planet."

Zola stared at me a moment longer, as if she was examining the edges of me. I looked to Hannah for saving, but Zola withdrew her hands. "Have you talked to Noah lately? They keep him so busy at the hospital."

My brother was a cardiovascular surgeon and by all accounts the love of Zola's life. I smiled. "No, but I think I need to see that ring in person."

Zola's whole face lit up as she extended her left hand. An oval-faceted natural emerald stone set in yellow gold and flanked by a round diamond on either side sparkled even in the low light.

"Oh wow," I breathed, "Noah did good."

Her smile brightened even more, if that was possible. "He did *great*."

Summer's voice came from the intercom. "Buckle up, buttercups. Our launch slot just opened."

Of course my seatbelt didn't work. "I didn't realize Summer was a pilot," I said, trying out another seat. Nope. Also broken.

Hannah beamed, a blush coloring her pale skin. "She's been training herself since her uncle left her this ship. I'm so proud of her. She's a natural. Try this one, Gem," she said, pointing to another seat.

Summer continued. "I need a quick roll call, people. I'm on the bridge with Eyre."

Hannah jumped up and hung on the intercom by the door. "I'm in the launch room with Gemma and Zola."

The same deep man's voice from before crackled over. "I'm in the med bay and still not happy about it."

"That's Beck," Zola explained, adjusting her scarf. "Our ship's resident male and klutz."

So it *was* the guy Hannah'd been bugging me about. Fantastic.

"He's not a klutz." Hannah's eyebrows pulled together, probably worried I'd lose interest. But I couldn't lose something I didn't have.

Zola leaned forward to look at Hannah. "I say it with love, but you know he's the first one to break a bone or get a second-degree burn because he accidentally touched the oven rack when he was baking cookies."

"He's really, really smart though," Hannah said in a rush.

"Smartest man I know," Zola said. "I'd say don't tell Noah I said that, but he knows. Beck's going to be the best man in our wedding. You're going to love him." Zola's smile was too big not to be suspicious.

Ugh. "That's what Hannah's been saying for years."

Hannah pulled her shoulders up to her ears in a dramatic shrug. "All I'm sayin', it's a long trip. You might get bored, be looking for someone—*things*. For things to do."

"Hannah," I said, an affectionate warning delivered with a grimace.

Zola smiled. "Don't be too hard on her, Gemma, she just wants you to be happy. Whether it's Earth or Gaia, love makes the world go 'round."

Maybe so, but only if you're not a monster.

Summer came over the intercom again. "Great! So that's six humans, plus a whole clowder of cats that I hope didn't escape their carriers.

Y'all better be properly secured with seatbelts on, because we're cleared. Launching in ten...nine...eight..."

As Summer counted down, I squeezed my eyes shut and breathed deeply, anticipating the twisting, hollow drag in the pit of my stomach that always comes before launch.

"...six...five..."

I couldn't swallow the sudden lump in my throat. We were leaving Earth for the last time. *The last time.* And I would never be back. I'd never see my parents' house again. Would never place another flower on their grave. *Wait!*

"One!"

The thrusters kicked in, pushing me back against my seat as the ship rose, creaking, into the air. My gut twisted like I was in an elevator powered by a jet engine, all the butterflies from before smashed against my stomach lining. Tears streamed down the side of my face, and not only from the launch. Out the high windows, dark clouds in a red sky bled to pink then white, and in under two minutes, the endless dark of space.

The air pressure inside the ship changed almost imperceptibly as the artificial gravity kicked in, and an indicator dinged. When the lit seatbelt sign on the wall flickered off, I unlocked my seatbelt and rushed out after the others into the lobby.

I pressed my hand against the window, my perfect pale pink nails contrasting against the dark. The rapidly diminishing Earth was a blue marble rolling away. That's what Mom used to call it. Then it winked out altogether in the vastness. Only Ceres, Jupiter, and Saturn—my favorite—bothered to show on our trajectory and bid us farewell.

I would never see Earth again.

A sob caught and tightened in my chest. I held my breath to keep it in, withdrawing my hand. Nothing good had ever happened on my home planet, but the tears still came. I lowered another steel door around my heart to block out the pain.

Good riddance.

"Gemma?" Hannah's soft voice caught my attention.

I wiped my tears and turned to where she stood with her arms wrapped around herself. In my eyes she'd always be a strange amalgam of grown woman and little sister.

"I'm so glad you made it," she said. "I was so worried you wouldn't. I missed you so much."

I pulled her into a tight hug. "I missed you too."

Summer's voice cut into the room. "Zola, Beck wants you in the med bay."

"He's probably looking for a 'get out of jail free' card." Zola laughed, wiping her own tears away. "If you need anything, Gemma, I'll usually be in the med bay on B1."

Before Zola had taken more than two steps, an alarm blared, and red emergency lights flashed on the walls. Summer's panicked voice thundered over the intercoms.

"Everybody to the sigil on Level 1, stat! We've got interference with the supercritical oxygen storage system!"

My heart went to my feet as I grabbed Hannah's arm. "The supercritical oxygen storage system that keeps the ship pressurized?"

Chapter 2

A Beautiful Marriage of Science and Magic

"I don't know!" Hannah cried. "I didn't help with that spell!"

Zola was already at a door beside the elevator. "I've got it, Hannah! Go help Summer on the bridge!"

As Hannah ran into the elevator, I ran after Zola. If something needed fixing, that's what I was here for. I tore open the door she'd just gone through and went up the stairs inside as fast as my heels would let me, my chest searing from the exertion and the terror. At Level 1, I burst out of the stairwell door and looked both ways down an empty hall.

Raised voices on the right. I ran toward an open guest room door. Panting at the threshold, I gripped the frame with both hands while I took in the scene.

Emergency lights also flashed in this room, and a pressure alarm blared. Zola stood on the outside of a circle painted on the wooden floor, holding a lighter to a smoking bundle of leaves tied with string. She blew them into a smolder and walked around the perimeter of the circle, step after slow, careful step. Burning rosemary sharpened the air.

On a folding table across the room, a cauldron bubbled on a hot plate. Beside it, a curvy woman in a short black dress over torn fishnets furiously ground a mortar and pestle, her long hair shimmering like the blue-black-purple of a raven's wing against her ultra-pale skin.

A tall, muscular man in a white T-shirt and jeans—Beck?—walked out of the kitchenette to the table and stood with his back to me.

"How many bay leaves?" he asked in the same, deep voice from the intercom earlier. He plucked leaves from a stem cluster and dropped them on the table.

"Three," the raven-haired witch said decisively. "No! Five."

"Remember we settled on four when the fifth leaf blew out a window," Zola sing-songed, her face placid as she paced around the circle, eddies of smoke following her.

Along the outer wall, an external window was boarded over.

"Four it is," Beck said. He turned toward me, and electricity shot through my body. He was obscenely beautiful, with dark, messy hair to his shoulders, muscular, tattooed arms—one bandaged—and a scruffy beard.

He picked a leaf up by its stem, brought it before his lips, and blew on it. It fluttered in his exhalation, and orange flames licked across it.

Power raced through my veins, my magic queuing up inside like a dog whose owner made the mistake of grabbing the leash. I balled my hands into fists, tightened all my muscles in a practiced tamping-down of my magic. Closed my eyes, imagined the fascia network under my skin choking off the power before it escaped its bonds. I didn't want to see magic, didn't want to feel magic, would never again do magic on purpose, not after what happened to my parents.

I opened my eyes again. Beck dropped a second burning leaf into the frothing cauldron and picked up another. He pursed his lips and lit it, then his head turned toward me. His light eyes locked on mine and widened. He took a quick breath, and we watched each other as the leaf was consumed by the flame.

He cussed and dropped the burning leaf to the floor, sticking the tip of his finger in his mouth while he stamped the fire out.

"Don't waste my leaves!" the raven-haired witch fussed.

He didn't reply, didn't look at me again, just lit another.

Zola chanted words in a language I couldn't match to any continent on Earth while the smoke trails of her ministrations whirled around the circle, picking up speed. A horrible whooshing noise rose to a low roar in the room. My head pounded like it was trapped in a tightening vice, and my magic surged again from my core, itching the inside of my skin, clawing to be let out. *Please, not now*, I begged it. A drinking glass on the table popped into shards.

Hannah's panicked voice came over the intercom. "Pressure's building!"

Beck looked up at Zola. "Shit. I think we did it counterclockwise." The roaring intensified, and he pressed his hands to his head. "Counterclockwise!" he yelled over the noise filling my ears.

"Where's the box of spells?" the raven-haired witch shouted.

I crouched close to the floor, aware of Beck's gaze on me, but too overwhelmed to care. Pressing my hands to my head, I desperately tried to hold the leash of my magic, to concentrate more on choking it off than on my fear of the faltering spell. I couldn't lose control of it, not here.

But the leash slipped through my hands, and self-protective magic swelled out of me in a crashing wave. More glass broke. Shouting filled the room. The pressure eased, for me. A crack and a whoosh, something—a crack in the windows, a crack in the wall—connected the little room to the sucking hell of space.

Muffled, echoey chanting beyond my bubble. More shouting. Quick directions being given and followed, but I was in a cocoon of my own making, crouched on the floor. For just a moment, taking a deep, unfettered breath.

Then adrenaline seared through my veins, fear and anxiety entwining like snakes in my chest. I curled into a ball. I didn't want to see the consequences of my cursed magic. All these innocent people on the ship, my Hannah, they'd *all* pay those consequences. And it wasn't fair.

I tried to dissipate my magic, my frenzied thoughts racing in a haze of self-hatred. *The window's broken it's all my fault we're all dead it's all my fault!*

My safety evaporated, and the roaring filled my ears again. Beck fitted an emergency seal across the window, chanting in that language while the raven-haired witch stirred her potion. Zola struggled to wave her smoking bundle, now walking counterclockwise around the circle.

After a few painful seconds, the pressure eased. The roaring softened, then died. I sucked a gasp of air into my lungs, and looked up to see the others' postures relaxing too.

Zola left the spinning circle of smoke and doused her bundle of leaves into a shell on the table beside the cauldron.

"It's ready!" the raven-haired witch called in a too-loud voice, stirring the pot with a huge wooden spoon.

Beck fitted one last seal against the window then ran lightly, barefoot, to the table. He pulled on a pair of potholders covered with pink cats—he was probably tired of burning himself—picked up the cauldron by its handles, and stepped over the spinning smoke without disturbing it. He sat the cauldron down without spilling a drop, right on top of a pentacle at the circle's center, and stirred the potion.

The two women staggered into each other's arms, whooping with relieved joy. Beck stepped over the circle and crouched into a fall onto his back on the floor near me, his arms out wide, panting.

I stood, wobbled, and sat heavily onto a bench beside the door. He looked up at the movement, and our eyes met. Normally I was too proud to show any weakness, any imperfection, especially around strangers. But I was going to hurl in a second, and I didn't want to do it anywhere near them.

"Oh my gods," the raven-haired witch said, "that was terrifying. What was that extra disturbance?"

I pushed myself to my feet and staggered out of the room, my hands shaking. Halfway down the hallway I pushed through the door of a restroom and threw up in the nearest toilet, tears streaming down my cheeks.

When nothing else would come up, I straightened and stepped to the sink with my legs shivering beneath me. The excited voices of the coven passing down the hall echoed under the bathroom door as I let cold water rush across my hands. I watched it drain into the sink, willing it to take the nausea and horror of the last few moments with it. If any of them noticed my magical disaster, I was completely sunk.

I wetted a paper towel and patted my face. I couldn't do much about my lipstick, but the cool towel revived me a little. I smoothed my hair, drank a little water from the sink, tucked my blouse back into my skirt, straightened my wide belt. My hands only shook a little now.

I paused halfway through the door with one foot in the hall. Beck stood against the wall, one bare foot up against it and his muscled arms crossed. He pushed off and took a step toward me, digging his hands into his jeans pockets, his expression serious.

"You okay?" he asked quietly, as if he really wanted to know the answer and wasn't making fun of me.

"I'm fine," I said, invoking every woman's sacred right to say it and not mean it at all. I crossed my arms, flustered by his presence and attention.

He extended his hand and continued in a quintessential New Orleans accent. "You must be Gemma, Hannah's safety-obsessed sister?"

I frowned and placed my little hand into his big, rough one, shaking it. "You're mispronouncing astronautical safety engineer."

He laughed without smiling. "You're right. I am. I'm Beck." He retracted his hand. "I hear we're gonna be working on the ship together. Wanna see the engine room?"

I nodded, and he led me to the central elevator. We stood in silence as the panel lights flickered from floor to floor. From the corner of my eye, I saw him check on me once or twice. But he didn't speak, and I wasn't about to. I was too busy feeling the intense embarrassment of an introvert having a very trying morning.

On the bottom floor of the ship, Beck led me through a door marked "Engine Room, Staff Only." I'd spent much of every work day inside simulations of engine rooms, and I was almost looking forward to the familiar hum and crunch of the machinery and the clean, working smells of finely tuned engines. But one step in told me the room was too quiet, and smoke dirtied the air.

I pushed past him, rushing toward the flickering light of a fire. I ran down a row of terminals on my toes over the metal grating, cursing my narrow, French-heeled shoes. Rounding the corner, I stopped short, my heart in my throat. In the command circle of the engine room where there should have been terminals and machinery, was instead the guttering light of dozens of candles, their flames flickering and throwing thin wafts of black smoke into the air.

"Oh my God!" I fell to my knees and blew them out.

"No! Don't!" Beck's footsteps were behind me, but no way would I stop. But the moment I blew out another fat one, something overhead emitted a horrendous metal-on-metal screech, clunking like a monstrous metronome. The ship pitched, throwing me back against a row of metal cabinets and to the floor.

"Jesus, do you wanna kill us all?" Beck threw himself into a crouch between me and the candles, his back to me. I was a turtle on its back, trying to right myself and keep my skirted knees together. Lighter already out, he relit everything I'd blown out. The engine overhead spat a shower of sparks on us and ceased its screech-banging, returning to its customary, humming purr.

"We're in a powder keg of carefully controlled gases and circuitry," I sputtered, trying to stand and keep my knees together, "and an open flame, much less sixty open flames—are you *trying* to blow us up?" I yanked my heel out of a grate, cringing before I made sure it wasn't broken.

"These candles are part of an intricately calculated spell system," he said, tucking his hair behind his ear. The muscles in his broad back shifted under his shirt as he touched candles here and there, adjusting a couple only by a quarter turn. "And they're keeping us hurtling the right way through space."

He stood to his full height and turned around to face me, arms back and palms behind him in an attitude of protection over the candles. "Please don't touch them."

He sighed and dropped his lighter back into his pocket. The ship lurched. I yelped and tumbled into him, my hands against his chest. He grabbed my elbows and kept us both from falling into the sea of candles behind him. The motion stopped abruptly, and he let me go as I took a step back, my face stinging with a blush.

I stood to my full height, hands on my hips. He towered over me. Sizing me up? I was certainly sizing him up. He smelled like clean laundry and smoke, which I knew because I was still standing far too close to him in the cramped space.

"Beck?" Summer's voice crackled over the intercom. "What in the actual fuck was that?"

He cleared his throat and reached sideways to press a button on the nearby steel column. "We're good now," he rumbled in his deep voice. "Just an accident." He let go of the button with a purposeful flourish, a bracelet on a black cord glinting in the candle and halo lights.

Summer came right back. "Don't let it happen again! Loki was on my lap, and he scratched the shit out of me."

"Is there a cat on the bridge?" I balked. Images of my childhood cat, Bella, ran through my mind, sprawling across my tablets and making things happen with her pink toe beans.

He closed his eyes and rolled his neck in a resigned fashion, leaned back, and pressed the button again with a sigh. "Aye-aye, captain."

He smoothed his face to a neutral expression and walked away, motioning with his head for me to follow. "You're exactly what I expected," he said, lobbing it over his shoulder like an insult.

"What's that supposed to mean?" I followed him, walking on the toes of my shoes across the grated floor and down a set of steps.

"Hannah warned us about your attitude toward magic."

I turned the corner in time to see him grab a caulk gun of adhesive. He applied it in a thick, uneven circle to the bottom of a fat cluster of amethyst, which he placed within a plotted collection of crystals and candles on the spoke of a six-pointed star painted on an empty expanse of concrete floor, where the shield generator should be.

The hair on the back of my neck prickled up. "Where's the shield generator?"

"This," he said, grabbing a hunk of turquoise out of a box and slathering adhesive on it, "is the shield generator." He plunked it beside another hunk of turquoise and smooshed it against the floor. Adhesive oozed out from the sides.

I had never, to my knowledge, *ever* fainted, not even when Noah and the officer came to the door to tell us about our parents' hover crash. But a wave of weakness roiled through me now. I sat on the steel steps, still gripping the railing, and pressed one hand to my stomach.

"How?" I didn't even know what to ask.

"It's a beautiful marriage of science and magic," he said, patting the nearest metal casing, "keeping a shield around this hunk of junk so we don't break apart in space. It kept us safe in that room upstairs when the window blew out."

I stared at him, taking deep breaths to try and dispel the tightness in my chest. *The shield generator.* This disparate collection of candles, crystals, and arcane markings.

He picked up a water bottle from the worktable behind him. "Here, this might make you feel better." He tossed me a bottle of water.

I caught it and opened the cap, hesitated. Did he drink out of it already? Whatever. I had worse problems. I took a big swig. "I thought you were an anthropology grad student."

He didn't look up from his work. "I am."

"But you're also a— What's a male witch? A wizard?"

He huffed what might have been a laugh, except he didn't smile, and pulled out a little pot of blue paint and a brush. "Witches don't have gendered terms. That's a flawed mythology based on a late twentieth-century children's author. I'm an eclectic witch, and I dabble in artificery." He settled cross-legged on the floor and thickened the lines of the pentagram with the paint.

"Which of those things makes you the right person to arts and crafts a shield out of paint and crystals?"

"I'm the only one here with an advanced degree in astro-engineering, so the job became mine by default."

"How many degrees do you have? You can't be much older than me?" I asked breathlessly, eyeing his handiwork on the floor.

"I'm twenty-eight," he said, his attention focused on his painting.

I looked around the engine room from my step, playing a frightening game of "what's wrong with this picture?" Strings of lights crisscrossed above the life support system, and someone hung a crocheted, rainbow-yarn spider web around the upper half of the recycling apparatus. Round paper lanterns painted with symbols hung all around the wastewater system.

Too much. I forced my eyes back to him.

He pointed his paintbrush at me. "You look exceptionally nervous. But look, we ain't breaking apart in space, so I must be doin' somethin' right."

Neither of us spoke. He tucked his hair behind his ear again and leaned across a candle, swooping his paintbrush over a farther spoke of the wheel. He was, perhaps, even more handsome in candlelight with his eyes reflecting the flame, but thinking that addled me more.

After a moment, he glanced up from under thick eyebrows. "You okay?"

"Peachy." I was not.

He jogged his head toward a wooden box. "I've got another brush in there if you wanna—"

"Certainly not," I said, enunciating every syllable. "I don't have magic anymore." *That I'm willing to tell you about.*

He pressed his lips together and went silent. Impending doom settled on me, stealing around my headache and still-queasy stomach. I'd already been apprehensive about this journey with my sister and her coven. How would I get through it in a constant state of panic over how the ship was still sailing, fighting off my magic every minute of every hour? And now I had to work with a male witch who already hated me?

"Suit yourself," he said finally.

I felt his gaze linger on me as I stood, then perched on a stool, but when I looked at him, he was focused on his work again. What could I even say to him?

"I'm surprised you gave up your plush ride off-world with Noble Industries. Why are you here with us scrubs?"

I swallowed hard. "That's a personal question."

He stood up suddenly. "You don't look like you feel so good." He grabbed a package of crackers and a lemon-lime soda from a little fridge on his side of the room, placed them on a workbench beside me, and went back to sit on a stool across the area. He nodded at his offering. "You need somethin' a little stronger than water? I don't know what'll happen to my spell if you get sick all over it."

I stared at him as he threw back a swig of orange soda, my heart still stumbling in my chest. "Are you making fun of me?"

He shifted on the stool, hooking one bare foot onto a rung. "No! Sorry. I'm an Aquarius."

As if that was any kind of explanation.

"Well, I'm a scientist," I shot back, "and I don't understand how somebody with as much education as you could possibly believe this"—I waved my hands at the *shield*— "and what's upstairs is superior to science."

"Spoken like a true Sagittarius." He paused, looking down into his soda can. "But I know that's not the first time you've seen magic done."

I popped my soda open and gulped some down. The fizziness cut through the yuck in my throat and bubbled down into my stomach. Hannah must've told him what month I was born in.

"Not like that."

"You thought your sister and the rest of us were just dancin' around naked at the solstice, adorning ourselves with oils and sigils drawn on with lamb's blood?"

I shook my head, heat coming into my face. His voice wasn't unkind, but I couldn't meet his gaze. The way he laid it out sounded ridiculous. And now I was trying not to picture him naked.

"See, that's where you're wrong. We only do that at the spring equinox." He coughed what might have been a laugh without a smile and cleared his throat. "Just kidding about the nudity and lamb's blood." He raised an eyebrow and tilted his head to the side. "But there's a fair bit of dancing."

I dug in the packet for another cracker, saying nothing, unable to imagine the tall, smile-less man before me *actually* dancing.

"Magic's pretty powerful. Some people have a natural affinity for it," he mused. "Some people don't, and other people"—his gaze landed on me—"don't want to admit they have it. A lot of witches go into science." He shrugged. "Seems like the closest thing to magic, to me, but scientists almost never go into witchery." He gestured to my dwindling cracker supply. "Do you want anything else to eat, Gemma?"

I shook my head, eating another cracker. The soda bubbles were settling my stomach, starting to calm it down. I was trying to ignore the irresistible way his full lips formed my name beneath his beard, and how his words terrified me.

My magic came out roaring when I turned twelve. I'd embraced it, was drunk in love with it, until my selfish, irresponsible actions caused my parents' death. Tears pricked at the back of my eyes. Since then I'd devoted myself to science like a frightened child lighting candles against the dark.

I could have told him all of this. Some of this. Instead, I stuffed more crackers in my mouth so none of my thoughts would tumble from my mouth. He was a stranger I wouldn't know for very long.

I shook my head. "I can't...do magic. Anymore." Another lie. "And I don't want any part of yours."

He frowned and tilted his head at me, as if to say, *come on.*

I shook my head harder and chased the crackers down with more soda. "Regardless, I don't want the ship to break apart, because I'm one of the idiots in it. What happened up there, in that room? Do y'all not have all that written down somewhere?"

"We were so rushed to hit our new launch slot. We threw all our notes and things into a box. It's on the stage, top-of-ship. But no." His gaze snagged on something above him, and he stood and reached overhead to tighten a lug nut by hand. "We don't have it written down and organized by any means."

His muscled stomach stuck out the bottom of his shirt, and I instinctively followed the dark trail of hair from his belly button to where it disappeared in his jeans. I snapped my eyes up to his face, my insides twisting.

He tapped the side of his head. "But it's okay. It's all in here."

My stomach and my jaw dropped. "What if something happens to you?"

He shrugged, coming down from his reach and settling on the stool again. "What's gonna happen to me on the ship?"

"You might irritate someone to the point of violence, and then where would we be?"

Whatever he saw on my face seemed to reassure him that I was over halfway joking. His eyes crinkled slightly. "Well, not just me. The five of us worked on all the spells together, so between us all, we've got this."

"That's not good enough!" I blurted "Somebody needs to— You know what? I'm gonna do it. I'm gonna gather it all up, write out the components of your"—I paused, not wanting to say the word, but unable to find a suitable replacement—"spells down. What if they fail again? Shouldn't we at least try to replace as many as we can with hard science and engineering?"

"Yeah. I'll help you." His face was guileless, even agreeable.

I blinked in surprise. I hadn't even been trying to get along with him.

"For one," he continued, "I think you're right. We have two months till Gaia, and that stuff needs to be organized. But also..." He hesitated, picking at a fingernail. "We may have enough parts around here to at least build some redundancy into our spell systems."

"Okay. Good. We're agreed."

He shook his head. "You didn't let me finish. I'll help you, on two conditions."

I huffed and looked sideways away from him, half expecting him to ask me out, with all this extreme eye contact. That was going to be a hard pass.

"What are they?" I asked.

"First, we have to call it...what you're writing down? We have to call it the *Interstellar Grimoire*, because that sounds badass." His eyes wanted to smile, but they couldn't quite get his mouth on board.

I couldn't stop a small laugh from breathing out through my nose. "And the second?"

He rubbed his beard. Wet his lips. Readjusted his legs. Narrowed his eyes and studied me for long seconds. "You want to tell me about how you lost control of your magic up there?"

Chapter 3

Brilliant and Beautiful

I froze, panic flooding me. "What are you talking about?"

His eyebrows rose as he stared me down. "I'm talking about that self-defensive bubble you made that nearly took out a window. I'm willing to bet you didn't make that on purpose."

I shook my head, ready to lie, like the last time my magic took control of me. "I don't—"

He sighed, frowning. "Don't worry." He put a hand out like he was calming a spooked horse. "I covered for you with the coven. And I promise I won't say anything." He shook his head. "I don't know why you're lying to your family about your magic. It's not my business. But you've got to get it under control. You could've killed everyone on the ship. So my second condition is that you let me help you control that magic that you absolutely don't have."

My stomach tightened. I was cornered. Not by him, but by my own biology. Whatever damnable thing that made magic course through my veins. I downed the last of my soda and stood up, tossing the can into the recycle bin.

"On second thought, I'd rather work alone." I took a few steps toward the stairs and stopped short. I was stuck on a ship with him for the next two months. I should say something to make nice, but what?

"Gemma, are you in here?"

Saved by the ringing of Hannah's voice through the room.

"I'm over here!" I called, moving toward her voice.

She rounded the corner. "Oh good!" She was beaming. "I'm so glad you guys met!"

My back to him, I glared at her.

She glanced between us uncertainly. "I was gonna offer to help you get your things to your suite. Are you busy? I can come back if you two are getting to know each other." She smiled broadly.

"We're not. I mean, I'm not busy." I walked past her toward the steps. *Manners, Gemma.* I turned back around. "Thanks for the crackers and soda."

"Anytime," he said, settling back down to his work and not sparing a glance for me.

Back in the lobby, Hannah detached my hovercart from the wall. "I'm so excited that you met my coven!" She leaned in. "What do you think of Beck?"

The arc of my eye roll stopped short at seeing a line of duct tape running along a window crack. No, *several* window cracks.

"Holy shit, Hannah! You can't use duct tape on spaceship windows!" I stepped back from the bank of windows, fight-or-flight kicking in. "The pressure alone should have taken those out, not to mention the radiation seeping in!"

Hannah waved her hand dismissively. "It's okay, Gemma. We have it covered. Sure, it's been a blur since this launch slot opened up, but we've got it all under control."

"Things weren't under control with that spell on Level 1," I fired back. My heart pounding, I scanned the lobby. Everything was intact. Not a single leaf fluttered on the small trees dotted down the walk, except for one under a vent. No crushing force of the vacuum of space, no flesh-melting radiation. No new cracks breaking out across the windows.

I breathed deeply, willing the hormone spike to pass so I could think more clearly. As bad as the cruiser had looked from the outside, the inside was so much worse than I'd imagined. And my sister and I were stuck on this deathtrap, hurtling through space with—

"Are those solar sails?" I cried, pointing out the window at the large, fabric-like structures jutting out from the side of the ship. "Hannah, those were recalled twenty years ago!"

"Welcome to the *WitchCraft*!" Hannah said, grinning from ear to ear and throwing her arms wide in an attitude of proud ownership. She laughed. "Get it? It was Beck's idea. It used to be called *The Shooting Star*, but we renamed it."

I was still pointing at the sails, my face slack with horror. Hannah gently pulled my arm down and turned my panicked face away from the window by the chin. "We're in good shape. I promise. I know you can't do magic anymore, but trust me. We've got it covered."

I pressed my hands to my chest, ignoring Hannah's oblivious mention of my lie, willing my heart to slow to normal. I needed to be alone. This was it. This was my limit.

I let her lead me to the elevator, her long, flowered skirt swishing.

"You're on Level 2, Suite 205. Right around the corner from me and Summer."

The copper elevator doors parting before me were carved in an intricate, swirling lotus mandala. Lovely, but I'd bet the machinery was old enough to be hydraulic.

The elevator chimed, and the doors slid apart like an old man struggling up from his chair. A whoosh of manufactured air prickled my skin as I pushed my cart in after Hannah.

"So the tech in this ship is, at best, fifty-one years old? And at worst"—I gestured at the old-fashioned bank of depressible floor buttons as Hannah pressed two—"eighty-five years old?"

She cocked her head. "Yeah, I guess that math tracks. It was the height of luxury in its day. Isn't it beautiful? It's got four roomy suites, plus eight other rooms for guests and staff. Most of those are full of luggage and backstock now. But the ship itself was free. Can you believe that Summer's great-uncle left her the whole junkyard and this ship too?"

"Imagine that."

Hannah picked at her chipped purple fingernails, ignoring my sarcasm.

"It took us almost two years to muck out the rats and roaches, clean it up, prune the ship's forest, figure out how to make it run again, and move in."

"You know that shooting stars are just dust and rocks that burn up in Earth's atmosphere, right? Are you sure this junkpile can survive entry on Gaia? Not to mention getting through the Bifrost."

The most frightening prospect of our journey was the manmade traversable wormhole that the International Council named after the Rainbow Bridge from Norse mythology. "You think a shield made out of paint and rocks is gonna get us through that unscathed?"

The elevator chimed, and the doors opened on a hallway lit with retro incandescent lighting. Hannah stepped out first, waving her hands dismissively.

"They've almost figured that out."

I sputtered, trying to speak. My cart dipped low over the threshold onto the carpet, and I wanted to sink to the floor beside it. "So in two months, we're either going to break apart in a wormhole or burn up in a fiery crash onto Gaia?"

"Psshh, no. Neither." She rounded a corner and pulled a metal key from her pocket—an honest-to-God metal key on a long, purple velvet ribbon necklace—and turned it in the lock on Suite 205.

"Hannah," I demanded, following her into the room, "this is serious!"

My sister sighed, her voice rising. "Summer and Beck are working on it, and I have full confidence in them."

"But Summer's a geometry teacher, and Beck's—" I didn't know how to finish that sentence. "What do those two know about ships entering the atmosphere?"

"Something even more powerful than science is running this ship, Gemma. Besides, all five of us knew what we were getting into."

"But you didn't bother to tell your sister, the sixth?"

"I'm sorry, but at least you're here now to tell us all what to do," she said in a huff, jerking the cart over the high threshold.

"Uh...you begged me to come!" I spluttered. "Guilted me into coming! Made me think you'd float off into space without me!"

I stepped into my suite, my home for the next two months until we all died in a horrific fireball that, judging by the size of the ship, would take out a small country when it crashed. Unless we were shot out of the sky first. Or would breaking apart in a wormhole be preferable? I didn't know anymore.

The corners of her mouth turned down. "Gemma, I'm really sorry. Please don't be mad at me."

Her penitent pout deflated my frustration, and everything I'd been through in the past few days rushed out in tears. "I'm so sorry, Hannah."

She rushed in to hug me. "It's okay, Gem, don't cry!"

"It's not you." I sniffed. "It's just...this is all a lot. Losing my job, leaving the planet, and I didn't expect the ship to be this bad off."

Hannah pulled me toward a wooden farmhouse table near the door and sat me down beside her in mismatched chairs. "You remember what Mom used to say?"

I nodded and pulled back, my face and nose a running mess. I grabbed a tissue from the box on the table. "'It's just something else we have to get through.'"

She put her head against mine. "Sometimes life feels like one thing to get through after another. But things'll get better. Gaia will be better. I have to believe it. And look, if you're worried about the wormhole and entry, you can work with Summer and Beck on it. I'm sure they'll be glad for your help."

I wiped at my face, nodding. "I'll help." A long, jagged scar along her forearm caught my attention. I grabbed her arm and turned it into the light. "What happened?"

"It's nothing. I wiped out on my bike last year at Christmas. I shouldn't have been riding through the junkyard. Oops!" She jumped up to grab the hovercart, which, although I'd disengaged it, was drifting across the room. While she grabbed its handle and set the kickstand down, I stood up to look around my room.

It must've been freshened up in the updates, because it had the same bamboo floor and similar wallpaper to the lobby. A kitchenette opened off to the right of the open foyer, a lounge area was just ahead, and around the right-hand corner, a big bed. A darkened doorway beyond led to a bathroom. Someone had set a devil's ivy on the counter height farmhouse table I was sitting at. The table didn't quite go with the rest of the decor, but I loved it. I ran my fingertips across the warm, comforting grain of the wood.

"None of the hotel's furniture survived," Hannah explained, "which is a shame because it was all art nouveau revival. So we brought our homes with us and decorated our own rooms. Beck made you a table, and we moved a bunch of your old things in from the house. All heirlooms and baby pictures are accounted for."

"He's a carpenter?" My eyes snagged on a sofa in my room's sitting area that I'd last seen in my parents' sunroom. I used to love to curl up on it to read. In the bedroom area, my own king-sized bed from my parents' house sat, dressed in the plush, pink velvet comforter I had as a teenager. It brought no good memories, only a twist in my stomach, and a past I'd do anything to forget.

"Yes, he's very talented in a variety of things. It's disgusting. We took pretty much everything from the house. We're not only traveling in the ship but living in it too, at least until we get settled. The rest we furnished from scavenging abandoned houses."

The ditsy floral pattern on the worn throw pillows broke a dam in my mind. A rush of memories poured out, happy ones painted over with guilt and anguish churning at the edges of my defenses like the gulf on the other side of the levees. I pressed my knuckles to my lips, curling into myself.

"It's almost only the dead who are still in New Orleans."

I turned at the wistful sound of her voice. Bright tears tracked down her pink cheeks. She wasn't talking about the vast, ancient cities of the dead at the base of Canal Street. She meant Mom and Dad. Each time I thought of them was like entering a new nightmare. I'd give anything to wake up and find them alive and well.

Hannah rubbed her whole face with both hands and took a big breath. "I'm so glad you're here."

"Me too," I said, pulling boxes off the hovercart. She joined me, and we worked in silence unloading the meager belongings I'd packed the night I'd left.

"You never answered me. What do you think of Beck?" she asked with a grin.

"Nannapie, don't you start with him again."

"Okay, but I wasn't lying when I said he was gorgeous, right?"

I sighed. Heavily. "He might be, if he ever smiled once in a while."

She eyed me like I'd grown a second head. "Almost all he ever does is smile."

"Then he just doesn't like *me*. All I got was fussed at for blowing out candles."

Her eyes went round. "You blew out candles?"

"I didn't know any better! What was I supposed to do, with a ton of open flames in an engine room?"

"Oh Gemma." She sighed. "We have to teach you a few things. He was probably just worried. I promise he's the biggest softy, nicest guy ever. And he *can't* not like you. I mean, look at you!" She came up and took me by the arms, gently pushing hair from my forehead. "Beautiful face, beautiful figure. I love your skirt, by the way. And I don't know how you get your brows so perfect. I wish you'd stop straightening your hair though. You know I'm jealous of your curls."

I sighed at her familiar lament. "Your hair's curly."

"My hair's *wavy*," she corrected. "It's totally different. In fact, I know he thinks you're cute. Do you know what he said when he first saw your picture at our house? He said, and I quote, 'Well, *shit*.' And it was the good kind of 'well, shit,' definitely not the bad kind. Then he immediately asked who you were."

"This is the same guy you've been trying to talk me into for years?"

She grabbed a box and disappeared into the kitchenette. "Maybe."

"He's so not my type," I said, dropping a box of shoes on the floor.

"How is brilliant and beautiful *not* your type? Not to mention, as I said, that he's the sweetest guy ever?"

"If he's so wonderful, why isn't he taken?" A valid point. But also, witches preferred to be with other witches. That's how their community was, Zola and my brother being one of the few exceptions. "That beautiful raven-haired witch seems more his type. Seriously, she's gorgeous. She'd probably hex me if I looked at him the wrong way."

Hannah rolled her eyes. "Eyre is his oldest friend, and believe me when I say she is *no* competition for you."

"She's not competition because I'm not competing."

"Come on! You need to put yourself out there! I haven't heard anything about you dating in years."

"All I want is time alone. I'm not looking for a relationship right now." My ex-boss came to mind. His thick dark hair and sexy smile...his look of terror when I tore his office apart with my magic.

"But Beck is—"

"Brilliant and beautiful, I know, you've told me. Look, I'm sure he'd be very nice if he ever smiled. And okay, so he's pretty easy on the eyes."

She leaned her head back, laughing. "I told you so."

I talked over her, louder. "He's just a nice view on the way to Gaia, okay? That's all."

Hannah narrowed her eyes at me, mollified for now. She glanced at her watch. "Alright. Well, it's been a long day, but at least it's time to eat. Eyre's got a late lunch-slash-dinner planned on the Star Deck. Our little first-night-in-space celebration. You'll come, won't you?"

"Yeah," I said. "I'll meet you there after I freshen up."

She smiled. "Sure." She pushed the now-empty cart out of the room ahead of her and closed the door.

I took a deep breath, turning into my suite. It was much smaller than my old apartment, but it was far quieter, and my family was near. Honestly, the longer I was away from San Francisco, the more relieved I was.

Except that I still had to get through dinner with the coven. But first I desperately needed the restroom. I walked past the row of drawn curtains that I didn't have the stomach to peer through, lest these windows be sealed with duct tape too, and flicked on the bathroom light.

A massive clawfoot tub buoyed a little bubble of joy in my chest. Adding that to the list for tonight. My heels made soft clicks on the green penny-tile floors as I availed myself of the amenities, washed my hands in the bronze sink, and studied my hair and makeup. What a mess.

Everything was a mess.

Chapter 4

The Star Deck

The ship-hotel's hand-carved wooden directional signs still hung at every juncture and elevator, all the way up to the top level of the ship. When the central elevator doors opened on the Star Deck, a grand room surrounded me on three sides. The expanse of star-speckled space sat cold on the other side of the windows stretching up the walls and part of the ceiling. According to the sign, the mezzanine behind me had a swimming pool and a hot tub.

Just one dinner to get through, and I could be alone.

I followed voices around the corner to my right. Hannah and the raven-haired witch—had they called her *Air*?—bustled around a table covered with retro metal lunch boxes in the middle of a worn parquet dance floor. Behind them, a plum-curtained stage sat empty except for a cardboard box overflowing with rolled-up papers.

This room must've really been something in the ship's heyday. Couples in suits and cocktail gowns must've danced among the stars while servers in crisp white uniforms brought steaming platters of delicacies to tables decorated with linen tablecloths and fine bone china. The vast room was empty now save for the food table and a cozy area of floor cushions and pillows tossed on a variety of mismatched rugs just beyond the dance floor.

I sat on a green velvet pouf in the cozy area and studied my nails to wait for whatever this was going to be. A friendly brown-and-black tabby cat approached me, sniffing the fingers I held out, then rubbing its nose across them. I smiled and petted him, delighted when he began to purr.

Elevator chimes sounded from two directions. Zola and Summer entered from the stern elevator, their laughter echoing up the high windows, and Beck headed in from the main elevator. The three of them met in the middle and went straight toward the table, bypassing me altogether. I put my head down and concentrated on giving the cat scratchies on his fluffy scruff, eliciting a purr that could wake the dead. My stomach knotted up again. I was good with groups of three, but anything above that tended to shut me down.

The others gathered around the table, their conversations and merriment ebbing and flowing like a family preparing for a holiday meal. I ran my finger along the fuzz of the cat's nose, painfully aware of my interloper status in the tight-knit group.

Hannah and Summer stood with their heads close, talking softly together. Summer's eyes focused on my sister as she spoke, and she reached out and tucked a lock of Hannah's hair behind her ear so gently. A soft jealousy twinged in my empty chest. I'd been too lonely for too long.

I glanced at the others. What was the protocol here? I was hungry, but if I went over for something to eat, I'd have to make small talk. I hated small talk. Stay here being awkward was clearly my only option.

Social situations with new people were the worst. I felt farther away from home than ever, and except for my siblings, who were both happily paired, and apparently this cat, who was now making a tentative approach to my lap, I was alone in the universe. The sprinkling of stars wheeled outside the bank of windows, and it made me long for home. Real home with my family, years ago when my parents were still alive.

"Hey Gemma! I didn't see you come in!" Summer sat on the rug beside me with a lunch box, and my furry friend scampered away at the movement. Hannah sat on her other side.

"Oby," Hannah called to the cat, "you don't have to run away! He's so scaredy," she said, shaking her head.

At the smell of food, my stomach growled so loud I think everyone must've heard it. I pressed my hand to my belly and tightened my muscles to shut it up.

"We didn't get to talk much before launch," Summer said. "How was your trip in?"

"Oh, it was fine." I shrugged. "It was the Tube."

She laughed and nodded. The Tube was good for only one thing: getting somewhere in a hurry. Otherwise it was an uncomfortable, no-frills, miserable little train with bad food and too few windows.

"How've you been?" I asked, remembering my manners.

"I'm great," Summer said. "Excited to be off and running finally!" She lowered her voice and leaned toward me, eyebrows drawn together. "Are you okay? Hannah told me about your job. I'm so sorry." She squeezed my arm, then unpacked her lunchbox.

"Sorry about what?" Beck sat beside me on the rug—at least at a respectable distance—and held two worn metal lunch boxes out toward me. "Would you like *Star Wars* or *The Incredible Dragon*?"

All I saw when I looked at him now was my engine room mistake and my secret uncovered. I frowned at him and grabbed one of the boxes with both hands. "*Star Wars*, thank you, because that's what we're going to have if you don't mind your own business."

Beck only nodded and handed me the requested lunchbox. Wise choice.

Summer sighed. "I swear he's got preternatural hearing, but he means well." She reached across to gently backhand him on the shoulder.

"I didn't mean to offend," he said, opening his lunchbox and unwrapping a sandwich. "I just thought I ought to get to know my chore-mate."

"Chore-mate?" I glared at Hannah.

"I decided to station you both in the engine room for the whole trip," Hannah said.

I glared at my sister, the maker of schedules and misery, but she was picking a subpar piece of bread off her sandwich, smiling like a Cheshire cat.

No one said anything, and it was awkward, especially the tension between me and Beck. "Thank you for the table," I blurted. "Hannah said you made it?"

His head turned to me. "Yeah. You're welcome. I made it for you last summer."

"Last summer?" I decided to come on this ship only two months ago.

He peered down into his soda can as if trying to gauge how much he had left. Or how much he should say. But I felt exposed, like I'd stepped out of the house in my underwear, and he was politely averting his eyes.

He shrugged. "I dabble in divination."

With nothing to say to that, I turned my attention to my lunch box. Tucked inside was a ham-and-cheese sandwich on homemade bread wrapped up in beeswax fabric, and my stomach urgently reminded me that I hadn't eaten since that morning.

"This looks so good," I said. "I can't remember the last time I had a real sandwich." I balanced the box on my lap and took a small bite, careful not to drop crumbs.

Beck frowned. "What have you been eating out in San Francisco?"

"Fresh food was getting pretty scarce. Let's just say I've eaten more than my fair share of FFPs in the last few months."

Eyre approached, her skin flawless, her winged eyeliner sharp enough to cut glass, and her wavy, raven's wing hair the epitome of a gothic princess. She sat beside Beck and leaned her head into the group, insinuating herself into the conversation. "What are we talking about?"

"Fortified food packet yumminess," Beck said, with no trace of making fun of me in his voice.

"Ugh," she groaned, tucking an iridescent strand of hair behind her ear as her big brown eyes widened at me in apparent sympathy. "We ate too many of those after Hurricane Macaron King, so I feel for you on a deep, spiritual level. I'm Eyre, by the way."

I reached out and shook the hand she offered. "Air?"

"Eyre, as in *Jane Eyre*. My parents are English professors," she explained, opening her lunch box.

Zola joined the group, dropping to the carpet between Eyre and Hannah with the grace of a ballerina. "Well folks, we made it into space, and all our spells are holding...sort of."

Sort of? I was a deer in headlights, but laughing, whoops, and applause broke out around me. How could they joke about our casual relationship with dying in space?

"Oh, so let me fill you in on our little crew's roles and responsibilities," Summer said, briefly touching her hand to my arm. "Hannah and I are co-captains, Eyre's our navigator. The three of us'll trade off shifts on the bridge, but I've got the lion's share since Hannah's helping Zola with general management, and plus she made all the shift schedules.

"Zola, of course, is our badass high priestess, spiritual advisor, chief séance officer, and resident doctor *and* energy healer." Summer paused to place her palms together and incline her head to Zola, who returned the gesture.

High priestess? Séance officer? I looked around at my crewmates. Did they all have stupid titles or just Zola?

"Eyre's also our head chef and kitchen witch," Summer continued. "Hannah said she told you how hard we worked on the spells that're keeping the ship flying. It's crucial that you don't disturb them."

Beck and Hannah occupied themselves with their meal, neither revealing a morsel of guilt at betraying my stupidity to Summer.

"If you see duct tape holding something together, don't remove it. Crystals in odd places?" Summer shook her head. "Just leave them. You'll see strange markings and candles lit. Please, for the love of Hestia, your rule of thumb on this ship is going to be: if it's lit, don't do shit. If you don't understand why it's there, leave it. Turn nothing off that's on, and turn nothing on that's off. Our collective survival depends on this."

I nodded, my cheeks burning. "Got it." All I wanted was to curl into a ball and hide. I couldn't bring myself to look at the windows lining the wall, at the brutal expanse of space. I wished the solid Earth was still beneath my feet so it could swallow me whole, and I missed not feeling like my death was imminent.

Eyre spoke up. "We've been growing food on the ship from almost the moment we got our hands on it," she said, "and we went into debt to buy the things we couldn't grow. I'll cook daily, and we'll all have shifts in the kitchen and the garden in the ship's forest. I'll post menus on the Common network."

"And that just leaves Beck, our renaissance man," Summer said, "who as you know will be in the engine room with you."

Zola leaned forward, looking at Beck. "How are you feeling? Don't think I didn't notice that you escaped the med bay without my permission. Is your arm giving you any trouble?" she asked.

All heads turned worried faces toward Beck. He waved them all off. "I'm fine."

"Okay, tough stuff!" Zola exclaimed. "Y'all don't let him fool you. It was a bad burn."

"Who gets a second-degree burn making cookies?" Eyre cackled, falling into Beck.

He laughed back in the same fit of hysteria. "You know if somebody's gonna do it, it's gonna be me."

Laughing harder, Eyre wiped tears from her eyes. "You even burned the cookies!"

"Yeah, because I was too busy hollerin' and running water over my arm."

While everyone else snickered at the exchange. I was judging how many chips I had left. Just four more, plus one little pot of pudding that I was hellbent on finishing, because chocolate. Then I could feign being too tired to socialize with people like Beck, who could apparently smile at anybody but me.

"Zo, the eczema on my fingers has been crazy since we made all that soap," Eyre said. "Can you help me out?"

"Of course! When we're done eating, let me fix you up."

I didn't want to know more about Zola's alternative healing credentials, but having a real doctor on board was a blessing. Even though a cruiser this old must have an AI nurse, it could do only so much.

"What's the plan for tomorrow, Captain Beautiful?" Summer said to Hannah.

Hannah's face lit up. "Well, Co-Captain Beautiful—"

"Get a room," Eyre teased.

"Now that we're in flight," Hannah said, wrinkling her nose playfully at Eyre, "we could use a good inventory, go through the packing lists."

"You just want to play in the spreadsheets," Summer accused with a smile.

Hannah laughed, nodding. "I do!"

Beck cleared his throat. "I've been thinking that someone should go through the spells in the box, write 'em all out, keep a grimoire for the trip. I thought Gemma could help me with that, if she doesn't mind?"

He'd asked the question innocently enough, but I knew the full context of the request. I turned a fake smile his way.

"Sure," I said through gritted teeth.

Hannah's smile perked up into full bloom as she looked between me and Beck. "That'd be a huge help. The box of spells is over on the stage. It's a mess. It'll take you a long time to go through it together."

Beck spared a glance for me. "What's our first order of business tomorrow, co-chief engineer and grimoire writer?"

I swallowed my last spoonful of pudding, considering a civil reply. "I guess go through the spell box. And has anyone inventoried the engine room yet?"

He shook his head. "I did one early on, but the past few weeks flew by. I grabbed as many promising-looking parts I could find at Al's and threw 'em in the storage area. Getting everything organized would be a great place to start."

"I'm sorry to interrupt. Eyre, I'm done if you want me to help with your hands," Zola said. "But catch me right now because it's been a long-ass day, and I'm already ready to go to bed."

Eyre scrambled up with her dinner things and nodded her head to the other side of the seating area. "Thank you! I'll meet you on the poufs."

"Good deal," Zola said. "I'm about to try and catch Noah over StarTalk again. The network's been out since yesterday, but maybe it's back up again. Anybody who wants to talk to him, let me know."

I said nothing. My big brother was the last person I wanted to talk to. I didn't need him evaluating my life and asking a million questions, uncovering the truth about my job.

Hannah turned to Summer. "When Eyre's done, let's go over the overnight checklist with her and make sure we're not missing anything. After that, I think we're done for the night. Oh, and Gemma?"

I looked up at the sound of my name.

"I've got stuff to do tonight, but I hereby claim sister time with you tomorrow. Deal?"

"Deal." I smiled into my sweet sister's face. I'd missed her so much.

Hannah hurried off, and I lost track of the others' conversations as I watched Zola sit across from Eyre on a cushion on the other side of the rug. Eyre put her hands on her thighs, palms down, and closed her eyes. Zola held her open palms above Eyre's hands without touching them. She held her hands there for several minutes, and every so often she waved her hands to the side, as if wafting something away from Eyre's body.

"Can I get you anything else?"

Beck's voice startled me. I turned to see him standing before me with his hands outstretched. He pointed at my lunchbox and dishes.

"Oh!" I scrambled to pack everything neatly into the lunch box for him, and handed it off as I stood. "No, thank you. Is there anything I can do to help?"

"Well, Eyre's got dish duty," he said, loading our things onto the cart. "But do you wanna go look at the box of spells?"

"Sure."

He placed all the items on the cart and headed toward the stage, scooping up my friend the tabby on his way. He kissed his head and held him against his chest.

"Who's this?" I asked.

"This is my sweet boy Oberon Galileo Breaux, but his friends call him Oby. He's a real love machine." Oby sniffed Beck's face, nose to nose, before Beck poured him onto the stage and pulled the beat-up cardboard box to the edge.

Oby came to me and rubbed his whole body against my hand. "Hey Oby," I cooed, "you are a sweet, fluffy baby." Oby purred like a '56 Vespian hovercycle.

While I was giving Oby scratchies, Beck pulled the box, overflowing with rolled up papers and notebooks, off the stage and sat it on the floor, crouching in front of it to lift some papers out and show me the contents.

"We were in such a rush. It's a big mess."

Oby jumped down from the stage and proceeded to bite tiny holes in the open box flaps with his sharp little teeth. Crystals rolled around in the bottom of the box, which was filled with drawings and sketches on loose-leaf paper, and more than a few candy wrappers.

"Oby, stop that," he gently admonished, pulling the tabby away and dropping kisses on his head. "Go eat your chicken nums." I followed his gaze as he looked around. No one else was in earshot.

"My offer still stands," he said quietly. "My whole family's on Gaia, and I want to get to them in one piece. I want *everyone* to get to their families on Gaia in one piece. I'm sure you want to get there safely too, right?"

"Obviously," I bit off, a little too forceful.

"I tell you what. I'll take this down to the engine room, and we can talk in the morning. Why don't you go get some rest?"

His face was impassive, no trace of kindness to match the kind-ish words. Smiles all the time, my ass.

"Sounds good." This day couldn't end soon enough for me, anyway.

He nodded and hefted the box into his arms. "'Night," he said. "Come on, Oby! Time to make *do-do*!" He went off toward the elevator, humming, his cat trotting behind.

Fais do-do. I smiled, and a twinge of homesickness skipped through my chest. My grandma used to use that old Cajun term for going to sleep. It was time for me to make *do-do*, too.

Chapter 5

Let Me Help You

My first night in my old bed in the ancient space hotel was full of tosses, turnings, and bizarre dreams on the edge of nightmares, punctuated by twice waking up in a panic in the dark. A light dawned through the transom above my suite door against a duet of synthesized birdsong, disorienting me. But at least the night was over. If only the chirping wasn't exacerbating the wicked headache I'd spent all night cultivating. Relieving headaches was the one thing I missed about my magic.

I stumbled into the shower, and in under thirty minutes, I flawlessly straightened my hair, did my makeup, and dressed in an ironed silk tank dress.

After a quick breakfast in the kitchen, I walked toward the engine room, watching the soft rows of ruffles at the knee line of my skirt kick out at each step. Food hadn't helped my headache at all. I didn't know why my first couple of days in space always brought on this much pain, but as a consolation, it was something I could always rely on.

I pushed my hand against the engine room door, and I could already hear Beck singing soulfully along with music playing inside.

"'—my future in your eyes; I thought you were just a dream.'"

Was that *Dream Girl* by R&B legend Maasai Malone? Beck had a nice voice. At least it was better than talking to him, and at least his singing made him easy to find. Downstairs, just past the "shield generator," he stood with his back to me in a workspace area, chucking bits of machinery into wooden crates already partially filled with cords, tools, bits of metal, and dials. A turntable and a battered pair of speakers sat near him on a worktable, and not far behind him, a hammock with a blanket hung above a cozy rug tossed with pillows and anchored with books.

"*'Then you walked into my life!'*"

He turned and startled at seeing me, eyes wide and hand over his heart. "Jeez, you scared me half to death!" No smile accompanied his laugh. "I didn't hear you come in. I thought I'd get an early start and pull all the extra tech together for an inventory, like we talked about last night. How's this for a perfect spot to gather everything?" With bits of spaceship in either hand, he held his arms out to show a run of mismatched wooden shelves against the wall that hadn't been there yesterday.

"Did you just build those?"

He shrugged and tossed the items in his hands into two different crates, then wiped his hands on his jeans. "I was too wound up to sleep last night."

"Looks good," I allowed. I surveyed the broken bits and baubles on the shelves, most of which didn't originate on a spaceship. A stark contrast to the stockroom at Noble Industries with its embarrassment of spare parts. Given an hour and a shopping cart, I could've found not only replacements and patches for every missing and broken item on the ship, but I could've even brought everything up to code.

"If you want to keep working on that," I said, forcing my thoughts back to the tasks at hand, "I thought I'd start organizing the spell box and inventorying the ship's systems. See which are working properly and which are being held together with washi tape and happy thoughts."

"She's coming out of the gate strong this morning," he said, almost an actual smile playing about his lips as he polished a lawn mower transmission with a dirty scrap of old T-shirt.

I shook my head and rubbed the back of my neck. "I just have a headache. Happens every time I go into space. It'll wear off in a day or so."

His eyebrows lowered. "Go see Zola. She'll fix you right up."

I scoffed, thinking of the energy healing from last night. "No thanks. I'm not dancing naked around a ring of candles or sleeping with a sprig of chamomile under my pillow."

"I'd have to check with Eyre, but I think you'd want lavender, not chamomile." He raised his eyebrows. "Zola's a doctor, remember? She's got ibuprofen or whatever you need."

My cheeks flushed. "You're right. Thanks."

He pointed right. "I put the spell box over on the drafting table, just on the other side of the wastewater system."

I started to walk off to berate myself in private for my awkwardness, but I turned around, remembering I had a question. "What's with the birds and the artificial sunshine in the hallways?"

"Summer rigged the interior lighting to cycle on and off, like day and night. She's trying to give us some normalcy. Plus, because she's clever, she rigged it to gradually adjust to the different day length on Gaia. She and Zola think it'll help us adjust better when we get there."

Very clever. I nodded and walked off.

"Lemme know if the music bothers your headache!" he called after me.

I didn't answer, just waved behind me as I walked away.

Cleaning out the spell box and organizing its contents took most of the morning. I pulled everything out, threw out the trash—somebody had an addiction to Chewy Bears, judging by the surfeit of wrappers—and began organizing the contents into piles, by spell and by my best guess. I also started gathering information about the systems in the engine room to prepare for my audit.

Beck and I managed to stay out of each other's hair in the vast engine room, which wasn't surprising considering it had dozens of alcoves, metal staircases, balconies, and catwalks over multiple open-air levels. Thank God most of the systems I'd checked so far were intact and functioning properly, as far as I could tell. I missed having access to Noble Industries' databases, but the Common had more manuals than expected. At least someone recently updated it. My main concern was trying to set those makeshift fixes to rights if I could, and make backup plans for when the spells would inevitably fail. Magic, in my experience, was too volatile for these fixes, even for as short a term as two months.

A few hours later, I was trying to read the model number on one of the evaporators, but the tiny thing was stuck on at an odd angle and higher than I could read from the narrow catwalk. Worse, strapped to the pole between it and me was a shelf with three candles burning. A ladder wouldn't fit—did we even have one?—and I wasn't about to stand on the railing without a safety harness and in my skirt. I eyeballed the height. Maybe Beck was tall enough to read it.

"Beck! Can you come see?"

"Coming!" He appeared a minute later with a new grease smudge on his shirt.

"Can you read the model number on that evaporator?"

He scaled the few steps toward me, and I pressed myself against the metal wall to let him pass in the narrow space. Again the whiff of soap and candle smoke from him, and also, slightly, motor oil. He stepped onto the first rung of the railing with his bare feet, hanging onto the catwalk's pole and stretching over the candles toward the label.

"Don't stand on the railing! You need a safety harness!" My hands reached out on their own volition to grab his legs, but I pulled them back into fists.

He ignored me. "It's Model 24-XRTC."

"Ok thanks please come down?" I blurted. If he fell, his body would catch fire and bounce off two different railings before he hit the concrete below.

He climbed down, agile as a cat, then gave me the tiniest smile as he edged past me. And it was...nice.

Okay, it was *really* nice.

He stepped to a respectful distance. "Thanks for not disturbing the candles this time. They're arranged at perfect harmonic intervals to activate the filtration system." He leaned against the railing and crossed his arms.

I scribbled the model number in my notebook, our conversation and his two conditions from yesterday hanging in the air between us. Much like the crocheted netting I'd been trying to ignore all morning.

"Still thinking about my offer?" he asked.

At least a dozen witchy fixes were set up throughout the engine room, not to mention the ones I'd passed in the ship this morning and last night. I'd started a section in my notebook listing them out, but the ratty collection of information in the box didn't give me much to go on.

When I didn't answer or look up, he went on. "I'm willing to drop the first condition, even though, c'mon." He leaned slightly toward me. "What a badass name would that be? *The Interstellar Grimoire*. The other name I thought of is nowhere near as cool, but it's not bad. Here, maybe you'll like it better: *The Book of WitchCraft*."

He nodded, eyebrows raised, looking thoroughly pleased with himself. I sighed and held the notebook to my chest, cocking my head to the side. I thought about his conditions all night. Well, not the first one. That was silly. But the second? I'd been struggling to control my magic for all of my adult life, and it had cost me more than I'd ever told anyone. What would learning to control my magic with him look like? And would it be worth working on when I was just going to have it taken away once I reached Gaia?

"I'm not tryin' to tell you what to do, I promise. But I think you ought to consider taking me up on that"—he held up two fingers—"second condition." His hand dropped to his thigh.

I didn't answer. My head hurt way too much for this conversation.

He persisted. "You know, Hannah said you got her into magic, but she thinks you don't have it anymore."

He was a snuffling bloodhound on a trail. "Maybe that's not your business." I sidled past him to go down the stairs.

"It's my business when you almost blow out a window on the spaceship I'm in."

I whirled around to retort, but what could I say? He was right.

He leaned over and placed his forearms on the railing. "Please let me help you, Gemma?"

I frowned at him, confused at his gentle tone and open expression. For a hot second, I thought he was trying to be my friend, and I almost replied.

But he cleared his throat and straightened his body and face into a more serious demeanor. "For the sake of all our lives on the ship, of course."

Nope, no friend here. Only more reminders of the losses my magic had caused. My dead parents, my doomed relationships, my lost career. Tears pricked behind my eyes. "I think I'm beyond help at this point."

I turned, and he said nothing as I walked away.

A couple of hours after lunch, Hannah texted me to meet her in the med bay for tea with Zola. Eager for both headache medicine and my sister's company, I left my work and headed straight there.

The double glass doors opened at my approach. The lilt of their conversation drifted into the reception area from the staff rooms beyond, and I followed the sound to find them in a long, wide room with a dozen open patient alcoves around the edges. Instead of a nurse's station, several long metal tables filled the space, some empty and some filled with supplies. Mismatched wooden china cabinets and armoires with glass doors had been conscripted from their civilian homes and lined up along the one available wall, and a narrow bookshelf in the corner was stuffed with medical books and romance novels.

"Gemma!" they exclaimed in unison.

"We waited for you." Hannah jumped up and grabbed three mugs as Zola took a tea kettle off a hot plate. The latter studied my face a fraction longer than normal. What did she see when she looked at me?

Hannah dropped tea infusers into the mugs as Zola poured. "Earl Grey alright?"

"Sure, that's fine." I slid onto a stool beside Hannah.

"I'm so glad you came with us, Gemma." Zola reached across the table and grasped my hand. "I've wanted to get to know you better for so many years, and I'm relieved you and Beck are writing up the grimoire. I don't think I can perform another spell under pressure like we did yesterday."

I tried to hide my inward cringe at the word *grimoire* while Hannah fixed mischievous eyes on me, murmuring, "You and *Beck*."

Zola's mischievous demeanor was a clear sign of her matchmaking complicity, but I ignored Hannah's implication. "You didn't seem ruffled at all," I said to Zola. "I don't know how you were so calm."

"Blame it on my balanced chakras." She laughed, holding her arms palms up on either side of her head. "Some of my notes are already in the box, but I've been writing down my other contributions to the spell systems." She grabbed a stack of papers and sat them near me. "I have a little more to go, but this is most of it."

"Thank you." I gathered the stack before me, trying to decide how to ask my question so as not to offend. "Beck mentioned that he's an eclectic witch who dabbles in...arti-something and divination. What kind of witch are you?" I asked. "I know that's not how to ask that question, but—"

"That's okay. I work with auras and energy healing."

Auras. That explains why she kept looking at me off-center. I've always been rubbish with auras, even as a teen when I was actively trying to develop my magic. I flipped through the stack of papers, seeing references to several spells interfacing with mechanical systems. "How do you do aura work on machinery?"

She smoothed her pink sweater where it hung off her dark shoulders and smiled like a cat with a canary. "Your first mistake is separating animate beings and inanimate items in your head, when the truth is that the whole universe—every element—is made of energy. Down on its most basic level, every atom is a mini-verse of spinning energy. It's the concept behind a lot of healing work, like Reiki, and if you're clever, you can do healing work on more than people."

"Energy healing, like when you helped Eyre with her eczema."

"Exactly." She scooped three teaspoons of sugar into her mug and expended a little bit of magic to set a spoon stirring on its own. "Gemma, I know we don't know each other well yet, but I'm worried about you. I can't help noticing you're carrying around a lot of negative energy in your aura."

Hannah looked between us. "Zola's the best with aura cleansing. She can make you feel so much better, Gem, maybe make you even open to loooove," she said, drawing out the word as she shimmied her shoulders.

Zola watched us over her mug as she took a sip, a gleam in her eyes.

"She's relentless," I said to Zola. "She's trying to hook me up with Beck, but it won't work." The absolute last thing I needed was to get involved with a witch while I was on my way to get my magic removed.

Zola leaned toward Hannah, smiling at me. "They *would* make such a cute couple."

"Right?" Hannah said. "The *cutest*."

I leaned my elbows on the table and rubbed my forehead with both hands. "Not you too, Zola. Can't I have one sister who's not trying to pair me up? This headache's punishment enough."

Zola popped up from the table while Hannah tried to defend her position. "I'm just saying, as someone who knows the both of you, I think it'd be a great match. Zola, don't you agree?"

Zola returned with two small bottles of medicine. "Here, take your pick. You should've told me sooner you didn't feel good."

"Thank you." I picked up the ibuprofen and downed two with my tea.

"I think he likes you," Hannah insisted. "He was acting all kinds of weird around you last night."

Zola was no help, watching me with her full lips pressed together in a barely suppressed smile. She shook her head, tassel earrings swaying, and brought her mug to her lips. "He was acting suspiciously weird. I've never seen Beck so...subdued."

"Not. Interested," I repeated, sipping on my tea again. "I've been through a lot lately, okay? And I don't have a good track record with men, and I'm gonna have to look for a new job when I get to Gaia—" I looked at Hannah. "You told her about my job?"

She nodded, and I turned to Zola. "Please don't tell Noah. I'd like to tell him myself."

"I understand," she said. "I didn't tell him, and I won't. But you look like you've had your own personal Year 2020, and I do want to help you, if you'd let me. As little or as much as you want."

"I don't know, Zola. It's really sweet of you, but I don't believe in any of that."

"I can give you some options," Zola continued, leaning back toward the table against the wall and picking up a bundle of dried leaves tied with twine.

"This is a bundle of herbs used in smoke cleansing."

I nodded, acting as if this was new information. I used to make them in high school, growing my own lavender, thyme, and peppermint in the backyard, twisting them in twine, hanging them in my room to dry.

"It's just sprigs of mugwort tied together and dried out," she said. "When it burns, it increases the amount of negative ions in the air. And even though it's a small thing, it might give you a lift. You know psychologists have proven that even a temporary lift in your mood will lead to better choices. It might give you some space to feel better." She held the bundle out to me. "Want to smell it?"

I shook my head. "That's okay."

She reached back to the table again and grabbed a wooden crate filled with carefully packaged leaf bundles. Hannah *oohed* softly and pawed through the box.

"I've got all kinds. You have to match the plant to the need. I've grown all these myself. So if you ever want to talk about what you've been through, or even tell me what you think you need, I might be able to make a better choice than mugwort." She studied the bundles, an artist selecting her brush. "Mugwort's a good all-purpose herb for smoke cleansing, don't get me wrong, but—" She turned and studied Gemma for a minute. "I've just got this feeling lavender and rosemary would be best for you. It's to inspire calmness and heart opening."

I exhaled a small laugh. "Two things I'm pretty short on. But...I don't know."

"Or maybe you'd rather a ritual bath?"

"Ooh." Hannah nodded vigorously. "She wants a ritual bath."

I shook my head. "I don't know what that is."

"It's not magic, per se, just negative ions and good intentions. I've taken a suite on Level 1, kind of above where we are now, this corner of the ship. I chose it because it has both a shower and a deep bathtub. The whole bathroom is *ti-dy*. And I'd love to set you up."

"What would I do?"

"First, you take a shower and get clean. Because a ritual bath isn't about getting clean, it's about getting *right*. Then you put goodies into the bathwater as it fills, all with good intentions." She swayed to the music of her words, opening her palms with each item on the list. "You light some candles, you pick some crystals, you cleanse yourself with smoke before you go in, and bam! You soak for thirty minutes. It can be life changing, even if you only believe the effects are psychological."

I *was* a sucker for a long, hot bath. But even though what she suggested wasn't *too* witchy, and her intentions were good, it was still too magic-adjacent. "No thank you."

She leaned back in her chair. "What is it you've got against magic? If you don't mind me asking."

I opened my mouth, took a breath. How could I explain that my magic paced inside me like a tiger in a cage, ready to pounce and devour me whole? That I once used it without reserve and with the joy and naiveté of a child, and that it turned on my family, destroying it?

"Oh Gemma, you look so sad," she said, reaching over and giving my arm a squeeze. "You don't have to tell me if you don't want to. I just ask because I don't understand." She looked at my sister. "Hannah said you got her into witchcraft."

Zola had been whittling at my wall, but that statement rolled me up tighter than a closed exhaust system, and my outward-pushing defenses went up. With them came my sharp tongue. "I don't know. I guess I just grew up."

Zola and Hannah both flinched, and I instantly regretted my words.

"I'm sorry." I reached out with both hands to grab one each of theirs. "I didn't mean to be insulting, it's just...I can't do magic. Anymore. And it upsets me to talk about it."

Hannah's face crumpled in sympathy, but Zola simply nodded, compassion glowing from her perfect complexion. "Fair enough. I have another option. Do you like aromatherapy? It's science-backed too. Scents travel up your olfactory nerve and act on your amygdala to improve your mood. I've got some good-smelling candles you might like."

Candles seemed innocuous enough, if burned properly and not en masse in an engine room. "Sure. I like things that smell good."

Zola rubbed her hands together, her emerald engagement ring flashing. "Yes! Come see my collection."

Hannah popped up too. "Can I have a candle too, Zo?"

"Of course, after you burn down and bring back the one you have now." She led us to one of the wooden cabinets and pulled the double glass doors open wide. Inside were dozens of candles, grouped by color and formed in a wide variety of containers: baby food jars, mason jars, tin cans, shot glasses, drinking glasses, and repurposed commercial candle jars.

Hannah dove right in, grabbing things and smelling them.

"How about you shop for what you want? No spells or anything on them. Just good smells and pretty colors." She left me and Hannah to peruse and went back to put the bundled leaves away.

I surveyed the selection, a myriad of colors and shapes, some even stacked in colors visible through their glass jars. A little yellow one in a baby food jar drew my attention first. It was sharp and citrusy, like a popsicle on a summer day.

"Ooh smell this one," Hannah said, holding a purple one under my nose that smelled of lavender and some sort of woodsy note.

We took candle after candle from the shelf, sniffing them, replacing them. A blue candle in a painted flowered jar caught my eye. I lifted it from the shelf and inhaled. It reminded me of a yoga studio I used to go to, when I first got to San Francisco, that always smelled so peaceful. It brought to mind a brave, happy memory of starting over.

"I'll take this one if you're sure you can spare it."

Zola put down the bandage she'd been wrapping and cocked her head. "Now you see? Your amygdala knows what you need. The blue ones are excellent: frankincense for peace, myrrh for clarity, and palo santo—sustainably harvested by Summer's extended family in Ecuador and included with her blessing—helps you heal from emotional pain."

I inhaled it again, and I felt a soft peace settle onto my shoulders like a cozy shawl.

"Those sound like just what I need. Thanks, Zola."

"Anytime."

Chapter 6

The Palm of a Witch

A week after takeoff, my headache was nearly gone, and I'd finished organizing the box of papers according to spell. I was even almost finished copying them over into my notebook, leaving spaces for the components that weren't in the box or that I couldn't divine by looking at the physical spells themselves.

The ship was running smoothly, and the smile-less man and I were minding our own business, both in and out of the engine room. He hadn't mentioned my magic since the day I'd asked him to get the model number off the evaporator. And even though he held the secret of my magic in his hands, he wasn't holding it *over* me. He was quick to offer help if he saw me struggling, and once or twice he walked past me to drop just the tool I needed on my worktable.

Was I starting to see him less as an adversary and *maybe* more as a potential ally? My head said I should avoid him because of what he knew, but I was drawn to him. I couldn't deny that my magic quieted when he was near. His presence calmed me, and his offer grew more tempting with every day that passed.

Even though the past week had been uneventful, and it was easier to contain my magic when life was even-keeled, the pressure of it built deep in my bones. During the day I kept my mind busy enough to quell my magic's siren song. But almost every night I'd wake up sweating from a nightmare that I'd blasted a hole in the side of the ship or wrecked the engine room, spiraling all of us into the abyss of space. I'd wake up with my magic practically crawling out of my skin, with such an unbearable restlessness that I'd throw my running shoes on and do laps around level B1 where I didn't think I'd disturb anyone.

I didn't know what haunted Beck, but on my middle-of-the-night runs I'd often see him through the window of the ship's gym, lifting weights or bare chested on the salmon ladder. I'm not too proud to admit that I went past the gym twice that night.

Sitting at the drafting table this morning, I almost felt as if things were normal, and that I wasn't hurtling through space on a deathtrap with barely contained, destructive magic in my body. This pressure spell had taken me days to transcribe and pull together, but I almost had the whole thing written down—

An alarm blared, and Beck sprinted past me to an open terminal on the wall, typing and tapping his way through the ship's systems.

I pushed my chair out and jogged up to him. "What's wrong?"

"Feed system on the antimatter drive." He slammed the terminal shut. "Help me?"

I shut the drive down, and he started taking apart the feed assembly.

"Here." He passed me an old rag and held another beneath the panel, pulling it open. When he pulled a gasket out, sludgy gunk and oil glopped out onto the floor. "Damn filter must be busted. I hope we have another one."

"I saw a screen filter in a box earlier," I said, sprinting down to the work area. I hunted through boxes and shelves, grabbed the filter, and ran back.

He was already cleaning off the second gasket, so I pulled the pieces of the old filter out, the slimy mess getting all over my hands. Lucky I'd worn leggings and a T-shirt today instead of something nice. After cleaning out the assembly the best I could, I slid the new filter in.

"It isn't quite right, but it's better than nothing," I said. "We'll just have to remember to clean it out every few days."

"Whatever works. We can figure out a spell backup for the filter if we need it."

"We won't need it," I said firmly, hastily wiping my hands off on a rag and switching the alarm off on the panel.

He closed up the assembly, locking each of the two closures with a zipdriver. "That ought to do it. Fire it up."

I reset the parameters and switched the drive back on. He stood back, his hands and shirt covered in gunk, and I held my breath.

The drive lumbered back into play, whirring smoothly. Beck breathed out heavily. "Bam," he said, sticking his fist out at me.

I looked at it in surprise, and he smiled at me, an honest-to-God smile. So he could form one with his face muscles after all. It was casually devastating. It lit his whole face and the room too. Right now, telescopes on Gaia were mistaking it for a supernova.

Damn it all, he was far too good looking to be allowed.

"C'mon, Gemma," he said, "don't leave me hangin'."

I bumped his fist, messy hand to messy hand, and he laughed. An honest-to-God laugh, and no one else was even around. It made me crack a smile.

Eyre's voice crackled across the intercom into the engine room. "Summer wants to know if the drive's back up."

Beck jogged over to the wall and pressed the response. "Yep! Gemma's got us back on track. We're good to go."

"Thanks, guys!"

He followed me to the sink. "We made a pretty good team back there," he said.

I had to look up while I scrubbed my hands to make sure he was talking to me. "Yeah, I guess." This was the friendliest he'd ever been. If Hannah or Zola told him something about acting weird, they were both going on my shit list.

"Look," I said, "I know Hannah has us working together for the next couple of months, but it's okay. You don't have to pretend to like me."

"What do you mean?" he asked, stopping with his hand halfway to the pumice soap I'd just put down. "I like you. You think I don't like you?"

Great. Now I made it weird. "I've just never seen you smile much before." I shrugged, not daring to look at him. "At least not at me."

His shoulders deflated as he picked up the soap and started scrubbing his hands. I regretted saying anything. Leave it to me to make an awkward situation way more awkward. And yet I pressed onward.

"I just figured you either thought I didn't know what I was doing, or you were still mad about the candles or the window. Or...I don't know." A rebellious corner of my lip tugged upwards. "Maybe smiling wasn't covered in any of the many degrees you have."

He paused, grabbing the bottom hem of his dirty T-shirt and narrowing his eyes at me, a smile playing about his lips. "Are you teasing me, Gemma Abadie?"

I shrugged. "Maybe."

He chuckled, his many large muscles rippling as he pulled off his dirty shirt and tossed it into a hamper. Heat rose into my face. I'd never seen a body like that up close and in person, only in movies and magazines.

"I'm sorry if I didn't make you feel welcome," he said. "And I've never doubted your capability. I guess I was just nervous about meeting you."

I remembered what Hannah'd said about him seeing my photograph, then looked up and caught the full display of his muscular chest as he dried his hands on a towel, a few tattoos winding down his arms. Those two thoughts jangled against my suddenly pounding heart. I swallowed hard and averted my eyes.

"That's okay." I busied myself with polishing the extra bits of grease from my nails with a rag.

"Was I rude to you?" he asked, worry coating his words.

"No, not at all. You were really sweet, offering me food, offering me help. Just not...smiley."

"I *am* sorry. I don't want you to think I don't like you. Because I do. Did you ever hear that if you meet someone and you like them straight off, even when you don't know them yet, it means your auras are harmonious? But if you instantly dislike them, and you can't put your finger on why, it means that your auras create static together?"

"Sounds familiar." I smirked. His aura was a magnet to me.

"I can't see auras for shit, but I feel them very acutely. Some people? *Beaucoup* static."

I hadn't heard anyone throw the French word for *a lot* into casual conversation since before I left for California. His voice always transported me right back home.

"You?" he continued. "No static."

"Well I guess that's good, since we'll be working together so much."

"Yeah, and we're both the odd ones out, with everybody else paired up on or off the ship." He stepped around me and picked a clean white T-shirt from the top of a stack of them, shaking it out and stretching it up over his head. His stomach muscles were halfway to mesmerizing me when he pulled his fresh shirt down. "At least I thought. What about you?"

I snapped my eyes up to his face, my heart pounding like the lecherous, guilty human I was. Did he just ask me if I liked him? Did he catch me checking out his abs?

"Oh, um, I suck at auras too," I said.

"No." He didn't look at me as he cleaned up the sink area. "I meant, are you seeing anybody? I haven't heard you talk about a girlfriend or boyfriend. Hannah didn't say you were."

My skin prickled with the pleasure of his interest, and I tried to keep a neutral smile. "You throw me a few smiles, and you get cheeky all of a sudden. How about I go back to the spell box, and we can each mind our own business?"

He laughed. "That works. Listen, you wanted to know about sigils and crystals. I asked Summer and Eyre to sit with you tonight on the Star Deck to go through things for the grimoire."

I made a "sounds good" face at him and went back to the spell box. But I smiled all the way there.

"Hannah did *not* want to jump off the cliff with me," Summer said, her deep brown eyes glimmering with happy memories in the low light of the Star Deck after dinner. Summer's aura—if I even believed in that stuff—was a cozy blanket in a cold world. I was almost glad Eyre was running late to our meeting so I could spend this time getting to know her.

"She agreed to hike up to the falls, she was happy to watch the rest of us jump, but *no way* was she going to do it herself. But when we got up there—and I don't even know what changed her mind—she jumped right off after Beck and Noah." She laughed, continuing the story. "After, she said we were right. It was amazing! The churning waters break your fall."

She looked down and back up. "While I have you, I wanted to tell you how much I love your sister." She smiled soppily, stars in her eyes. "Hannah's my forever," she said, pressing her hands to her heart. "It'd mean the world to me if you and I could be close too."

I smiled and hugged her. "I would love that."

The elevator dinged. Footsteps mingled with voices approached us. Eyre's voice. And Beck's? I sat up straighter and adjusted my hair. He hadn't said he was coming.

They walked up, each holding a little mismatched ceramic bowl with a spoon in either hand.

"We thought ice cream would make this a party," Beck said, his smile settling on me like warm sunlight. I couldn't help but smile back.

"Zohmygod," Summer exclaimed, bouncing on her cushion as she reached up for the bowl Eyre offered her. "Are those chunks of chocolate chip cookie dough?"

"For sure." Eyre settled onto the rug on my right with a wink and a grin at me. I had to admire her. I thought I was careful with my appearance, but even I'd resorted to leisure wear on the trip. Not Eyre. Every day she dressed like *Vogue Witch* was coming for a photoshoot. Tonight, she wore a corset top that hugged her figure and a long, black velvet skirt, her makeup perfect.

Beck sat close to me, his wet hair pulled into a messy bun. "When's the last time you ate real ice cream?" he asked, handing me a bowl.

"A really long time," I breathed, taking it carefully from him like the priceless work of art it was. I dug my spoon in and took a bite. The chocolate and vanilla ice cream was stuffed with brownie pieces and chunks of cookie dough. I forgot all my manners and spoke with my mouth full. "This is phenomenal. Thank you."

"Eyre makes the best ice cream," Summer said.

I couldn't disagree. I savored several chilly, delectable bites, but still no one spoke. Maybe they were waiting for me?

"So I won't keep you all too late," I said, balancing my ice cream bowl while I pulled out my notebook. "I just want to know more about your contributions to a few key spells around the ship."

"We mainly worked on sigils and crystals," Eyre said, waving a red-tipped finger between herself and Summer, who was already almost scraping the bottom of her bowl.

"We collaborated on the sigils with Beck. They're the primary function by which the spells tie into the machinery. And crystals are Eyre's thing."

I'd had a fondness for working out sigils when I was a teenager. There may have been infinite ways to make the symbols that focused magic, held spells together, but the ones I'd found in the box didn't look anything like what I used to make.

"My sister Portia helped us kickstart the forest not long after we got the ship," Eyre continued. "She's a very talented green witch, which is funny, considering her aversion to putting down roots."

Summer gave Eyre a sad smile. "Kickstarted our forest, and then went dark again. Do you think she and Juliet already left for Gaia?"

"Who knows." Eyre rolled her eyes, but her expression was pained. "I guess she'll deign to contact me again, one day. But I do miss my niece."

The silence after Eyre's family drama reveal was even more awkward than the ice-cream-eating silence. "Can you tell me more about the sigils?" I asked. "I found some sketches in the box, but they didn't all match up to spells I could find on the ship."

Eyre pulled out a tablet. "So a sigil is a line drawing, basically," she said, misinterpreting my question as complete ignorance. I wasn't going to let her think otherwise.

She tapped at her screen until she got to a canvas. "But it carries a lot more meaning behind it. They're usually short phrases, or intentions, that when activated by magic, make something come into being."

"Or repel something," Summer cut in, "whatever your desire."

"Our coven's settled on one main way to draw them that works best for us." Eyre unhooked a stylus from the tablet and began writing on the screen.

"So if you wanted to manifest more joy into your life, you might write out 'I AM JOYFUL' in capital letters." She illustrated her process with artful strokes. "Then you scratch out all the vowels and break the remaining letters into pieces, making a bank of shapes to draw from." She drew lines about the same sizes as the letters: four vertical, four slanted, four horizontal lines, and one gracefully curved J shape. "Once you have those broken out, you arrange them in a manner that's aesthetically pleasing to you."

Her stylus flashed as she made a fanciful symbol from the components, finishing with something that looked a little like a pyramid and a little like a W. "Then if you want to embellish it with a strategic rune or two to give it an extra oomph, like a couple of *wunjo*"—she drew an angular P shape to either end of the symbol—"that can strengthen it too."

"You can draw personal sigils on your body with makeup or even a marker," Summer said, "or write them on paper and burn them."

Beck held up a finger. "My personal favorite."

The image of Beck blowing onto the bay leaf blazed through my mind and sent a shiver across my skin. I tried not to look at him and concentrated on Eyre's drawing.

"Or, like we've done, you can just paint 'em and leave 'em," Summer said, "and activate them with spellwork. We worked with Beck to determine what shapes might actively interface with the machinery. Then we combined my knowledge of geometry and Eyre's artistic talents to select the best medium, color, and placement for each of them."

I thought about the blue sigil in the engine room. "Would you draw the ones you used in the spells in my notebook? I don't think I could recreate them properly. And shouldn't we keep track of the original phrases or intentions?"

Eyre nodded. "That's a great idea. I have all the original paper sketches. I can bring them to you to put in the grimoire."

"Thank you." At Eyre's use of the word *grimoire*, I glanced at Beck, and he wiggled his eyebrows mischievously at me.

"I see the name Beck gave this thing is catching," I said.

Eyre shrugged. "He isn't wrong. *The Interstellar Grimoire* is pretty badass."

Beck leaned near me, and I caught a waft of woodsy soap. "When Eyre gives you those sketches, I can write up anything that needs to be captured about how they intersect with the machinery."

"Thanks," I said, looking to Eyre to try and focus on something other than him sitting next to me. "Perfect. And the crystals?"

"The crystals prime their surrounding environments into the most advantageous atmosphere for the spells to work," Eyre said. "I charged every crystal on the ship under the last full moon, but they all need to be recharged periodically. Depending on whether they're fixed or moveable, I recharge them by laying them in the running water in the forest, or smoke cleansing, or singing bowl, or even my own magic."

"Eyre's got this super cool approach to magic. She likes cascading systems. Like you set up one spell to make another thing naturally happen, and that sets off the thing you actually wanted to happen. Like the crystal environments."

Eyre shrugged. "I find the elements work best when they think it's their idea, so I set things up and let them all roll downhill."

"Roll downhill," Beck repeated, laughing and pushing his palm down away from him, mimicking going downhill, making Eyre laugh too. "She's been like that ever since I've known her. I've never known such a chill toddler."

"As if you were such an old man when we met. You couldn't have been any more than what, six?"

"I didn't realize y'all've known each other that long," I said.

"My family and Beck's go way back in the New Orleans witching community. I moved in with the rest of the coven when my grand-mère passed away a few years ago."

"I'm so sorry," I murmured.

Beck gave Eyre a sad smile. "I miss Grand-mère." To me, he said, "I studied under her for a while. I've been staying with the coven for a couple of years, since my parents went to Gaia."

The silence lengthened just long enough for me to feel awkward. So not very long. "So this might be a stupid question, but how do you activate your spells? What makes them...work?"

"*We* do." Summer shrugged. She waved her hand across her empty ice cream bowl, and it and the spoon lifted into the air, circled around each other, then set back down.

I edged away from the display of magic, remembering the days when I, too, made things move around in my room.

Beck leaned back onto a floor pillow. "Depending on the spell, it might be our own magic that activates it, either individually or in some combination. Some are potion activated, some require intricately worded spells. You'll have to see your sister for those. Some are elemental."

"Fire, earth, water, air, spirit," Summer explained.

"It must've taken a long time to figure out how to make some of these spells work. You couldn't find the parts you needed?"

"Or couldn't afford them. My uncle giving us the ship and the junkyard was a huge boon. We replaced and repaired everything we could, raised money selling things we didn't need. But ultimately, when the whole planet's evacuating, there's just not enough to go around. Then the surprise launch slot." She shook her head. "That was *crazy*."

Beck shrugged. "Some of the parts we did have, other people needed worse. If we could figure out how to make do with magic when they couldn't, we let 'em have it. Ya gotta help one another, you know?"

I nodded silently. I did know.

It was getting late, and Beck's eyes were bleary, as if he might fall asleep any minute. I knew what my trouble sleeping was. What was his?

"Thank you. I think I have enough to go on for a bit more, until Eyre brings me the sketches. If y'all think of anything else I need to know, send it my way."

Eyre picked up the dirty ice cream bowls and gracefully got to her feet. "Anytime! I'll grab these. See y'all tomorrow."

"Night," we chorused.

Summer stood, jerking her thumb toward the bridge. "I'm going to see my lady love on the bridge before I go to bed. G'night!"

Beck yawned and arched his back over a pouf, stretching so wide his shirt lifted over his belly. Somebody needed to get this man longer shirts because I didn't need to be wanting all of that.

He pulled his shirt down and got up. "C'mon. I'll walk you home," he said, leaning toward me with his hands outstretched. I let him pull me to my feet and walked with him to the central elevator.

He pressed the down button. "So Gemma. Do we have an accord?"

I glanced up to see him side-smiling at me.

"I don't know. You snuck condition one past me. I thought you said you could do without it?"

He belly laughed, pressing a hand to his chest. I'd never seen a man laugh like that, unfettered and uncaring what he looked like. Watching Beck laugh made me laugh.

"Yeah, I decided it was too awesome to give up on. Figured if I snuck it past you, you maybe wouldn't mind?" He rocked from his heels to his toes and glanced back over either shoulder. A co-conspirator checking for eavesdroppers. "Where are we on the second condition?" he asked quietly. "I've been good. I haven't asked you in almost a *whole week.*"

The elevator doors opened, and he followed me in, saying nothing further as the elevator descended. It was ridiculous of me to pretend that he hadn't seen me do magic in the pressure room, ridiculous to push away an offer to quell the one thing I'd never been able to tame myself, especially because it endangered everyone on the ship.

I'd thought I was doing a good job of pushing all my emotions into the corners of myself, thinking that would prevent my magic from exploding out at all the wrong moments. But not only was it not working, as I thought back to my most recent outbursts of power, they were also getting more and more destructive. Until I got to Gaia and had my magic taken away, it might be best to get help controlling it.

"I've been thinking about it," I admitted when the elevator doors opened on my floor. I walked out and pressed my hand against the elevator doors to keep them open. He still stood to the back of the elevator. "You coming?"

He pushed off the back wall and followed me out and around the corner to my door. I fumbled with the key around my neck, trying to get inside my room before anyone overheard us. I held the door open, and he followed me in, shutting the door behind us. I tossed my key on the table on my way to the couch.

He made a soft noise and rubbed at the spot on the table where my key had hit. "Are you being good to my table?" he asked.

"*Your* table? I thought you built it for me because you gazed into your crystal ball and knew I'd need one?"

He chuckled. "I did. But I didn't use a crystal ball." He sat a little ways away on the couch and pursed his lips, studied me for a minute.

"Why are you looking at me in that tone of voice?"

He shrugged. "I was wondering if you'd let me read your palm."

I made a face that I hoped matched my playful mockery. "Like some Fat City vagrant?"

He scratched his beard, which wasn't as scruffy looking since he'd trimmed it a couple of days ago, and sat up straighter on the sofa. A little closer. "I probably look like one." He grabbed a purple throw from the back of the sofa and laid it over his head like a veil.

I snorted. He looked ridiculous, and this was probably just a scheme to hold my hand. But I didn't call him out on it. Except for his intelligence, he was definitely not the kind of guy I would have ever gone for before. He was less captain of the soccer team and more harum-scarum rock god. Less polished and more real. Maybe that was a good thing.

"Now then," he said in an approximation of an old woman's voice, "can I read yer palm, young lady? It's free today, but only for women with brown eyes."

"Oh!" I exclaimed. "In that case, a bargain!" I stretched out the hand closest to him.

"Now tell me, child, are you left-handed?"

I smirked. "You're a terrible palm reader. I'm right-handed."

"Ah." He placed my hand carefully on my bent knee and took my right one instead. "We have a skeptic. That's alright. I'll win you over, dearie." He turned my palm up and held it toward the light.

He peered intensely at my hand and ran a finger down the center of my palm to my wrist. I took a breath, trying to ignore the shiver that went through me at his light touch.

"Your fate line..." he said, turning my hand this way and that in the scarce light, "...is broken."

I laughed an unfunny laugh. "That seems about right."

He shook his head and resumed in his normal voice. "It's not a bad thing. It usually means a career change, a change in life direction. Some kinda change. Ooh—" He paused, looking up through his long lashes. "I hate to tell you this."

I scrunched up my face. "Oh God. What?"

He looked down, licked his lips, and looked back up. "This is the palm of a witch."

I shook my head. "If you're trying to get my buy-in, you're not gonna get it."

"No, really. Look." He pointed to the base of my pinky. "Over a dozen lines. It's a Samaritan sign. You're a great healer."

I narrowed my eyes. I *did* used to do healing magic. Little things, like zits and scrapes. Some bigger things, too, like a twisted ankle from volleyball. Hannah must've told him. I leaned in closer to him, peering at my palm.

"Psychic cross under your ring finger—*somebody's* gonna be lucky in love." He grinned, and my heart sped up. "One under your index finger too. Ever consider teaching?"

It was hard to return his gaze with my brain caught on the words *lucky in love*. He really sucked at palm reading. I shook my head to answer him.

He dragged his fingertip from my ring finger to the center of my palm. "You've got a mystic cross. Did your magic come in at a young age?"

"I was twelve. Is that young?"

He nodded. "A lot of people don't get theirs until they're thirteen, if not older. And ooh, this is rare. Your life line meets up with three bracelets on your wrist. That indicates a long, healthy life, and a lot of happiness."

"When's that supposed to start?" I scoffed.

He smirked and released my hand. Sitting back and resting his elbow on the back of the sofa, he sat his chin on his hand. I pulled my own hand back awkwardly into my lap. His green eyes were bright, and he spoke gently. "You know, having magic is more of a blessing than a curse. Is there a reason why you're trying to shut it out?"

I nodded but didn't answer.

"That's okay. You don't have to tell me. But can I at least try to help you?"

I tucked a foot up and peered down at my hands, at the lines at the base of my pinky that supposedly proved I'm a witch. "I can't control it," I said quietly, willing the tears not to come. They came anyway, slipping down my face. I wiped them away. "I'm sorry I put us all in danger. I didn't mean to."

"I know," he said. "It's alright. We're all okay."

I risked looking up at him. His eyes were soft as he waited for me to go on. He genuinely meant what he was saying. The open kindness on his face cracked my shell open.

"I've tried to hold it in, honestly I have. For years. But it keeps breaking out of me at all the wrong times. I do okay when things are going okay. When I'm calm. But if I'm scared, or angry, or upset—really any strong emotion—it barrels out of me." I took a deep, shaky breath. "If you can help me control it and keep the ship safe, I should let you. Do you really think you can? For the sake of the ship?" I added hastily.

His smile was almost fond. "Does bionic electro-plasma resynchronize erbium microfilament?"

I laughed through my tears. "Yes. Yes it does."

"But just so we're clear," he said, sitting up and taking on a more serious tone, "the only way I know to help you isn't by getting you to suppress it. Tell me if I'm wrong. I definitely don't know all the answers." He tilted his head. "You seem like you just want it to go away."

I looked down, nodding, crunching my face up against the tears falling faster.

"I'm sorry. I just don't think—" He breathed out heavily. "Trying to subdue it is like trying to shove down all your feelings. Or mixing dry ice and water in a closed container. It's gonna explode out."

I cried harder at his apt description. The harder I pushed it down, the wilder it came back up.

"Aww, Gemma," he said, scooting closer and laying his hand briefly on my forearm. He jumped up and came back with a tissue box, handing it to me and continuing softly. "I think maybe that's why you're having so much trouble. From what I know about it, the only real way to control magic is to use it. If you focus it in ways you want it to work, and don't let it build up unspent, it won't come barreling out when you don't want it to."

It was on the tip of my tongue to tell him about Madam Indigo. But no, she warned me the process might be painful, and I didn't want him to try and talk me out of it, or even worse, tell Hannah about it, who'd tell Noah and anybody else who'd listen.

"I really don't want to use it," I cried. "Isn't there anything else we can do?"

He bit his lip, frowning empathetically and rubbing his upper arms like he didn't know what to do with himself. "I don't think so, but maybe we'll come across something. I hate that you're so sad, Gemma, I just wanna hug ya," he said. "Can I hug you?"

I nodded, still crying, and he stretched his broad arms around me, resting his chin on the top of my head. He murmured softly, "Hey, it'll be okay. I'll help you. I promise."

I leaned against his chest, and the persistent pressure of my magic eased. Gradually, my sobbing calmed, my tears lessened. Being in his arms made me feel protected. Cared for, even, like when I was a child, and my mother would rock me to sleep. I couldn't think about what that meant, that being near this witchy man who finally started smiling at me brought me so much comfort. Even a few days before, I couldn't have imagined talking so honestly to anyone about my magic, especially him.

Did I overshare? Embarrassment washed through me, and I pulled away. His shirt was wet where my face had been. "I'm sorry," I said, avoiding his eyes. I was such a pain, such a burden. Such an embarrassment.

"Sorry for what? You don't need to be sorry for anything."

"Sorry for being such a mess. You would've had a peaceful trip if I hadn't been here."

"Nah." He chuckled. "It would've been boring. I'm glad you're here."

His smile was genuine, and warm, and I ducked my head, feeling even more embarrassed and not knowing why. "Thank you." I pulled out another tissue and cleaned up my face. "Okay. I'll accept your help. But can we start in the morning?"

"Of course! Whatever you want." He yawned. "It *is* gettin' late. I'd better go check the antimatter drive before I go to bed. Probably shouldn't have bothered with the shower." He stood up but narrowed his eyes at me. "You good?"

I nodded. "I'm okay."

He patted my head twice on his way out the door. "Sleep tight."

I missed him the second the door closed.

Chapter 7

A Small Grace

After lunch, Beck and I sat cross-legged on the rug beside his hammock, facing each other with a spare candle sitting on the floor between us. The engine room purred and hummed around us.

"I had trouble controlling my magic too, when I was thirteen," he said. "But my grandpa worked with me to harness it. Lighting a candle by blowing on the wick requires a lot of focus, which makes it good practice."

He held the candle in front of his lips and blew as if trying to snuff out a candle. Instead, the flame leapt to life out of nothing, and his minty breath wafted my way.

"Amazing." No less miraculous than the first day I'd seen it.

He blew it out and pinched the wick. "Here, you try."

I took the candle from him, my fingers grazing his. The black wick was an island in a little pool of wax. Dead and lifeless. No way could I coax a fire from it. I looked at him doubtfully.

"Ok, position it right here." He put his hands around mine and brought the candle up so that it was in front of my lips. "And close your eyes. Reach in and grab onto the first bit of magic you find."

I complied, finding it hard to concentrate beyond his hands over mine. But once I went looking for my magic, it sprang right up like it had been expecting me. I bit my lip, trying to keep it in check.

"Don't bite your lip," he gently admonished. "You wanna channel it, not choke it off. Envision this candle, show your magic in your mind's eye that you want it to light the wick, only the wick, and when you're ready, open your eyes and blow out. Let your magic ride on your breath to accomplish your task."

My magic danced inside of me, a dog eager to grab a treat from its mistress's hand. I cleared my mind, focusing on the image of fire lighting a candle, opened my eyes, and blew.

A bright orange flame was born on the wick, but it flickered and went out. Its ghost curled into the air between us.

My shoulders slumped, but Beck whooped.

"I saw it! It almost caught. I'm impressed. It took me a whole day to do what you just did."

I relaxed a little, pleased that he was pleased with my efforts.

"Okay, now try it one more time," he said, not lowering his hands. "Then we'll try to replace the crocheted net with that stuff you found yesterday. You don't want to try too long in one sitting. It can be frustrating, and you have a much better chance of it all going sideways."

"Wait, there's no danger I'm going to set you on fire, is there?"

"Nah, you won't. Try again."

But now that I'd thought of setting him on fire, I was too nervous, and my second attempt produced even less than the first. He patted my hands before taking his away.

"That's absolutely alright. It's not a linear process. Let's go see if we can fix the life support system."

The past two days had been a mix of working to negate the need for the crocheted netting and sitting down to try again on the candle. Even though I was never able to even repeat my first small victory of the ember, Beck neither lost patience nor faith in me. But we'd been at it so long tonight that I was starting to lose my cool.

"I can't do it, Beck, I just can't." I rubbed my forehead.

"It's okay. Maybe I've been trying to get you to focus on the wrong thing. What if your magic doesn't work this way?"

I folded my arms tightly across my chest and bent in on myself. "The thought of forging out in a new and equally fruitless direction makes me sick to my stomach."

He leaned forward, catching my eye. "But we can't get to where we need to go if we're going the wrong way. What kind of magic did you do when you were first learning?"

I sighed, thinking back. "I don't know. Um...I used to move things with my mind. I dabbled a little in sigils. I had a tarot deck."

He nodded, pleased. "Divination."

"I also used to...you know, I was pretty good at healing."

He cocked his head. "Still think I'm bad at palm reading? What did you heal?"

I smirked. "Small things. Cuts, scrapes—I was the only girl in high school who never had a breakout."

"So you'd heal anything that came along back to perfect health?"

"You're making a lot out of it, but kind of," I said through a yawn.

"So what if we—"

"Please, not tonight. I can barely keep my eyes open, and I just feel like screaming."

He rubbed his beard and glanced at the clock. "Tell you what, lemme think about your healing magic, but I don't want to send you off to bed all aggravated. Hey, you wanna see my favorite place on the ship?"

I loved how his face lit up whenever he was excited about something. I nodded.

"Come on. Let me show you." He got to his feet and started out the door, crooking his finger at me to follow.

I went with him into the elevator and all the way up to the mezzanine of the Star Deck. A tarp stretched across the pool, filled as a reservoir for laundry and sanitation and not for swimming. He walked me past it to the diving platforms, a higher and lower one set at one end of the pool. I hadn't paid attention to the higher one before, but now I noticed it was blocked off at the diving end with metal bars and hemmed in on three sides with wood and rugs.

At the top, the entire platform—about five by eight feet—had been cozied up with rugs, blankets, and pillows. He walked a few steps onto it then crawled down into the area, flopping on his back amongst the soft things. I had to hand it to these witches, they didn't just dabble in comfort, they made it a high priority.

He patted the rug beside him. "Come see."

I hesitated a second. Where did he think this was going? I lay a body's width away from him, but he didn't even turn toward me. His hands clasped on his belly, he gazed out of the overhead window into the dark wilderness of stars.

"You ever study astronomy?"

"Not really. Only the extreme basics I needed to work on ships."

"Well we're just over a week into FTL travel, and it's so hard to know which star is what without a detailed star map, but look over there." He pointed to a spot on his far right. A nebula shimmered in beautiful, vivid brightness like the eye of a god. "That one's a collapsing star. You can tell by the concentric shape of it. But just look at it, Gem. Red dwarfs, white stars, there's a blank space over there, maybe a supervoid"

"What's a supervoid?" Him using my family's nickname for me was...charming.

"They form when a bunch of smaller voids coalesce together, like soap bubbles. Or it could be an advanced civilization that's cloaking its stars in Dyson shells, mining them for energy."

I turned my head to him. His eyes were lit up, roving all over the great beyond.

"It blows my mind that we haven't encountered another civilization by now. Especially when we were looking for Gaia. No way we're all alone out here."

Eyelids heavy, I gazed out, looking for the beauties he described. Listening to his warm voice ebb and flow, the music of him sharing what he loved the most, with me.

He pointed suddenly. "Ooh, look at that emission nebula! Did you know there's a nebula close to the middle of our galaxy that tastes like raspberries and smells like rum?"

"Huh. So that's where Raspberry Nebula Soda gets its name."

"That's exactly where. It's an ethyl formate gas cloud, mostly. You know, everyone always thinks about the stars and how their alignments affect you, but so few people ever work with the influence of nebulas. That's my mom's special interest. She's been working with the Witches'

Interstellar Astrological Association, WISTAA, to chart the stars, work out what new influences we'll have because all the zodiac constellations will be different. What will our children be born into? Will our old alignments still affect those of us born on Earth?

"And you have to think about the movement of the other six planets in the new system. See the Helix Nebula was in Aquarius. That's me. They call it the Eye of God, or the Eye of Sauron if you're into the *Lord of the Rings*."

"I always wanted to be an elf, but I've come to accept I'm a hobbit at heart."

He laughed. "I'm totally the same. They say that nebula's what makes some Aquarians adept at divination. And do you know what's in the middle of Sagittarius? Sagittarius A, a massive black hole at the center of our galaxy."

I spoke through a yawn. "I'd hate to know what that's supposed to mean about me."

"Nah, there's nothing more magnetic than a black hole. Nothing can escape it, although it does spit things out from time to time. You know what *else* is in Sagittarius?" He barely paused to take a breath, his voice dripping with awe. "The Lagoon Nebula. Right on the archer's bow. At least, it was on Earth."

"I'm very impressed with your knowledge of space...stuff. Were you interested in it all your life?"

"When I was a kid, I wanted to be an astronaut."

"You seem like the kind of man who could've been an astronaut if you wanted to. What changed your mind?"

He still smiled, but his eyes grew guarded. He looked into the depths of space above our heads. "Nah, you're gonna laugh at me."

"What? No, I won't. I promise."

He bit his lip and studied my face. "I hate being in space. It's fucking terrifying."

I shifted my whole torso to fully look at him, but I didn't laugh. "Really?"

"Yeah." He winced, looking back at the stars. "I found out when I went to Summer in Space camp. It was everything I thought I wanted. But when I got up there, out here"—he waved his hand across the windows, gesturing at the universe beyond our ship—"surrounded by the vast nothingness, I couldn't handle it. I was terrified. When the panic attacks got too bad, I almost left early, but the counselors were awesome. They helped me get through the summer. I had so many opportunities to teach other people that summer, and I realized that's what I was meant to do. The anthropology degree's for fun, but I plan to teach astronomy."

I studied him, still surprised at his revelation. So that's why he wasn't sleeping.

He turned to me, eyes guarded. "You want to laugh, don't you?"

I laid flat on my back. "Not at all. I'm just thinking that this must be hard for you, this journey." And that I'd never known a man who'd have admitted something like that to anybody.

He rubbed his eyes. "I've barely been sleeping, and I have to meditate a lot so I'm not screaming in fear all of the time. Spending time in the gym helps. And I don't think I could make it if I didn't have the forest."

It was a proven fact that humans went a little crazy in space without something green and growing to be around, hence the potted trees in the lobby and the little devil's ivy in my room. Maybe I should go visit the forest on B1. I hadn't spent more than thirty minutes in there harvesting tomatoes with Hannah one day last week.

He spoke after a while, still gazing at the stars. "You're helping a lot too, you know."

"Me?" My cheeks heated, and a buzz of anticipation fluttered in my belly.

"Yeah." He raised his hand from his stomach, holding it open with his elbow resting on the rug.

I considered for a few heartbeats. His face was hopeful, on the verge of a smile, and lit with an honest vulnerability. He was, frankly, irresistible.

I lifted my hand from my belly toward him, and he scooped it into his larger one, intertwining his fingers with mine and dropping it to his side with a satisfied sigh.

He didn't rub my fingers or take any other actions. He just seemed to need the comfort of human touch, and that was something I was happy to provide and even take in return. A small grace I hadn't expected to find on this ship, or in him when we first met.

"We'll all get through it together," he said, as if reassuring himself. He closed his eyes and took a deep breath.

I squeezed his hand once. "Yeah. Together."

We were silent for a few moments. Vulnerability in a man was more attractive than I'd realized. I'd been so closed up with him, but he may as well know all my secrets.

"You asked me about my plush ride offworld with work," I started. "I didn't get a leave of absence. Actually, I'll be lucky if they don't have people waiting to arrest me when we land."

He furrowed his brow and turned to me, looking both confused and slightly alarmed.

"And I don't exactly work there anymore." I took a deep breath and explained what happened in my boss's office the morning I left San Francisco. The truth about it. As I spoke, his features expanded more and more in outrage. I ended my story with, "But you can't tell anybody."

"So that asshole assaulted you?"

"That's what you're taking away from it?" Protective male vengeance glimmered in his eyes, and I didn't hate it. "He didn't assault me. I wanted to kiss him. But instead, I wrecked his office and exposed him to the toxic San Francisco air. Busted a glass door, or two. I'm not looking forward to dealing with that when I get to Gaia."

He turned back to the windows overhead. "Sounds like he had it coming. You were his employee, and he shouldn't have come on to you."

"He's really a great guy, and his attention wasn't unwelcome. And it was flattering to have the company heir interested in me. He's tall, and cute, and smart. My work friend, Imani, never understood why I didn't seem interested."

"I'm just guessing here, but I'm thinking it's because he was a dick?"

I smiled but ignored him. "Evander was the kind of guy my parents would've chosen for me. A wealthy scientist whose father was at the top of every circle: social, business, academic. Why wouldn't I be interested?"

"Because he's a predatory dick," he stated flatly.

"Because I don't date," I blurted, watching his face for a reaction.

He nodded, but his face remained impassive. "Why's that?"

God this was embarrassing, but I was the one who'd opened this door.

"I used to. I want to. But the longer I've been away from home, the more anxious I am, the worse my magic busts out at—" I paused, struggling with how to put this delicately. "*Really* inappropriate times. I haven't been on a date in years."

He nodded, still impassive. "You mean during sex."

My whole body cringed, and my hand in his grew sweaty. "Yeah, that's definitely...one of the times. Yep." I fixed my eyes on space. "Maybe you can help me with that too?"

He lowered his eyebrows with a bemused sideways smile. "What exactly are you asking me for, Gemma?"

Heat shot up my face. "I meant by helping with my magic." Could I crawl into a deep, hidden compartment of the ship? Jump out of an airlock?

He laughed. "Yeah, I can help. Like I said, when you're using your magic in small ways, it doesn't build up and bust out all at once in ways you don't want it to." He blinked and half shrugged, mischief all over his face. "Although magic during sex can be fun."

The curve of his smile sent a visceral, desirous shiver through me. What was he thinking about over there? Because breaking things did *not* sound sexy to me, but the sudden throb between my legs wanted him to show me.

My hand in his felt slippery. He held it loosely, and I could've taken it back if I wanted to. But now I was mortified into indecision.

The silence lengthened. Did he think I was coming on to him? That I was testing the waters to see if he was interested in me? Was I?

"I mean, it's not just the magic, that I don't date. I don't ever feel like I measure up in relationships. It's exhausting. I'm probably better off alone."

"What do you mean?"

Crap. Why did he have to be an emotionally mature man who was interested in what I had to say?

"I mean, if it wasn't the magic, it was something else I wasn't enough of. Depending on the guy, my hair wasn't long enough, my stomach wasn't flat enough, my boobs weren't big enough. I don't know if I'll ever find love."

His bright eyes turned to me. His nostrils flared slightly, betraying a touch of anger on an otherwise placid face. "Actual men have told you those things. About yourself." More of a statement than a question.

It did seem kinda shitty, now that I said it out loud. "Not in those exact words, just the suggestions." I deepened my voice in an unflattering mimic of a guy I'd had one date with when I first got to San Francisco. "'Have you ever thought about getting a boob job, Gemma?' That kind of thing."

His eyes still searched the cosmos, but a muscle tensed in his jaw as he shook his head slightly. "Gemma, you're—"

I cut him off. "I'm not fishing for compliments."

"I didn't think you were," he said, an edge to his voice. "I just—"

He shook his head, his mouth open, like he was struggling for words. I both wanted him to refute the things those men said but also not to be another man passing his opinion over my body.

He continued more softly. "I think your real problem is that you've been dating men who aren't good enough for you."

Disappointed, relieved, and pleased all at once. "Maybe so."

"Definitely so."

The silence lengthened again, grew more comfortable. His breathing got slower and slower, until I almost thought he was asleep.

"Hey Gemma?" he asked suddenly.

"Yeah?"

"If you ever want to talk, I'm here."

I smiled, pleased to my core. "Thanks, Beck."

It was a quiet afternoon, for once. In the past several days, we'd had two near-emergencies that had been neatly handled by the organized beauty of *The Interstellar Grimoire*. I definitely wouldn't trade the past several boring hours of sorting and cleaning mechanical parts with Beck for a life and death emergency, but this task was wearing thin. It was far past lunch, but we were so close to the bottom of this box. I sighed and tossed another lost-beyond-hope piece into the scrap metal bin, stretching my neck and back.

Beck sat on the floor across from me, cross-legged and barefoot as usual, polishing what appeared to be a particularly ornery manifold until it shone. He looked up. "You okay?"

"Yeah. Just a little drained." At two weeks into travel, my thoughts were less and less occupied with the debacle that was San Francisco, and more and more with where to find a job while I waited for my appointment with Madam Indigo. I'd waited tables in college. Summer probably wouldn't mind if I stayed on the ship for a few months. I could earn enough money to pay Madam Indigo and to live on while I figured out what the hell to do with my life now that I'd killed my professional career.

But could I stay that long with my family without them finding out about my magic? Could I stay that long around Beck? Since the dam had broken on whatever he'd been holding back, he'd been the kindest friend, attentive and caring, funny and wonderful to be around. When we worked together, we were as harmonious as a perfectly functioning antimatter drive. There was no drama, only flirting and the best conversations.

Was what I was starting to feel for him real and important, or only fueled by proximity and his potent pheromones, which were custom-blended to turn my body into one big pleasure ache? His presence distracted me from figuring out my future. Clouded my thoughts and stacked my opinions into the wrong boxes until my brain felt like it'd been wired by a drunk electrician.

I caught him looking at me. "Give me twenty minutes," he said, standing up, "then meet me in the forest."

My stomach politely growled. "Will there be food involved?"

"That's the idea." He winked and was gone.

Twenty minutes later, I pushed open the door to the forest, the spot on B1 that was a small farm and orchard. I still hadn't spent much time in here. The bright light hurt my eyes after so long in the relative darkness of the rest of the ship. When my eyes adjusted, I took in the vegetable garden and a Celtic knot herb garden to my right, the flower gardens to my left. Lilacs were on the cusp of blooming, and roses and lavender swayed in the artificial breeze.

Dozens of trees grew close together in a mini-forest and stretched tall toward the blue sky of sun lamps on the ceiling. A manufactured breeze skimmed across my bare arms, through my hair, ruffling the leaves. I sighed and turned my face up to the fake, warming sun, eyes closed, and pulled my ponytail out to let the breeze in. The room was far lovelier than most of the other enclosed forests I'd been in on Earth. This one had been tended with love.

I followed the sound of Beck singing "Dream Girl" again through the grove of trees before me, my tennis shoes crunching through the mulchy ground as I passed apples and oranges, a few elms. I found him in a small clearing in front of a mini waterfall and lagoon. He sat cross-legged on a quilt spread over the ground, his hair pulled up in a messy bun and his plaid flannel shirt lying on the ground beside him. I tracked the sinuous lines of his black tattoos, down his muscles to where his hands dug inside a picnic basket. Beside him, Oby rolled around in the sunny grass with all his white belly fluff on display.

"Where did you find a picnic basket on the ship?"

"Ah-ah!" He held one hand out to stop me as he put another plate on the quilt. "You don't come into the forest with shoes on."

"Oh! I didn't know that was a rule." I slipped off my shoes.

"Socks too!"

"Really?" I reached down to remove one sock, then the other. The grass in the clearing was soft and feathery on my feet. I almost forgot I was on a spaceship.

He chuckled. "It's not a rule. I just thought some grass underfoot might do ya some good."

"You're probably right. I think that little Devil's Ivy on my table is keeping me sane."

He looked pleased with himself. "You're welcome."

Of course that'd been him. I settled on the quilt across from him and swept my hair back up in a ponytail. "Did you make me lunch?"

"Yes ma'am." He sat a sandwich on a plate and handed it to me, keeping it out of the way of Oby's interested pink nose. "I even have these chips I made last week," he said, handing me a pouch. "But the pièce de résistance"—he pulled out a drinking glass and dropped some ice cubes into it before handing it to me—"is this." He pulled a soda can from the basket. "One of the precious few Diet Coke cans on this ship."

I took in an excited breath, glorying in the snap of the tab, unlike any other sound, the fizz in the air, the bubbles rushing up as he poured it into my cup. I hadn't had any since I was on the Tube from San Francisco.

"How did I rate one of these?"

"It's from my private reserve. I heard you bemoaning the loss of Diet Coke this morning at breakfast, so I figured you deserved one."

He popped a stainless steel straw in my thermos, and I took my first glorious sip: sharp, sweet, delicious.

"Oh my God thank you. I feel like an addict who finally got a hit."

We exchanged smiles and ate companionably. Did I even need to include Beck into my decision to stay or leave the ship once we got to Gaia? For all I knew, he was planning to take off once we landed. His friendliness toward me could be only because of his friendship with Hannah and Noah. The thought left me cold, but it'd make my staying on the ship less complicated.

"What are your plans when you get to Gaia?" I asked. "You've talked about teaching, but that won't be your whole life."

He gulped down his last bite of sandwich, took a swig of his own Diet Coke, and lay down on his side across the quilt, his elbow crooked to support his head. "I've got a teaching gig already lined up at the university near my folks. I've gotta finish out my anthropology degree too. I figure I'll build me a house on the land my folks set aside for me." He closed his eyes and grinned, lying on his back and turning his face to the sun. "Settle down with a smart, beautiful, dark-haired witch, and spend my days neck deep in kids and kin."

A conceited rush of hope sparkled through my chest. He lay there with a smug smile, both hands cradling his head, his muscular arms on full display. Since his eyes were closed, I took the liberty of scanning down his body, the muscles in his chest and stomach, belly button exposed and shrouded in dark hair that led down and down. I brazenly stared at the enticingly large bulge *just there* in his jeans.

He cleared his throat and my eyes snapped to his—still closed, thank God.

I cleared my own throat. "Let me guess, you've already divined that she's dark haired?"

He shrugged and waited a beat. "That's just my type."

I took my last bite and wiped my hands on a napkin, wrapping everything up and putting it aside so I'd have a place to stretch out too. "That sounds like a pretty tame existence for a world traveler like yourself."

"No doubt I want to get around, check out the new planet. But my folks grabbed a rural spot where the sky will still be dark, and that's where I want to settle. Thinking about nights around a campfire, under the night sky, teaching my kids about the stars. Sounds like heaven to me."

That plan was a far cry from what I'd imagined for myself in San Francisco. If I'd stayed at Noble Industries and settled down with another engineer, even on the new planet, mine would've been a sterile existence of city penthouses, nannies, and upper crust friends whose smiles couldn't be trusted. Playdates with other mothers and kids who also hadn't seen the sun in weeks, trying to measure up to a moving target of perfection. But boarding this ship set me on a different trajectory, even though I had no freaking clue where it was heading.

Beck's plans sounded perfect. Dirty, muddy feet, grass on the kitchen floor, wildflowers in a jar by the sink. Messy little chocolate faces huddled up in blankets by a campfire, their bellies full of smores, listening to Beck tell them about the stars. I sighed. Why was I not surprised to see Beck show up in my reverie?

"What are you smiling about over there?" he asked.

I opened my eyes to find him looking at me. "It sounds lovely, that's all. I can almost smell the firewood burning."

He sat up in a rush, sniffing the air and looking around.

I sat up too, alarmed. "What is it?"

He rubbed his beard. "I think I'm still traumatized from our little fire last week." He stood up. "Come on." He held his hands out to me, and I let him pull me to my feet.

He took my hands and raised them to my eyes.

"What are you doing?" I pulled my hands away.

"No peeking!" He placed my hands back over my eyes. "Count to ten, then...come find me!" His footsteps retreated and went silent.

I laughed. "Hide and seek? Really?" But I covered my eyes and started to count. "Fine. Whatever. One...two...three..."

At ten, I uncovered my eyes. "Ready or not, here I come!" I couldn't see him anywhere through the trees.

"Where are you?" I called, walking around, feeling foolish. I went into the little shed by the garden, but he wasn't hiding there among the shovels and rakes. He wasn't behind the little hillock that the waterfall came down from, or behind the tumbled rock retaining wall that held it together. The trunks of the old trees were wide enough for a man to hide behind. They must've grown wild for years before the coven took the ship over and pruned everything down to a manageable level. It must've taken a ton of work just to get this one room cleaned up. Sometimes I didn't give them enough credit.

"Are you up a tree?" I wandered through the forest, looking through the branches. A real bird fluttered across and I gasped, surprised at the movement. A little sparrow. I stopped and watched it eating from a bird feeder hung on a tree. Two others joined it, and more birds sang in the trees. When was the last time I'd seen a real bird? I couldn't remember. Had I wasted the last several years of my life, holed up in the San Francisco tunnels, the laboratory, my sterile apartment, exiled from what was real?

"Did you give up?"

I jumped and whirled around at his voice right behind me, squealing, my hands up in an attitude of defense. He brought his hands up too, my surprise having startled him too. We burst out laughing, gripping our hands together.

"You scared me!" I accused. "Where were you hiding?"

He pointed behind himself. "Behind that apple tree."

The door to the forest opened. Without thinking, I pulled him against a tree to hide and huddled close to his chest. His arms were around me, hands on my back. I stifled a giggle and shushed his.

"Eyre," Hannah called from the door. "Are you in here?"

We leaned together, shaking with silent laughter.

"Why are we hiding?" he whispered into my ear, sending a thousand electric shivers down my back.

The door closed, and we busted out laughing aloud, leaning together for support.

"I don't know!" I squealed. But my amusement sobered up. I was standing in his arms, my hands on his chest. If I wanted to, I could stretch right up and kiss him. Just plant one on him here, barefoot in the forest. He had nice lips, full and usually smiling. Kind things came out of them.

I remembered myself and looked up into his eyes. They were focused on *my* lips. His lips parted as he met my eyes, and warmth pooled in my belly.

I shouldn't. What would he think of me after I had my magic taken? He'd said he wanted a witch to settle down with, and that wouldn't be me.

I lowered my head, and he let go of me as I stepped back. He crossed his arms across his chest, his cheeks flushed above his beard.

"I brought that last piece of coffee cake too." He cocked his head toward the clearing. "I'll race you for it."

He didn't start running until my brain caught up with what he was saying, and I took off. We raced through the trees and both hit the quilt at nearly the same time. But I zigged when I should've zagged, and he tripped over me at the last minute, tumbling into the grass, laughing.

"Beck! Gemma!" Summer's voice came over the intercom. "We have a problem! We only have a half hour until we need to change course at the next dynamic vector, but our propulsion system's too weak to make the adjustment!"

Beck dropped the cake back into the picnic basket and took off running. I ran barefoot after him out of the forest, skidding to a stop in front of the floor's master panel where he was already tapping through the systems.

"Everything in here looks fine."

He scanned through panel after panel. Everything *looked* fine. Except—

I grabbed his arm. "There! Go back!"

He flipped back a panel, and I leaned past him to zoom in on a schematic of the external components of the propulsion system.

"Gah," he muttered, now seeing what I'd seen. "The Lichtenstein drive. And of course it's only accessible from the hull."

My brain pivoted into problem solving mode. "Okay, so we send the astromech out to fix it."

Beck shook his head, agitated, but not at me. "We don't have an astromech."

All the hairs on my neck stood up. "We don't have an astromech?" How had I not asked that question before on a ship this age?

"We have one, but it's missing its CPU. We tried to spell him back together, but we can't control him well enough from inside the ship for him to do that fine an adjustment." He slammed his fist on the nearest column and stormed toward the elevator.

I trailed behind him, a formless worry starting to claw its way up from my stomach. "Where are you going?"

"On a spacewalk," he said quietly, pressing the up button five times.

Chapter 8

A Spacewalk

"There has to be something else we can do." I thought about the room full of astromech scraps I'd left behind at Noble Industries.

"We don't have time to think of anything else."

"Well you're not going alone. I'm coming too."

"Absolutely not," he said, stepping in as the doors opened. "Your sister needs you, and Noah'd kick my ass if I let you go out there." He pressed the intercom on the elevator wall and leaned in to speak. "Prep for a spacewalk."

Summer responded. "Shit. Ten-four."

"*Noah* recognizes I'm a grown woman who can do what she wants," I huffed. "You don't get to decide what I do and don't do. And it's not protocol for only one person to go. Why are you talking like this? Do you think I don't know what I'm doing?"

"Obviously you know what you're doing." He pulled his hair up with a pink hair elastic. "But Gemma, the suits we have are old. Not everything works on 'em. And I think you're more crucial to the survival of this ship than I am."

"That's the sweetest line of bullshit I've ever heard." I laid my hand on his arm. "Why are you throwing up ridiculous excuses?" I asked quietly.

His eyes on me were full of fear and something else. "You want the truth?" he asked, just as quietly, placing his hand over mine, moving closer to me and sending shivers skittering under my skin. "I care about you, okay? I don't want anything to happen to you."

My heart thudded, but I could only blink at him as the elevator dinged. He squeezed my hand and walked out, and I trailed after him.

Summer met us on our way to the dock off the bridge. "Are you sure there's no other way?"

"I'm sure. Unless we want to overshoot our adjustment by twenty parsecs," he growled.

I hadn't been in the dock much, just long enough for Summer to prove it'd been thoroughly inventoried. Two airlocks, each not much wider than a gondola car, sat along the outer wall, and the side wall held cabinets of gear and tools. Beck pounded his fist once, hard, against the locker labeled "shitty astromech—RIP."

Summer pulled a suit from another locker and handed it to him. "This is the best one we have. It looks like crap, but everything's been tested to work."

"I'll need a suit too," I said, digging through the lockers. Two doors down, I found a suit tagged "second best." Comforting.

"Wait, you're going too? No, no, no. I can't have both of my engineers going on a spacewalk."

"You don't have a choice. It's a two-person job, and anyway, EVA protocol is two people." I whirled around to see Beck stripping down to his underwear. Damn, he was fine. I averted my eyes. "Don't you want some privacy?"

"No it's not," he said. "Extra-vehicular activity protocol allows for unnecessary redundancy, especially with a crew this size. It's a one-person job. And if you weren't where you shouldn't be, I wouldn't need privacy. Summer doesn't care."

"Well *I* want privacy." I stomped off to the cubicle curtain in the corner and yanked it shut around me. Why was he being such an ass? I rushed out of my clothes, not trusting him to wait for me.

The silence from the other side of the curtain was punctuated by the clicks and snaps of straps and locks, the hissing autofit adjusting the suit to his size. I tucked behind my ears stray hairs that'd come out of my careful bun, snapping them down with pins, and stepped into my suit.

My autofit hissed around me as I inspected the propulsion, the com links, and the fastenings.

Beck looked up at the sound of my curtain rattling open, and our eyes met. His terror was plain on his face, and my anger softened.

"Look, I can go by myself," I said, "even if it's against protocol. I'll reset the hyperplumb and be back before you know it."

Hannah walked in while I was speaking, with Eyre right behind.

"You're going out?" Hannah asked quietly, slipping a Chewy Bear into her mouth and the wrapper into her skirt pocket. She began to check all my seals and straps.

"Yeah." I smiled. I'd caught the Chewy Bear bandit at last. "But don't worry, Nannapie, I'll be back before you know it."

The corners of her mouth rose at the nickname. The room was a nervous kind of quiet as Hannah double-checked my suit and Eyre helped Beck load up his toolkit. Oby kept rubbing against Beck's legs, as if he knew what was up.

Summer approached, pulling at straps on my suit. "Gemma, I can't promise you that everything works right on this suit. I think this is the one with the latching issue."

"Latching issue?"

"Yeah, the strap where the toolkit latches in is busted, so it's compromised the rigidity of that area. It'll hold, just don't mess with the tether after you hook in, or you might have a real problem." Summer positioned my helmet over my head as Hannah gave me a quick kiss on the cheek. "Ready?"

"Let's go." The vacglass came down, separating me from the others in my own life-preserving cocoon.

I joined Beck in the airlock where he was already attaching his tether, and Summer shut the vault behind me. The roaring hiss of the airlock depressurizing and our suits' responses sent my heart pounding. Just minutes ago, I was inches from kissing Beck in the forest. How were we about to go on a spacewalk?

Summer's voice appeared inside my helmet. "Can you guys hear me okay?"

"Yes," we replied in unison.

Beck threw a thumbs up at the camera then ran his finger along the tablet embedded on his suit's arm. "Gemma, I'm sorry I'm being an ass. I'm just scared. Thank you for coming with me."

I glanced up from checking my tether to recognize he was only talking to me. I adjusted my own tablet to the private channel. "Of course. We're in this together, right?"

He reached out with his fist, and I bumped it. He exploded his on the way back, and I chuckled as I set my tablet back to all comms.

"Are you tethered?" Summer asked.

"Yes," we both answered.

"Okay, those suits will last you an hour, but we've only got fifteen minutes until we overshoot our course correction. Airlock opening in five...four..."

I glanced up at the monitor to see nearly all the denizens of the ship standing around in the bridge, including three of the cats. Zola appeared beside the others, one hand on her hip as the other gesticulated wildly at us.

My hands were ice, and my heart skipped and bounced around in my chest like I'd downed two cans of Berserker Energy Drink. I took deep breaths and stepped beside Beck, resisting the urge to grab his arm for comfort.

"One!"

With a grating hiss, the airlock opened. My feet left the ground, my stomach lurched, and I checked my tether on reflex. Beck had already propelled himself out of the ship. I followed, trying to ignore the hazy glow that marked the boundaries of our shield, about two hundred feet away, and the stark dark of space beyond. Squeezing the propulsion trigger at my thigh, I shifted my direction to land beside him on the hull, reaching out for the metal rungs of the access ladder. I grabbed on, suddenly enamored with the rivets of each rung, those beautiful fasteners that gave me something solid to hold onto with the vast nothingness of space at my back.

"Don't look out, don't look out," Beck repeated quietly.

"I'm not."

"I'm reminding myself," he said.

It took us a few minutes of climbing to get to the hyperplumb panel. We hooked our arms and feet around the access rungs, and he pulled the powered screwdriver from his pack. Within seconds, he'd unscrewed all six screws from the panel, and I lifted it off.

"There's the problem." I reached down into the box to disconnect the wires of the broken plumb and pulled it out. He stuffed it into his bag and came back out with the replacement, which I took and carefully attached.

I hooked the meter to the panel and watched the numbers fluctuate on the screen. "It's got electricity, but it's not calibrating."

The formless worry that I hadn't been able to name barreled up my throat. We looked at each other and spoke at the same time.

"Interference from the solar sails!"

"Shit," he said. "I was worried that was gonna happen."

"So what about the solar sails?" Summer said over the coms. "I don't want to rush you or anything, but we've got ten minutes till."

"Alright." He crunched his eyes closed.

I did the calculations in my head. The numbers on the screen were what I'd expect to see if the sails were shorting. But should they detect the sails?

"Are the sails serving any functions still? Our antimatter drive's working, and we're on the highway, so we shouldn't need them, right?"

"I was thinking about that," he said. "But I'm afraid to detach them. If we upset the balance of the ship, we might have adverse effects to the shield, based on the spells we have supporting those systems."

"What if we disconnected their power supply?"

One side of his face pulled up. "That might work, but I can't remember if it's upline from anything."

"It shouldn't be. Even these old ships weren't primed for electromagnetic navigation, so the connections on the sails shouldn't affect anything, right? What am I missing?"

"You're not missing anything," he said, "you're a freaking genius. Yeah, this ship is about twenty years newer than that tech. We'll be okay if we detach the power, but not the sails themselves. Let's do it."

We reattached the panel and started toward the power supply to the sails. Cold sweat dripped down my back. I gazed longingly at the airlock as we passed it again. Several rungs later, I looked back and shook my tether experimentally, then looked past him to where we were going.

"Beck, our tethers can't go that far."

He turned around to judge for himself, when Summer's voice piped into our ears.

"Seven minutes! And that's to get you back in too! You have about four minutes to do whatever you're gonna do!"

Beck shook his head, frowning. "You're right. Look, we're at the switch. You stay here so you can ground it after I disconnect the supply."

"Okay, but let me go back and unhook my tether to give you twice the length."

I turned to go, but he gripped my arm.

"There's no time, Gem, and you have that latching issue." His face was pale. He chewed his lip, looking back and forth between the sails and his tether. Finally, he shook his head and gripped the access ladder, unhooking his tether with his other hand.

My heart dropped to my feet, and I grabbed his arm. "What are you doing?" The only thing keeping him from interstellar nothingness was his hand on that ladder and the propulsion in his suit.

He took a deep breath. "My propulsion works. Yours might not. I'll go to the sail, disconnect it, and I'll come right back. I promise."

"No way!" I said, my grip on his arm solid. "There's gotta be another way. Just gimme a minute to think." The sails were only about sixty feet away, but if he slipped outside the shields, the ship would leave him behind, and we may never find him.

He swallowed hard. "We don't have a minute." He smiled bravely, his eyes seemingly full of unsaid words. "If I don't make it, tell my family I love them."

"Beck, don't talk like that," I pleaded, my voice trembling.

He licked his lips, and his eyes locked on mine, brighter and softer than usual. "And I want you to know, Gemma, you're *amazing*."

He faced the sails and pushed off.

My heart pounded. Gray edges around my vision threatened to take me over as Beck sailed untethered in interstellar space. I had to calm down. I'd ruin the whole mission if I didn't get my nerves under control. This was fertile ground for my magic to ruin everything.

I took a deep breath, gripped the panel where the switch was, and reached in, closing my hand around it, ready for his command. I couldn't take my eyes off of him. He sailed the sixty feet, and with perfect aim, latched onto the ladder at the base of the sails. Once he took out the screwdriver and began working, I started breathing again.

Just a few more things to get through, and we'd be safely inside. Then I'd yell at him for telling me I'm amazing, then scaring me half to death. I tallied what we had to get through like a to-do list in my head, like I often did when I had to get through something upsetting. Just five more things to get through.

He removed the two screws and flopped the panel open. That was two; just three more. He reached his hands in. The switch would be three.

"Now!"

I pulled the switch back on his call. Sparks traveled away from me, mini shorts flashing in a line straight to the sails. "Let go!" I shouted.

But too late—electricity moves faster than human reflex and reaction. The surge reached him, and his shout echoed over the comms. He shot away from the sail base, streaking toward the abyss.

"Beck!" My voice, Summer's voice, shouting over the din of my heart in my ears.

I fumbled at my tether connection, disconnected, and pushed off hard in his direction. In seconds I was nearly to him, but my course was in a different vector. I grabbed my propulsion and steered myself toward him.

I was approaching him too fast. I stretched out my arms and legs. A crack splintered across his vacglass, and I slammed into him, throwing all my limbs around him.

We somersaulted too close to the shield's edge. Seconds went by like ages. The din of the crew shouting was in my ears, and he wasn't grabbing me back.

I dispersed my propulsion, slowed our flipping. As we evened out, I located the ship and got my bearings, tried to orient myself in the most advantageous position to get us back to the airlock. I glanced into his helmet. His eyes were closed. I was alone, one life responsible for two.

I pivoted and grabbed the shaft of my propulsion. Just a quick release in the right direction would get us there. I squeezed.

Nothing.

I gasped for air, blinked away tears. Icy sweat slipped down my back, and spots threatened my vision. I squeezed again, inhaling a shuddering sob. Nothing. We'd drifted even farther away.

This wasn't happening. Nothing made sense but the ragged beating of my heart. I reached down for Beck's propulsion. Dead like mine. His eyes were still closed. More cracks in his vacglass.

Then I made the worst mistake I ever could have. I looked out.

The French call it *l'appel du vide*, the call of the void. I looked into the eyes of infinity, and it looked back at me with billions of glittering stars, vast clouds of dust and gases, the spirals and bright smudges of other galaxies. It was a siren, seductive, dangerous, and undeniable. I shifted my legs to move toward it.

A bulk between my thighs reminded me I wasn't alone. Beck was here. Beck, who was afraid of the dark, quiet hell of space. Beck, who I wouldn't condemn to drift in the abyss, dead or alive. I took a deep breath, the call of the void forgotten like a past shiver.

I repositioned him, freeing my hands to fiddle with the propulsion. I might be able to fix it with tools and time, but I didn't have either. All I had was Beck, and he was in trouble.

No. I had something else.

Deep in my marrow, my magic begged to be released. The power I'd been trying to coax out with lighting candles. I didn't need much propulsion, just a little.

My hand still on my propulsion, I shut my eyes and reached deep inside myself. I pushed out with my mind, just like with the feathers and pencils in middle school. But this time it was me and Beck, two adults drifting ever closer to the abyss. I opened my eyes. We were farther away. It wasn't working.

I took a deep breath to still the sobs shuddering through me, applying my scientific mind to the willing spark that awoke within me, ready to do my bidding. We were light as thoughts out here, and I was as strong willed as iron. I focused on the airlock, calculated the vector, emblazoned the image in my brain, and shut my eyes.

I coaxed the little spark into a flame, and *pulled*.

I opened my eyes. We were soaring toward the airlock.

Within seconds we were inside it. I smashed the close button on the inside of the doors as we passed them.

With a hiss, the airlock began pressurizing, and I fell softly to the floor, straddling Beck. I unlatched my helmet and threw it away, peeled his cracked helmet off, pressed my fingers to his neck. I couldn't feel anything through the damn gloves. I unzipped his suit down his chest and laid my ear against him. An erratic beat. But he wasn't breathing.

I sat up and began compressions, my magic wild and pushing into his body at each thrust, seeking something to heal. Tears streamed down my face as I gasped for air.

"Beck," I said weakly. "Beck, wake up!" *Save him*, I willed my magic.

I barely heard Summer's voice through the intercom over the roaring of the air.

"Gemma hang in there. Zola's almost in."

Beck gasped but didn't open his eyes.

Then Zola was at my side. "I got him, Gemma. It's okay."

I stumbled off of him at the touch of Zola's hand on my arm. She leaned over him, and a stretcher waited on his other side.

"He's breathing, heart's steady," she called.

I watched in a daze as Eyre dropped the stretcher, and she and Zola loaded him up. Zola slipped oxygen on him as Eyre pulled the stretcher up and rushed him out of the airlock.

Zola crouched by me, bringing her scent of jasmine. She peered into each of my eyes with a small light, listened to my heart as she squeezed my hand. "You did great, Gemma. I'm so proud of you. You saved his life, and we hit our course correction. Are you okay?"

I nodded, tears falling.

"Your vitals are good." She turned to Hannah and Summer as they rushed in. "Her vitals are good. Get her out of this suit and let me know if anything changes." She kissed the top of my head and took off.

Hannah ran up. "Need help getting up?"

I shook my head and tried to stand, but my legs quivered. I fell back down. Hannah and Summer each grabbed under an arm and pulled me to my feet.

My whole body shivered in paradoxical cold, like putting a hand under too-hot running water and having pain receptors unhinge, thinking it's cold. I closed my eyes only for a moment, but when I opened them, I was all the way in the dock.

"Never mind, she's up!" Hannah called across the room. She turned to me, her eyebrows drawn together. "You okay?"

I reached up and patted her face. "I'm alright, Nannapie. I told you I'd come back."

"Girl, that was epic," Summer said. "If I was a real captain and had a medal of honor to hand out, I'd give it to you."

I leaned my head back against the wall. "Is it just me, or is it a thousand degrees in here? Or negative eight? Definitely one of the two."

"Let's get you out of this suit." Hannah waved her hand and closed the cubicle curtain between us and Summer. She knelt beside me and began unfastening the locks.

"What happened out there? Did your propulsion die?"

"For a minute," I lied, "but it kicked back in long enough to get us back."

Hannah brushed tears from her cheeks in between undoing my zippers and snaps. "I don't think I'm gonna sleep tonight. When I close my eyes I just see you drifting away."

The suit slipped off my torso and cold goosebumps rose all along my back and neck. She lifted me. Shivering, I threw my arms around her neck, letting her pull the suit off my bottom and legs. She left it in a heap on the floor and grabbed my tank top, slipping it over my head and pulling my arms through it as if I was a child.

I couldn't stop shivering, but my arms were working better, and at least I felt honestly cold now. I grabbed my leggings and slipped them on, leaning on Hannah to stand.

She waved her hand across the curtain, and it opened. "Do we have a blanket?"

Summer flung open a cabinet door and pulled out an old airplane blanket. She sent it flying through the air on waves of magic to envelop my shoulders.

"What do you need, Gem?" Hannah asked. She slipped her arm around me, and I rested my head against her shoulder.

I breathed and thought a moment, snuggling close to her. Then my stomach twisted with a cross between hunger and nausea. "I might throw it all up, but suddenly, I'm starving."

Hannah laughed, relieved. "She's okay."

Eyre rushed into the room and ran right up to hug me.

"Beck's still unconscious, but Zola says he's going to be fine. Thank you for saving him, and all of us," she said.

"Thank him. And thank God it worked," I murmured.

Two hours later, I'd stuffed my face with the most delicious hamburger and fries I think I'd ever had, courtesy of Eyre's appreciation. I'd taken a bath, slipped into my favorite silky nightgown, and had a chance to calm down. I pulled back the velvet comforter on my bed, eager for sleep, but my tablet buzzed on my nightstand.

Zola: *Hope I'm not waking you. Beck's doing great. He's up and asking for you. I promised I'd tell you.*

I marked the message with a heart and threw my fuzzy purple robe on.

Zola looked up from her novel as I walked into the med bay.

"*Gemma.*" She exaggerated my syllables in an awed tone. "That was"—she breathed out hard—"foolishly brave of you, and an impressive act of CPR. I don't know how he survived it, but it's not an exaggeration to say you saved his life. Beck's one of my favorite people on the planet—" She caught herself. "On any planet. Thank you for bringing him back to us."

I smiled. "He's growing on me. You said he was asking for me?"

"Yes!" She pointed to a glass-enclosed patient alcove draped in closed curtains. "He was awake a minute ago when I went in to check on him."

I peeked through the slightly open curtain. One soft lamp cast its shadow across the small room, and Beck lay in the bed, eyes closed, hooked up to monitors. His arms rested on top of the covers, an IV in his hand and his tattoos peeking out from beneath a home-sewn, blue-flowered hospital gown. Oby lay half-asleep, curled up in between his legs. He opened one green eye then flopped over half on his back, his paw over his face.

I stepped just inside the room and watched Beck's chest rise and fall for a moment. Thank God he was breathing so easily. I'd been replaying everything in my head. The moment he pushed away from me. The moment the electrical short shot him off the sail. Him and me, drifting into the cold abyss. My magic flooding his heart. I took a shaky breath.

His eyes fluttered open and found me. "Hey," he said quietly, smiling and taking a long, slow blink. "I'm glad you're here." He opened his hand and reached out.

I padded into the chairless room and perched on the side of his bed, taking his outstretched hand in both of mine.

"You look so beautiful, like a space angel."

I tucked an errant curl behind my ear as a blush warmed my cheeks. I'd left my room with my hair loose and un-straightened, and no makeup on.

"I was about to go to bed when I got Zola's text. How are you?"

"I never knew your hair was so curly." He reached up, tugged on a curl, and let it go. "I love it. I'm glad you came," he said again, yawning. "I'm good, thanks to you." He took a big breath, and looked at me solemnly. "Thank you for saving my life. Twice over. I swear I thought that was the end."

"Of course. And thank *you* for saving the ship."

"Only because of your brilliance. Gem, I can't—" His eyes filled with tears. "You risked your life to save me. Zola said you untethered."

I smiled through blurred eyes. "You risked your life to save the rest of us. Besides, we're supposed to finish inventorying the storage rooms this week, you know. You'll have to do better than almost dying in space to get out of it."

He chuckled softly. "I'm serious, Gemma, I owe you my life." His eyebrows went up. "I don't know how I could ever repay you."

I glanced down at his arms. I'd been curious since I met him. "You can tell me about your tattoos." I tilted his arm slightly so I could see the whole black design running down his forearm.

"Nah, now you've crossed a line and asked for too much," he said, rubbing the back of my hand with his thumb.

I caught the teasing in his voice, even as his caress awakened my whole body. "No really. Tell me about this one." I ran my finger down the black, runic design. "What's it say?"

He shifted his arm, looked at it himself. "A couple of years ago, when I was studying out at the Kerry Dark Sky Reserve in Ireland, I connected with some local witches, and I met this amazing woman, *Máthair Chríona Niamh*. It's Gaelic for Wise Mother Niamh. She was the coolest old lady I ever met. A divination witch, but not like anybody else. She wouldn't read for everybody, but when she agreed to read you—and she was *selective*—she'd go into a trance and tattoo what she saw, on the person, with her eyes closed. I kept seeing witches with these similar markings on their arms." He turned his arm to look at the tattoo. "And they were all beautiful."

I side-eyed him in amusement. "You let an old woman tattoo you with her eyes closed?"

"Well yeah," he said, as if I was the one being silly. "I figured if nothing else I'd get a reminder of my trip. But it came out awesome."

I traced the outlines of the black ink on the inside of his forearm. It was beautifully designed, artfully balanced, skillfully executed. And his skin was warm. Alive. My eyes teared up. "What does it say?"

"It translates to *love will save you from the abyss*."

A presumptuous little thrill skipped through me, and I shifted closer to him.

He caught me smiling at him, and his eyes twinkled with mischief. "She was Christian. I figure she meant I had to love my neighbor so I didn't go to hell."

I nodded, smiling. "That's probably it." We both knew it wasn't. "She did a beautiful job."

"I think she's already on Gaia." He yawned again. "I could put in a good word for you, if you want one. No promises, though." His eyes fluttered closed again. The clock on the wall read past midnight.

"I should let you get some sleep." I stood up, but he gripped my hand tighter.

"Will you stay until I fall asleep?" he mumbled, eyes still closed. A sweet smile lit his face. "I love having you around. Think you'll chase away the nightmares."

"Of course." I sat against him and pulled his hand on my lap. I loved having him around, too.

Chapter 9

Definitely the Right One

I waited for the consequences of using my magic to save myself and Beck. But three days had gone by, and...nothing. Beck was up and about. Nobody died. We'd caught our waypoint and were traveling on schedule toward Gaia. Everyone on board was well and in good spirits, and Beck was beyond pleased that I'd used my magic to save us.

"You ready for candlepalooza?" he asked, his arms outstretched over our project for the evening: rows and rows of fresh candles.

"As I'll ever be!"

"Speaking of which, you left your rose candle in here earlier. I can't help but sniff it every time I pass it, so you'd better take it before I steal it."

"Aww no. You didn't use up all the smells, did you?" I asked, feigning disappointment. I grabbed it from the table and sniffed it. I'd stopped by the med bay earlier to turn in my depleted candle and get a fresh one. Zola said the rose candle, which had appealed to me the most this time, was good for wellbeing, affection, and love. "Can't you go get one yourself?"

"Yeah, I probably could. It's just easier to mooch smells off yours."

"Gotcha. Let's get this thing over with." I settled down onto the floor with a lighter and held my hand out.

"Why, you got somewhere to be? An appointment in the Andromeda galaxy?" He brought over a crate of candles and crouched beside me, beginning to hand them to me one at a time to replace the guttering ones.

His hair smelled amazing, and just being near him put my whole body in a heightened state of awareness.

He elbowed me and raised his eyebrows suggestively. "A hot date with an alien from Messier 81? Come on, you can tell me."

"No," I said, bumping my shoulder against his. "Zola talked me into a ritual bath." I'd asked her, was more like. After all the magic I'd been doing with Beck and on the spacewalk, I decided it might help me.

"Really?" He said it with an air of surprise.

"Yeah, why?"

He looked sideways at me. "Is it your first one?"

"Yeah," I repeated slowly. "Why?"

"Your first one is always the best one. I mean you should only do it once a month, on the full moon—" He stopped himself. "Well, when we had *a* moon. I don't know what the recommendation will be when we have *three* moons. But it can be transformative. I swear the first one she set me up with took years of worries off me."

"Is that why you're so charming and lighthearted?"

"Oh, so I'm charming, am I?" His eyes crinkled with mirth as he nodded, lit by candlelight. "That's a nice compliment."

"Don't let it go to your head," I said, lifting my chin. "It's the same thing I told my alien friend on Messier 81 before I stood him up for a date with a hunky alien on Cygnus A."

He put his hand over his heart. "The Gemma giveth, and the Gemma taketh away."

I grinned at him. "Candle?"

He passed a candle to me, his fingers grazing mine too much to be an accident. My cheeks warmed. "Do you have any advice for a first-timer?"

"Hmmm, let me think."

As I lit each candle and slipped it into place, he collected the spent ones and stacked them in the crate.

"She's gonna give you a smorgasbord of awesome stuff to choose from to throw into your bath, with *intention*. So my advice is twofold. First, think about three intentional statements, positive statements like affirmations. It's like a meditation. You're not gettin' in there to get your body clean, but to cleanse your aura and set intentions."

I felt a flush color my face when he said "your body," which embarrassed me, flushing me worse. He handed me another candle, and our eyes met, widening both of our smiles. My body was a waterfall of hormones walking around in a trench coat, masquerading as a girl, and this guy was definitely starting to make me have feelings.

"She's gonna have you put things into the bath in threes," he continued, "and each time you do, you're supposed to say a positive affirmation with it."

I laughed. "Like 'I'm beautiful, I'm wonderful, and everyone loves me?'"

"But those are truths, Gemma," he said, placing his hand on my shoulder as he got up for another crate of candles. "I mean you have to state *intentions*. They're not quite the same thing."

"Oh come on, sweet talker." *Really, go on.* "Just give me an example."

"Alright. Sea salt. That's a good choice. You'd grab a handful of sea salt, and as you spread it into your bath, you say something like 'I release all negative energy and associations from my aura.' With the second handful, you say something like 'I welcome only love and light into my aura.' Then with the third handful"—he kneeled down beside me with the next crate—"you might say something like 'Beck is the sexiest man alive.'"

I laughed so hard I snorted.

He affixed his face in a hurt expression, but his eyes twinkled mischievously.

"Aww, poor Beck." I leaned over and rested my head against his shoulder for a second. "You said the affirmations can't be truths. Do you need somebody to manifest that into being for ya?"

He chuckled, placing his arm briefly around me, squeezing me against him. "I need all the help I can get!"

"You really don't," I murmured.

He gave me a double take and raised his brows. "Wait, what?"

My whole body flushed hot. "Nothing." *He's just your friend, Gem, just your friend.* But the hormones rushing through me did *not* like the friend plan. I went back to my work.

He smiled silently for about a minute straight before going on. "Your last intention might be something like 'I release all negative beliefs and thoughts I'm holding on to.' Then if you use crushed rose petals, take three handfuls and repeat the same affirmations with each handful. She might have all kinds of other goodies, too, like bath bombs, or essential oils. You basically make a lovely soup and soak in your own good intentions."

"It sounds relaxing, at least, and I definitely need to catch up on my relaxing."

"It's probably more exhilarating than relaxing, but if you're doing that tonight, you're gonna sleep like a baby." He collected up the last of the spent candles. "Actually, none of the babies I know sleep all that well, so I don't know why people say that."

"Know a lot of babies?"

"My brother's kids. Charlotte's about to turn three, but I haven't met my nephew yet. Henry Beck. He was born in Nouvelle Orleans last summer." He placed his palm warm against my back, his eyes growing darker and more serious, though the familiar crinkling was there. "And thanks to you, he'll get to meet his Uncle Beck." He scratched my back once and stood up.

That simple scratch sent an avalanche of desirous shivers through my body that collected in an ache between my legs. "Maybe you can save my life once, and we can call it even."

Still holding the crate in both hands, he pointed his finger at me as he walked backwards a few steps. "Hey, I'm there for ya babe. But you better get going. Punctuality is next to godliness for Zola."

"Oh wow. I didn't realize it was so late!"

His voice came over from upstairs and around the corner. "Time flies when you're with the sexiest man alive."

I smiled, blushing, and hurried toward the door, but his heavy footsteps jogged behind me.

"Hey Gem—" He held my rose candle between us.

I reached for it, but he pulled it back. "Hang on, one last drag." He inhaled it deeply, then breathed out a heavy, contented sigh. "That's some good shit."

I snatched it from him before he could trick me again. "Good night!"

He called out after me, his words all in a rush as the door closed between us. "Tell Zola I want a rose candle and a ritual bath appointment too!"

Thanks to Zola's text of what to bring, I showed up right on time to Suite 107 with all my bath and nighttime things. The door was already open, and I found Zola in the suite's expansive bathroom. It was the loveliest place on the whole ship. Reclaimed wood covered the ceiling and walls, all whitewashed. A white, clawfoot tub stood against the wall, and beside it, salvaged window panes enclosed a double-wide shower. A tile floor overpainted with a soft, repeating mandala design and a few mismatched lamps completed the soft look.

"This might be the bathroom of my dreams."

"He did a beautiful job, didn't he? He far surpassed what I thought he could get done for me."

"Noah?" I didn't remember my brother being especially handy.

Zola smirked. "Oh heavens, no. Beck. I chose this bathroom to make a sacred space, not just for the journey, but also for the time we'll be living in the ship while we all build our houses. Beck overheard me lamenting to Eyre that I didn't know how I'd ever get it into shape, so he stepped in and offered to pretty it up for me. And you know he spent so much time fixing up everybody else's stuff, his suite is pretty plain. Well, he had your suite at first. But when he learned you were coming, he gave it up and moved downstairs so you could be closer to Hannah."

He'd never told me that. I ran my hand along a pipe and wood towel bar. "He thought of everything."

"He's a thoughtful man. And all with unclaimed property from abandoned houses in New Orleans. Beck practically lived on the road this past year, getting us all the best things he could find. Anyway, I've got everything all set for you."

She opened a tall wooden cabinet against the wall. Artfully arranged inside were over a dozen different jars and small wooden boxes of salts, flower petals, essential oil bottles, mini bath bombs, bath melts, and a selection of crystals, all labeled with their names and supposed benefits. A smoke cleansing bundle sat in an abalone shell on a small wooden stand.

"First things first. The bathroom has to stay scrupulously clean. So I need you to take a shower first to get *yourself* clean. Wash your hair and all. When you're done, place all of your belongings you brought with you—along with your dirty towel—on that stand outside the bathroom. Don't worry, I'm locking the door on the way out, so it'll only be you in here."

Then Zola proceeded to explain the ritual much as Beck had, even showing me how to light the smoke cleansing bundle that Beck had forgotten to mention.

"Got it?"

"I think so. Thank you for setting all this up. By the way, Beck's jealous. He wants a rose candle and a bath appointment too."

Zola cocked her head. "Okay. I can arrange that. I think he's about due for one. I'm gonna get going now. Eyre's waiting on me for movie night."

"Have fun!"

After Zola left, I showered quickly and stowed all my things on the stand outside the bathroom in the suite, including my judgment. Naked and bereft of everything I'd brought in with me, I started the bath water, lit the candles, and lit the smoke bundle, blowing on it until it was smoldering. I coated my whole body in the whirling smoke and let it drift through my wet hair, watching the patterns and focusing on cleaning and fresh starts.

As the water filled, I selected my three crystals and placed them on the bronze tray beside the bath. Grabbing my first handful of rose and herb sea salts, I spoke my first intention: "I release all negative beliefs that have been holding me back." A second handful, a second intention: "I attract only light and love into my life." A third handful, a third intention: "I welcome new joys into my life with open arms and an open heart."

I repeated the three intentions with the three mini bath bombs. The water was toasty and perfect, frothing with bubbles and colors. The moment I plunged my foot in, an exhilarating, overwhelmingly positive sensation effervesced out of the water and skipped across my skin. I settled under the surface like it was a warm blanket on a cold night, with only my face out of the water to breathe.

It was divine. I glanced at the clock on the wall to be sure I wouldn't overstay, and I repeated the three intentions aloud three more times, tasting them on my tongue, trying to deeply live in and believe them: "I release all negative beliefs that have been holding me back. I attract only light and love into my life. I welcome new joys into my life with open arms and an open heart."

I studied the pale rose quartz, touted for self-love and relationships. It was multifaceted, raw, and cool in my hands. Maybe it was okay for me to look for love. I'd been punishing myself for my parents for years, and it was hard to see anything redeeming in myself.

I set the rose quartz down and picked up the smooth, tomato-red carnelian stone, studying its orange-hued crackles and striations. Creativity, motivation, and a soulmate. I'd certainly need creativity and motivation to get by on Gaia without a job and probably blacklisted from my profession. As for a soulmate? Beck's face flashed, unbidden, through my mind.

I finished with the clear quartz, which was supposed to amplify the effects of the other stones.

Even though my thirty minutes were up too soon, I was eager and excited to get out. I got dressed, gathered up my things, and padded to the elevator with my damp hair clipped on top of my head and all my dirty clothes wrapped in a towel in my arms. Adjusting the sash of my fuzzy robe over my favorite silky nightgown, I felt effervescent and excited, like my life had so much to offer that I couldn't wait to dive into it.

I pressed the up button, and my thoughts turned to the nearest, most interesting good thing in my life. *Beck*. I let a smile overtake my face, gazing dreamily at the panel of little round lighted numbers as they lit the floors on the elevator's way to me. Beck and I had done some quality flirting earlier, and it was monstrously unfair that I had no excuse to see him until tomorrow.

A chime, and the mandala on the doors before me parted, revealing Beck. Too-handsome Beck casually leaning against the back wall of the elevator, hands on the railing.

My breath hitched, and my face broke into probably the sappiest smile in history.

He looked up and smiled broadly when our eyes met. "Well if it isn't Gemma, fresh from her ritual bath."

My whole body reacted to him, and my face went hot. If he could read my mind, he'd see daydream Gemma throwing her arms around his neck. He was still in his white T-shirt and jeans, bare feet crossed on the rug. I was scanning his whole body when he spoke again, leaning forward to catch the doors before they closed.

"Are you coming in?"

"Yeah." I giggled, ducking into the elevator. Giggling? Was I a teenager?

He held the door a moment more. "Heading home?"

I nodded, and he pressed the button for my floor and released the doors. They whirred and stuttered, taking a long time to close as usual.

He stood beside me, clasping his hands behind his back and turning slightly toward me, his eyes twinkling in the low light. "How was the bath? Damn," he said, not waiting for my answer and leaning closer. "You smell even more amazing than usual."

As the elevator lumbered to life, I looked up at him, and a thrill went through me to see his face so close to mine. "It was everything you said it would be."

He grinned and straightened but didn't move away. "So I was right about two things."

"Two things? The bath and what else?" I challenged, lifting my face closer to his.

"The bath, and"—his gaze traveled down my body and back up—"that you're the kind of woman who sleeps in beautiful night things."

"You've only seen me in my nightgown twice," I teased. "You don't know that." The elevator stopped, chimed, and the doors labored open. I leaned closer. "For all you know I could sleep naked."

A muscle in his jaw twitched, and his smile got bigger, more mischievous, maybe a little...embarrassed? Was he blushing? Oh God, did I really just say that to him?

He reached a long arm out and held the door open for me, kept his eyes on me as I stepped past him. "You're right. You could be just like me, and I wouldn't know."

He walked out beside me, and I could feel his body heat even through my own furious blushing. I tried not to picture Beck naked in my pink-flowered sheets but failed spectacularly. Daydream Gemma was about to get into mischief with a hot witch. My skin was hot and tingly all over, with more than my magic.

He shoved his hands in his front pockets as he walked beside me down the hall to my room. As I fumbled with the key in my door, he leaned in again.

"Do you smell like roses?" He pressed the bridge of his nose to my temple, and my insides turned to hot mush. "So much better than the candle," he said gruffly before stepping away toward the stairwell door beside my suite. "Night, Gemma."

"Did you get off on the wrong floor?"

He shrugged sheepishly with his hand on the stairwell doorknob. "Nah, most definitely the right one."

He smiled at me for a heartbeat more, then disappeared through the door. I scraped myself off the floor and smiled all the way to sleep.

Chapter 10

Refresh My Memory

Beck and I were nearly finished repairing the biofilter instrumentation that had flipped out on us a few hours earlier, overheating and smoking. We hadn't seen much of each other the past few days, with all our shifts in the kitchen and garden, so getting to spend this evening with him was a comfort. Even though we fought machinery, we were at least fighting together.

He reached down to me from where he stood on a catwalk ladder, properly secured this time because I made him. "Hand me a hex key, please?"

I placed the tool in his hand. He brought it up to adjust the fastener, and the indicator bulb in front of his face burst.

I cried out and turned my face away. Glass tinkled to the ground. When I turned back, he was looking at the broken bulb, a deep bleeding gash across his face. He turned, and a narrow sliver of the fragile glass caught the light from where it was embedded in his cheek. He raised his hand to his face.

"Don't touch it!" I grabbed his leg to get his attention. "You have glass in your cheek."

"Damn I got lucky," he said, wiping dripping blood from his beard below the cut. "That could've hit my eye."

It was a lot of blood. I pulled at his arm to get him to come down. "It looks pretty serious. Let me see."

"Shit. Is it deep?"

He came down from the ladder, and I stood on my tiptoes to look. "I can't tell, but it's definitely stuck in your cheek." I helped him get the harness off and led him down to the sink, dragging a stool over. "Sit down. Let me get a better look under the light. We might need to wake up Zola."

He peered at the mirror while I switched on the light over the sink.

"Come on, sit down so I can see."

He complied, hooking his heels on the rung of the stool and letting his knees fall outwards. I wet a clean towel and wiped his face around the gash the best I could. It was hard to see the wound under all that blood. If I used tweezers, I might accidently break the fine glass off in his skin. It would be mighty hard to get the rest out then. And he might need stitches. Right across his handsome face. That'd be a damn shame.

"Gemma," he said quietly. "Why don't you use your magic."

I lowered my hands, my stomach churning. Since I'd told him about using my healing magic on him after the spacewalk, he'd been looking for ways to get me to use it. But short of purposefully injuring one of us—which was out of the question—we hadn't had another opportunity. I was rusty, but if I used my magic, I might be able to get all the pieces out, even seal the wound so he wouldn't need stitches.

"You could maybe save me from needing stitches," he said, as if reading my mind.

I took a deep breath. "That depends." I was nearly at eye level with him, and we looked into each other's eyes for a moment. I trusted him. Whatever bond we were forming on this journey was not something I took lightly. I asked him the one remaining question.

"Do you trust me?"

"Of course I trust you." One eyebrow raised. "Are you gonna try?"

"I'm gonna..." What could I use to catch the glass? A soap dish sat beside the faucet. I removed the bar of soap, handed the empty dish to him, and pulled his hand to hold it over his left knee. "Hold this here. I'm gonna do a thing." I took a breath and laid my left hand along the jawline of his unhurt cheek, turning his head to a better position under the light. "Be still."

From the corner of my eye, I could see him watching me curiously, and it sped my heartbeat to be so close, to be touching him. It was already thumping at the thought of using my magic, like a bull with a rider eager to be let out of the gate. I studied his cut, then hovered my fingers over the glass fragment in his cheek, focusing all my attention on it. Emboldened by the rush of adrenaline, my magic sang through my veins, infusing my body with heightened awareness and the flush of power.

The magic in his blood rose up to meet mine. That didn't happen after the spacewalk. I wrapped tendrils of my magic around the waiting tendrils of his, as if I were threading my fingers through his and making our hands stronger together, helping his magic do what it alone could not. Our magic actually fused together, flooding me with warmth, confidence, and the sensation of being wholly connected to his very soul. This would be easier than I thought.

I sinuously pushed our magic—gently, gently—skimming around the surface of the glass, identifying it, matching its inorganic makeup to three other minor fragments embedded in his cheek. I drew them out with an invisible force—gently, gently.

He took a soft breath, and the fragments of glass tinkled as they fell into the soap dish. With our magic wrapped intimately together, I directed the mending of his cheek tissue on a molecular level, putting back to rights the chains of proteins, minerals, and cells that the glass had torn apart, layer by layer.

When I sensed that his injury was mended, the skin around it matched and whole, I opened my eyes, not quite breaking our magical connection. I stood in between his legs, closer than when I'd started, close enough to feel his body heat. He watched me back, a look of unadulterated wonder and adoration in his eyes, his lips parted. My hands were still on his jawline. I felt like I was glowing. Standing like this, I could bring him in for a kiss so easily. The earnestness in his eyes smoldered back at me. Flushed with magic and the nearness of him, I very much wanted to.

He tilted his head and looked down to my lips. My heart hammered. I didn't pull away. I couldn't pull away, not with his face so close, his magic still mingling so intimately with mine.

I slid my hands further along his jaw, cupping his face, and we closed the distance like magnets. His lips were warm and sweet on my mouth, his beard tickling my face. The clatter of the soap dish in the sink, then his hands were warm on my hips. He deepened the kiss, and I pressed closer—

"Beck and Gemma, are you in here?"

We broke apart like two halves of a wishbone at Summer's call, our bodies and magic sliced in two.

"Hey Summer, we're over here!" I rushed up the steps and toward the door, my heart racing.

"Oh good, you're both up. Can one of y'all come check the intercom switch on the bridge? It's sticking."

Beck bounded up the stairs behind me. No blood on his face. No cut.

"I'll go check it out." He turned to me, his face guarded but lit with something new. "We can finish with the biofilter tomorrow morning. Why don't you get some sleep?"

The rush of adrenaline from healing and—oh wow, that kiss—was plummeting now, and I recognized his words as good advice. And a chance, in the ice bucket bath of Summer's presence, to regroup.

"Yeah, thanks. I think I will." I yawned and ducked out the door.

Beck was singing.

I sat up in bed, confused and exhausted from too little sleep.

"—happy birthday to you!" His voice over the intercom continued. My clock said seven in the morning, just five hours after I'd left him in the engine room last night. Did the man ever sleep? I lay back down, snickering. He probably looked fucking adorable.

"Happy birthday dear Gem-ma, happy birthday to youuuuuuu! And mannnnyyy more!" he finished with a flourish. "Everyone is invited to a special celebration tonight on the Star Deck in honor of the woman, the myth, the legend, Gemma—" He paused and spoke more quietly to someone on his end. "What's her middle name?" Murmuring. Then Beck's voice boomed, "Gemma Louise Abadie!"

He mimicked the sound of screaming fans at a stadium, and I snorted and put the pillow over my head to block him out. It was time to get up anyway. I had chores to do, and we still had to deal with the biofilter indicator.

I smoothed down my fitted knee-length dress, adjusting the low bustier bodice for the ninth time as I stepped into the elevator to head to the fancy party that everyone insisted on throwing for me on the Star Deck.

They'd emphasized that this was a fancy dress party, but I still hoped I wasn't overdressed. My dress, a sheer black dotted swiss over nude crepe, didn't allow for a bra, and it showed a lot more cleavage than I was used to. But it was the last nice article of clothing I'd bought in my old life, before I'd started saving every scrap to pay Madam Indigo. I'd planned to wear it to a holiday party with a date who'd canceled on me because I'd scared him off with my magic. I'd stayed home that night eating ice cream, but I was excited to repurpose the dress now, overwriting a painful memory with what the excitement in my veins told me would be a good night.

The elevator chimed, the doors opened, and the rush of air fluttered the long sheer sleeves cinched at my elbows and wrists. I stepped out, happy to once again feel the stemmy height of my black pumps with every step.

The Star Deck appeared even more magical under the softened lights and with the curtains open to the stars. White string lights crisscrossed above the dance floor and dining area to create a little human universe under incandescent stars. Not everyone was there yet. Eyre and Zola flipped through a stack of records by Beck's stereo, and my eyes immediately sought him out. He stood with his back to me, talking to Hannah by the windows. My heart fluttered. He was wearing a dark suit, and that was my kryptonite.

Before I could decide what to do, Eyre and Zola appeared before me.

"Happy birthday, Gemma!" they chorused, attacking me with hugs.

"Holy Aphrodite, girl," Eyre said. "You look stunning!"

Zola hugged me quickly. "You look gorgeous."

"Me? You two are amazing!" I was relieved to see that my dress fit right in with theirs. Zola's skinny dress with a cowl neckline sparkled over her slim hips like black glitter, and Eyre, not wearing black for once, wore a shimmery blush spaghetti-strap corset dress with a tulle skirt, her raven-wing hair piled up on her head, colorful rose tattoos tumbling down her shoulders.

"Thank y'all so much for going all out for me. It's magical in here!"

The service elevator chimed.

"Dinner is served!" Summer announced, wheeling a cart toward the nearly empty buffet table.

Eyre whooped and walked that way. "Good! I'm starving."

I stepped forward to walk over and help, but Zola stopped me. "This is your day. You relax." She winked at me. "By the way, I have you seated at the table between me and Beck." She sashayed away with a smile, and my face went hot.

Were we that obvious, or did Beck tell her about the kiss?

He and Hannah had turned around at the commotion, both looking where I stood between them and the food. I tucked a strand of hair behind my ear and breathed deeply, straightening my posture and acting fascinated by the sight of dinner being plated across the room. As if I couldn't feel the heat of his gaze on me, and as if I didn't care if I could.

But I did. I was obsessed with that kiss. It'd been sweet, thrilling, amazing. The man himself—sweet, thrilling, amazing.

But the prospect of getting involved with a witch still felt dicey, at best. His constant encouragement to use the magic I'd tried to repress for so long—which was going well, all things considered—was a constant knot in my chest.

And doing magic in tandem with him had been intoxicating. It'd made me start to doubt my appointment with Madam Indigo. But I didn't want to be turned aside from a decision I'd already made. Beck was a permanent part of my siblings' lives, and I wasn't sure if I belonged.

My resolve not to look his way broke. I glanced past Hannah at him as she walked up, pleased to no end to see him standing stock still, looking at me. If I got involved with him, would he ever forgive me for having my magic removed? Would he still want me afterwards?

If I didn't get involved with him...Even after one kiss, imagining him with someone else made me sick with jealousy.

Hannah walked up, beautiful in a dark moss-green velvet dress draped off her shoulders.

"You look stunning," I said, hugging her.

"Thanks, sis. You're gorgeous and sophisticated, as always. I still don't know how you get your updos so perfect by yourself."

I shrugged. "Practice."

She winked at me and walked off toward the others, but I stayed where I was, sensing that Beck was just behind me.

"Gemma."

I turned to see him smiling at me, and my heart fluttered. That smile lit every room, and the effect was magnified by how ridiculously handsome he was in a black shirt and suit. His green eyes twinkled in the relative darkness of his trimmed beard and loose dark hair. He straightened his suit jacket as he approached.

"You look—" He broke off, shaking his head and blinking slowly. "Wow."

"That bad, huh?" I asked, twisting my fingers together. I glanced at the others across the room to judge their hearing distance—far enough—as his aura moved enticingly into mine.

He placed his hand gently against my lower back, just below the cut-out in my dress, and murmured in my ear. "If by 'bad' you mean breathtakingly beautiful, then yes. You look very, very bad."

Warmth flushed my skin, and desire twisted through my body, but I didn't have long to process it.

"Shall we?" he asked, removing his hand and offering me his crooked elbow.

"Let's." I slipped my hand into his arm and let him lead me to the buffet. I followed behind Hannah, adding New Orleans delicacies I'd missed to my plate: soufflé potatoes, red beans and rice, and fresh mini-French bread po-boys. I stopped still, jaw open, at the next small table where my cake was. The sides looked like a galaxy, with purple, blue, and pink smudges in a sea of black, speckled with white stars. A bouquet of buttercream flowers in the same hues sat atop the cake.

"Who made this gorgeous cake?"

Hannah slipped an arm around my waist. "It was a joint effort. Summer and I took a cake decorating class a couple of years ago. It's a lil' hobby."

"You never told me about that!" I said. "You're both so talented! Thank you. I love it." The evening just started, and I was already getting choked up over a dessert.

I sat next to Beck during dinner, soaking up his happy energy, jumping into conversations with the rest of the coven. After dinner, we feasted on the cake, which was as delicious as it was beautiful.

Eyre handed me a little package wrapped in art paper painted with flowers.

"What's this? You didn't have to give me anything."

"But I wanted to. We all did."

Eyre gave me the softest fingerless gloves she'd knitted in my favorite plum color, Zola gave me a spa package full of her best bath bombs and salts, and Summer gave me a warming pillow she'd sewn herself, filled with lavender flowers and flaxseed.

Hannah took a small, open-sided glass terrarium planted with succulents from the table and presented it to me with outstretched hands. "I couldn't wrap it, so I made it birthday table decor!"

"Thank you all so much. This is amazing." I blinked my tears away. They were treating me as if I was part of their family. I hadn't been part of a family in a long time.

"I don't know about y'all, but I'm gonna dance! C'mon Summer!" Hannah cranked up the music, spinning on her toes like the ballerina she'd been as a child. The party wore on, and the wine flowed freely. Eyre even convinced Zola to break out her violin to play along with the records.

I danced a little with the others, but no wine for me. I couldn't let my consciousness be altered by any kind of drug. That would just invite my magic to run wild.

Late in the party, after Beck slipped away to the elevator, I went upstairs to the mezzanine restroom for a refresh. On the way out, I stopped to watch from the balcony, my heart full. I'd dreaded spending time with this coven, but dammit, they'd won me over completely. Summer and Hannah were cozied up, talking in the corner, while Zola and Eyre laughed and shrieked, disco dancing together on the parquet floor.

Beck had returned, standing near his records. His back was to me, but as if he felt my eyes on him, he turned and looked right at me. He strode up the stairs to join me.

"You're not partaking either, I see?" He toasted me with his water bottle.

I shook my head, slightly moving in time to the song. "I'm not a drinker."

"Me neither. Listen, I'm sorry I disappeared, but I went to get your gift. I didn't have anything to wrap it in, so close your eyes and put out your hand."

I laughed and put my water down, complying with his request. Something small and hard dropped gently into my hand, and a delicate chain draped down beside my thumb, gently swinging.

"Okay, you can open them."

In my palm was a necklace with two pendants: one, a small burnished circle of metal, had tiny holes punched into a constellation, and the other was two small stones—a green one and a black one—entwined with wire. It warmed my heart to think about his big fingers putting this delicate thing together for me. Or maybe he'd used magic?

"It's the Sagittarius constellation," he said, pointing to the punches in the disk. "And the green stone's aventurine. It attracts luck, success...and love. It's good for growth and opportunities. The other's black tourmaline, for protection."

"You made this for me? It's beautiful. Thank you."

"You're very welcome." He smiled.

"Would you put it on me?" I handed it back and turned around. After a second, he passed it in front of my face, and I held it in place while his fingers brushed the back of my neck, clasping it. "I'd also like to give you a tarot card reading, if you're up for it. As part of my gift."

"Sure." I turned around, touching the necklace. "I love it, thank you."

"I'm glad."

The next song began, a slow love song that'd been released on Earth before we left. I'd skipped it each time it'd come on the radio on the

Tube down to New Orleans, but hearing the violins start up sounded so hopeful with Beck beside me.

He cleared his throat. "Do you want to dance?" He raised his eyebrows, gesturing with his eyes to the empty space behind us.

"Yes," I said, without even considering. He placed his warm hand against my lower back, leading me out onto our own private dance floor.

His hands slipped onto my waist, and I draped my arms over his shoulders. We danced without speaking, exchanging glances, smiling, then looking away. After a moment, he cleared his throat.

"Sooo, are we gonna talk about last night?"

I looked down, my face heating. I didn't know if he meant the magic or the kiss. Probably both, but I was mortified to talk about either.

"Gemma, you're amazing. You completely healed my cut with your magic. Not even Zola can do that."

I risked a glance up. He pointed at his cheek, and one of his winning grins brightened his face. "You didn't even leave a scar on my pretty face."

I shook my head. "I should've left you one to keep you humble."

He threw his head back and laughed. "You probably should've."

"Your magic helped."

"Yeah, I felt that," he said, twirling me around. "And I've never felt anything like it before. I've combined magic with other people lots of times, with the coven, my family, ex-girlfriends, but last night was—" He shook his head. "Completely different, and more beautiful than I ever could've imagined."

I was starting to be a little overwhelmed by the excitement blooming on his face and the feel of his hands, back at my waist. I wanted him to hold me closer. Was afraid to let him. I glanced at the stairs. No one was coming up.

He wrinkled his nose and side-eyed me. "If you'd be willing to talk to Zola about your healing magic, I think she could help."

"Absolutely not. I don't want anyone else to know." I gasped. "Wait, was that what her wink was about? You didn't tell her, did you?"

"No! Of course not. I wouldn't tell anyone unless you were okay with it."

I bit my lip. Of course he wouldn't. I was wrong for asking.

We danced a moment more, silently. He pressed his lips together. There was more on his mind, and I'd just made the mistake of looking at his mouth. God, I wanted to kiss him again.

"Something else I wondered about," he started, his gaze soft.

"What's that?" I tipped my face up to his. Dancing had naturally brought us closer. All my senses heightened with my chest pressed to his and his hands on my back.

He leaned in and spoke softly, his lips a breath from mine, his eyes dark and serious. "Was it that forgettable?"

"No," I breathed, "but refresh my memory anyway."

He kissed me, his hand slipping warm across the bare skin of my back. Excitement erupted like fireworks through my body. I melted against him, wrapping my arms tighter around his neck, wanting to get closer, closer. The kiss began sweetly, gently, like last night's, but then it amped up with an edge of hunger, mine matched to his.

Any doubts I had dissolved with his arms around me, leaving only a sense of rightness, of being exactly where I was supposed to be. I arched my back, pressing closer, grabbing his jawline as his hand caressed my back. He breathed a soft whimper against my mouth when I pressed my hips to his, and his hand slipped from my waist down my backside, pressing my lower belly against the hard line of his need. A delicious ache in my core, and I was kissing him harder, pulling him closer.

The women downstairs were calling my name.

Summer's voice rose above the merriment, singing to her own tune. "Gemma, Gemma! Where are you?"

I broke away, not wanting to stop, but not wanting an audience either. He kissed me again, quickly, then pressed a warm kiss to the crook of my neck, his tongue the epicenter of sparks shooting through my body and pooling in my core, weakening my knees.

"Captain Killjoy," he murmured in my ear. He flashed me a wicked grin before slipping into the service stairwell.

Heart pounding, I wiped my face. My lipstick was probably everywhere. Was the skin around my mouth red from the sweet abrasion of his beard?

"I'm up here!" I called, stepping to the top of the stairs and down. "I was in the bathroom," I lied. "What's up?"

Zola met me halfway down the stairs and put her arm around me, leading me to a table that hadn't been there before. "It's time for your birthday spell."

"Birthday spell?"

Hannah dropped leaves into a cauldron on the table, and the main elevator dinged. Beck walked out of it, hands in pockets, the picture of innocence.

"What's a birthday spell?" I asked, getting closer and suspicious.

"It's a potion that predicts your happiness in your next year." Zola looped her arm through mine. "Hannah's got it about ready, and all we need is a strand of your hair."

"A strand of my hair? Seriously?"

Eyre giggled over her pink drink. "You're traveling with a coven, and you're gonna ask a question like that?"

"Okay, so you put a strand of my hair in there, and what happens?"

"A multi-colored surprise!" Hannah said.

Beck arrived beside me and picked a card up from the table. "It's a divination spell we came up with, where the colors predict your year ahead."

Panic gripped my heart. What if it formed big red letters that read *Gemma's getting her magic taken away*? Or *Gemma and Beck were just making out on the mezzanine?*

"What if it's bad?" I asked. Beck turned the card toward me. I leaned in as if interested, but all I wanted was to get him alone again.

"Don't worry," he said, "it's all good things. See?" He pointed at the card. Beside each swatch of color was written a single word in Hannah's handwriting. "Gold for luck, orange for success, red for love..."

He met my eyes, the light of his desire still bright and clear, electrifying my skin.

A bright pinprick of pain stung my scalp, and Eyre walked away with one of my hairs. "Ouch! I probably have some on my dress. You could've asked!"

"Yes," she said, holding my hair up and appraising it carefully. "But it could've been Hannah's hair, or Beck's hair, or my hair—" She carefully handed it over to my sister, who also treated it like highly enriched uranium being transferred to a secure location. "Have to be sure it's yours for the spell to work right."

"You ready?" Hannah grinned.

"I guess." Their faces were so excited, but I was apprehensive. Beck put his hands on my waist and arm, and pulled me back from the table as the other witches backed off too. Hannah held safety glasses over her face, dropped in my hair, then scurried back ten paces, laughing, into Summer's arms. Eyre ran over and shut off the main lights in the room, until all that was left was the strings of lights and the light of the stars outside.

The cauldron bubbled, excitement tingled the air, but all my focus was on the warmth of Beck's hand against my back. I looked up at him. My magic had been more and more cooperative since he'd started working with me. I couldn't tell how much was his teaching and how much was just his presence. Even with this display of magic before me, my own sat contentedly in my body, just vibing, enjoying the evening. He caught me watching him, and his face lit up. He gave my back a gentle scratch with his fingertips that lit me up from the inside.

White bubbles frothed and overflowed from the mouth of the cauldron, crackling and snapping as white sparks fizzed out in all directions. A shimmering streak of white shot up toward the high ceiling with a sizzling whoosh like fireworks, and the witches cheered. The ball of white light burst open into a magical shower of purple stars and sparkles, and rained down on us like confetti.

"Travel!" they shouted, shrieking and squealing with joy.

The sparkles fell onto my outstretched hands where they tickled, bounced, and disappeared. Across the deck, Hannah stood in Summer arms, both of their faces lit up with the spell's display.

While the purple shower was still pouring from its source, another white ball rocketed from the cauldron, popping open into a shower of silver.

"Joy!" they shouted.

"One more," Beck said softly into my ear, sending sparks of an entirely different nature skimming straight to my core.

The last shooting star blasted into the air and burst open into a shower of red stars.

The crowd whooped and crowed. "Love!" they shouted.

As the word left Beck's lips, I felt his hand on my back softly caress me where the others couldn't see. Then Zola and Eyre pulled me to dance with them among the spellwork's still-bubbling, still-falling stars.

Chapter 11

Past, Present, and Future

When the spell had run its course, and the women were tired of dancing, I noticed Beck putting dishes on the kitchen cart, talking to Eyre. Through the music and the others' gaiety, I couldn't hear what they were saying, but Eyre said something to him, and he glanced in my direction and winked at me when he caught me looking at him.

"Well, girl, I've gotta go back to the bridge and keep us flying straight, since I *am* the designated driver," Summer joked, coming in for a hug.

"Thank you so much for everything!"

I approached Zola and Hannah where they were cleaning up the cauldron. "Can I help pick up anything?"

"Absolutely not," Hannah said. "Zola and I pulled dish duty, and we're gonna leave the decorations up for now. You go do whatever it is you want to do, birthday girl."

She hugged and kissed me, and went off with Zola and the cart, right behind Eyre, who disappeared onto the bridge.

Beck looked up from his turntable across the room, sleeving the record that had last been playing. "And then there were two."

"Seems that way. Need any help?"

"No," he said. "Absolutely not. I'll get this in the morning." He stacked his last record in its crate. "How about I walk you home, and if you're up for it, give you that tarot reading I promised?"

"Sure," I said, stars spinning in my heart.

As we walked side by side into the stairwell that let out nearest my room, he scooped my hand into his.

"Did you have a good time?"

"I did!" I exclaimed. "It was absolutely magical. My best birthday yet."

"I'm glad," he said, opening the door to my hall.

I slipped my key into my lock and flipped on the entry light. He followed me in and pulled off his jacket before sitting at the table he'd made and sliding the plant to the side. He pulled a black velvet pouch from his suit pocket, about the size of a wallet, and eased open its drawstring as I slipped my heels off by the door and headed into the kitchenette.

"Want something to drink?" I asked.

"Water would be great, please."

By the time I brought the bottles out, he had a stack of cards in his hands.

"How did you know to build my table? Really?"

He took a sip, eyes a little bleary under the drop lamp. "Hannah came to me back in August. She was so worried about you. Just had a bad feeling. She asked me to do an astrology chart and a tarot reading." He looked at me for a second too long for it to be casual. "I dunno. I just...sometimes I know things before they happen."

Sometimes, like now, I wondered if he knew more about me, about us, than he was letting on. I cleared my throat and steered the subject in a different direction. I wasn't sure I wanted to know if he did.

"Great, you can tell me what to do when I get to Gaia. I'm probably blacklisted from every astrotech firm on the new planet."

"You think so?"

"I do."

I drank my water as I watched him shuffle and riffle the cards. He riffled them so many times I started counting.

"Is seven times really necessary?"

"Sure, if you want the cards to be completely randomized. It's the Gilbert-Shannon-Reeds mathematical model of shuffling." He placed the deck on the table. "Think about a question you have about your life."

"That's the problem. Right now, my whole life is a question."

"Then try to narrow it down to one question, but don't tell me."

"Is this like a magician's act?"

He faux-grimaced. "No. It gives a cleaner, less-biased reading. If I know what you're asking about, I might try to address it directly, and that almost never gives you a creative solution or new way of thinking."

I bit my lip, thinking, while he watched me expectantly. So many questions about my life plagued me, but the one that made the most sense to ask was *how do I move forward?*

"Okay. I have my question."

"Ok. Now cut the deck."

I grasped about a third of the cards and set them to the side.

He put the part of the deck I'd removed beneath the stack and pulled a card off the top, laying it face down on the table. "This is your past." He laid two more face down after the first, in a row. "Your present, and your future."

I studied the lines of his face beneath the beard. He and his magic cards might be crazy, but he was beautiful. And kind. And sexy. I wanted him to kiss me again.

He reached out to flip the first card over, but I put my hand on his to stop him. "You know I don't believe in any of this, right?"

He chuckled. "You've made that *abundantly* clear." His eyes twinkled. "May I proceed?"

I removed my hand. "Carry on."

"Your past—" He flipped over the first card. "Five of swords."

Three witches stood around a cauldron—typical pointy-black-hat witchy activity. One seemed quite proud of herself and immersed in the spell where five swords floated up from the bubbling cauldron. The other two looked upset, even devastated by what was happening. One was even crying.

I shrugged. "So...what does that mean?"

He tapped his finger on the card. "You've spent a lot of time and effort trying to be the best. Trying to be perfect. Better than everyone else"

"So you're saying I'm a snob." My tone was accusatory, but I smiled at him. Probably accurate, but I'm sure he figured that out about me the moment we'd met.

He grinned and narrowed his eyes at me. "That's not what I meant."

When he smiled at me, I didn't want to look away. "Go on."

He tapped the card. "And you worked so hard to get everything you had. You built the perfect—by all appearances—life: perfect career, all the perfect packaging." His tone got softer. "But it was all a beautiful lie. You were so busy trying to build something to other people's standards that you were blind to what was going on around you, even blind to what you truly wanted."

I tried to keep a poker face. These were nearly all things I'd told him before.

His habitual smile was replaced with solemn eyes. "And it was all hollow, wasn't it? Your life was a beautiful facade. You should have had everything you wanted, but it only led to sorrow. Loss." He cocked his head to the side, considering me, looking so sad himself. "So much regret and pain. You didn't just lose your job. You lost your whole future, at least the one you'd planned, and that's what you're mourning the most. That perfect, planned future."

I couldn't look at him. All I could see were those three witches on the card, swimming in the vision of my tears. I blinked, and a tear streaked down my face. I quickly wiped it away. "Sounds about right."

He placed his hand over mine on the table, rubbing it gently with his thumb. "I didn't mean to make you cry on your birthday. Are you alright? We don't have to continue."

"No, I'm fine. Go ahead."

He frowned and watched me a second more before he removed his hand and turned over the second card. "Four of swords, your present." He let out a one-breath laugh but didn't smile. "I swear I didn't fix the cards."

A witch with long dark hair lay sleeping with her cat curled up against her. The four swords displayed beside her were full of cobwebs, as if the witch had lain there for a long time.

"Oh Lord, is she dead? That can't be good."

"No, she's just resting. Kinda recharging. Right now, you're going through a period of withdrawal from the world. A self-imposed isolation. An exile, while you convalesce." He tapped on the present card, then on the past. "But you have to learn to accept help from others. Tell what's real, from what's not real. That's what got you into that fragile life of the past. You had to break out of it pretty spectacularly. She may look asleep, but she's dreaming. Trying to sort things out."

"I guess leaving Earth in a spaceship through the middle of interstellar nowhere qualifies as exile," I said. "But what's my future?" I tapped on the third card.

He turned it over, nodding in approval. "Three of pentacles."

"That's good?"

He nodded. "It is. I don't think you've ever recognized your own worth. All that driving toward perfection might have been a way to keep up appearances for other people. But that's already changing. You have these extraordinary innate talents, beautiful abilities that you've been pushing down and hiding away."

Madam Indigo-related guilt tugged at my belly.

He wagged a finger playfully at me. "But no more bushels over your inner light. Your journey has a metamorphosis. You've got something really special, and you'll take pride in work that you wouldn't have been humble enough to do before. And besides all that, you've tried to isolate yourself from others, but not anymore. No more solitary work or life for you."

"But that still doesn't answer any of my questions." I folded my arms on the table. "What am I supposed to be doing in exile? Sleeping the whole way to Gaia? 'Cause I can do that, no problem, but that means you're on your own for the next candlepalooza."

He gestured toward the deck with a nod. "Cut it again."

I did, and he took the top card off and laid it on the table beside the others.

A witch with striped stockings stood astride a broom at the edge of a cliff, one foot on the ground and her arms in the air, triumphant. One of her feet was poised to step off the cliff, but her face showed only joyful excitement.

I did a double-take. "Does that say 'The Fool'?"

"*Yeah* it does," he said emphatically, his tone excited.

"First I'm a snob, now I'm a fool?" I balked, halfheartedly, and a little flirtatiously.

"It's a fantastic card. It's not about lack of intelligence. It just means you gotta take risks. You may not know what the next steps are, so have fun with it. You have to stop evaluating every possible outcome. There's no right or wrong. Maybe you'll fly, maybe you'll fall. Either way, you'll learn something about yourself."

I leaned in and spoke softly. "But taking risks is scary."

"I know," he answered, leaning in and matching my tone. "But no risk, no reward. Maybe think of it as a leap of faith."

He was entirely too attractive to be that close to. I pushed away from the table and went into the kitchen. "What if I don't even know what to believe in?" I drained the last of my water and set my empty bottle down.

He joined me in the kitchen and leaned back against the counter. "You can believe in anything you want. That's the beauty of starting over. You get to decide. But you might start by believing in yourself."

I turned to really look at him, smoothing down my dress. "Thank you."

He looked at me sideways from under a thick, raised eyebrow. "For what?"

That look always sent chills through me. He was always so respectful. Always so honest. But I didn't even know how to properly express what I meant.

"I'm so grateful to have a friend like you on this trip. I'd have been so lonely if you weren't here."

He peered into his bottle for a few seconds, then brought it to his lips. "Same," he said finally, taking a sip.

My heartbeat sped up, and I play-kicked his shoe with my bare foot. "What, you don't want to be my friend?"

He smiled, looked down at his water again, and was silent for an eternity. I held my breath, but then his eyes met mine.

"I'd be lyin' if I said I wasn't interested in more." He cleared his throat and dropped the smile, holding my gaze. "But Gemma, you put me wherever in your life you want to, and I'll respect it."

The look in his eyes laid his soul bare to me, vulnerable and honest. Maybe I *would* play the fool.

I took the bottle from him and set it on the counter. He stood up straighter, put his hands back against the edge of the counter, looking down at me curiously. I was hooked. I took a step closer, my face tipped up to his.

His presence was magnetic, and my heart beat stronger, all the surfaces of my skin electrified just being near him. I was the tide to his moon, and his gravity pulled me closer, a breath apart. He tilted his head, lips parted, glancing from my eyes to my lips. It took my breath away.

I slipped my hand along his jawline, fingernails through his beard, and I kissed him. Stood on my toes to wrap my arm around his neck as he melted against me, kissing me gently back. His hands settled warm on my hips—a perfect fit—and everything else fell away. Our auras melded with an electrified thrumming of belonging, transforming into something new and different, something real and palpable.

I broke the kiss, and he pressed his forehead against mine, his eyes dark and desirous. He was delicious, and now that I'd had another taste, my mouth was shaped for him, and hunger twinged low in my belly.

I went back for more, my arms encircling his neck to get my body closer to his, our kisses deeper, hungrier. He was the perfect blend of science and spirit, pheromones and enchantment, both existing in one earthly body I couldn't get close enough to. My back arched, and I softly ground my hips against his. He made a soft *mmmm* in his throat and leaned over me, enveloping me in his arms, his thigh slipping between my legs, his hands across my back and backside, pressing me closer to his hips.

Magic laced the hormones racing through my veins, revving up my desire, the soul inside me yearning for the spark of spirit in his eyes as we broke away, looked into each other's eyes, and fell into more passionate kissing. Both could exist while his mouth devoured me, trailing hot down my neck; both sides could thrive, neither disproving the other. The universe was vast and mysterious, and as his thumb skimmed along the side of my breast, nothing was black or white, right or wrong. Everything was an electrifying array of colors, and I wasn't going to question it.

I was half crazed with desire, and I could feel his frenzy rising too. Our arms, hands, and hips, leveraged for closer positions. Our hands explored, tugged and squeezed. Our mouths latched and broke away, roving for new slivers of skin to kiss. We took distracted, rushed steps out of the kitchen.

He pressed warm kisses against my breastbone, and I unbuttoned his shirt. His fingers found my zipper and slid it down.

He shrugged off his shirt as I tugged at the wrists of my dress, pulling it off and baring my breasts, letting the dress fall to my ankles where I kicked it off.

He breathed out, crushing me to him, skin to skin, his hands skimming across my back as his mouth nipped and kissed at my neck. I slid my hands along the muscles of his shoulders, dug my hand in his hair to bring his kisses closer. Up on my tiptoes to drape my arms around his neck again, I sighed at the delicious shivers his kisses sent through my body, delighted by the blissful warmth of his broad, bare chest pressing against my breasts. His strong arms encircled me, both comforting and intoxicating. He captured my mouth again and slipped his hands down to squeeze my bottom, and I hopped up into his arms, wrapping my legs tight around his waist.

He rumbled a deep groan and set me on top of the table, and I squeezed my legs tighter, bringing him closer, not able to get his clear desire for me close enough to my core, even through his thin dress pants.

He pressed his forehead against mine. "Do you want to make love?" he asked, his voice deep and ragged against my lips, his eyes searching my face.

He was worlds above any man in my past.

"Yes," I breathed, sliding my hands up his broad shoulders and pulling his mouth back to mine.

He captured my mouth in a soul-stumbling kiss, slow, whole-hearted, brimming with passion, cupping my face with both hands. Pausing, I felt, to lay bare his intention: to make something of substance, to *make love*, and not just satisfy a physical whim. It was reverent and sweet, and it made me want him more.

He climbed onto the table, still kissing me as he lay me beneath him. Tarot cards—my past, present, and future—stuck to the damp skin of my back. He slipped his fingers against my belly, under the top of my panties, and I lifted my hips to let him pull them off. Then he was back above me, one hand beside my head on the table, the other skimming rough fingertips across my eyebrow, cupping my face in a kiss. He trailed languorous kisses in a straight line from my lips to the valley between my breasts as his fingertips trailed down my neck and chest. He captured one breast in his hand, and the other in his hot, pinching mouth. I cried out his name and wrapped my legs around his back, desperate to get at the sweet aching between my legs that only intensified with each flick of his tongue and nip of his teeth. I twisted my fingers into his hair, pulling his mouth closer. He smelled like incense and engine smoke, and he was burning me up.

He kissed my mouth again, his hand still tormenting me. "Fuck, Gemma," he breathed against my neck. "You're so gods-damn beautiful. Beautiful face." He kissed my cheek, the edges of my lips, down my neck. "Beautiful breasts." His mouth found one again, and my breath hitched. "Beautiful belly," he breathed, splaying his hand low across it, caressing it as he came back to kiss my lips. "And beautiful..." his hand moved lower and lower down my belly, "...here." His hand slipped between my legs, dipping his fingers where I wanted him the most, sweeping them in a perfect circle.

"Beck," I whimpered, digging my fingers into his broad shoulders.

He chuckled. "I think I can make you moan louder than that." He abruptly took his hand away and scooped me up, slipping off the edge of the table with me in his arms.

He carried me like I weighed nothing, my bare thighs hooked on his hips, his hands on my bottom as I pressed my nakedness against his stomach, his lips buried in my neck. Tarot cards popped off my skin and fell to the floor, and he stumbled on the rug, cussing, on his way to the bed.

He laid me down and quickly pulled off his pants while I lay back on my elbows, watching him. I gazed hungrily down his exquisite nakedness, admiring how the muscles of his broad chest shifted as he stalked me. Now I saw where the dark hair below his navel led, and my breath caught in wanton hunger.

"Are you okay?" he asked.

"Perfect," I breathed, sucking his bottom lip into my mouth and reaching my hand down to his backside to bring him closer to me. All the impressive, rigid length and breadth of him pressed warm against my lower belly like iron. I wrapped my legs around him, reached my hand down to grasp him, desperate to get him inside me, but he slipped out of my hands, skimmed his arousal down past my thighs, kissing my neck. Clamping his hot mouth against my breast, teasing me with his tongue and teeth before kissing down my belly, his hands full of my breasts. He ran his tongue along the tender line where my inner thigh met my torso, dropping kisses there, and I gasped.

He slid his hands down to my hips and pulled me suddenly down to the foot of the bed. I laughed, throwing my arms up in surprise, but then he pulled me until my bottom was just at the edge, and he kneeled down and hooked my thighs on his shoulders.

I had a half-second to fret about not having showered first before his hot mouth latched onto the bundle of nerves between my legs. I cried out, twisting my sheets in my hands as his tongue skimmed lazy circles, sucking me softly, flicking his tongue across me, until I thought I would die of the pleasure.

My magic stirred, and my whole body stiffened. But he slipped his hand along my thighs and gently pushed my hips back down to the bed. "Relax," he breathed against me.

I willed all the tension out of my body and surrendered to his ministrations. For an eternity, his hot mouth sucked at the bud of me, his tongue flicking across and lazing in circles, building me, building me. His fingers slipped inside me, and intense pleasure swelled until I thought I'd burst.

My magic built inside me too, ready to explode. I tensed, started to sit up. "Beck, my magic. It's—"

He paused, easing me back down. "Do you trust me?" he rumbled.

"Yes," I cried out, completely undone.

"Meld your magic to mine," he murmured, his lips against me. His fingers still inside me, still circling me, his magic called mine there. It rushed forward to meet him, to join him in whatever adventure he had in mind. His mouth was back on me, tormenting me, building me, our magic buzzing me to heights of ecstasy I never dreamt possible, and then, he held me there. He held me there at the peak of rapture, crying out with each breath as the minutes slipped by. Then my wave crashed, one orgasm slipping into another and another.

I was hot and luminous as a star as he dragged his tongue up my body, clasping it at my breast. My core was ravenous for him. He pulled me higher up on the bed and let his blessed weight sink over me, his hand cupping my face, kissing me like I was water, and he was dying of thirst.

Just when I thought I'd die if I didn't take him inside me, he kissed me passionately and slowly thrust the hard length of himself in, inch by inch. I wrapped my legs around his waist and pulled his face closer, his body deeper.

"Gemma," he murmured, shifting his angle of penetration and reaching an untapped wellspring of pleasure.

I cried out his name, and he thrust harder, rhythmically, romancing that spot with the immaculate hardness of himself, over and over, ratcheting me to a height I didn't think was possible, until I came, my body crashing again on his shore.

He thrust faster, harder until he cried out. I felt his relief follow mine. He kissed me hard and withdrew, collapsing beside me on the bed and drawing me into his arms.

We lay together, panting, my heart beating nearly out of my chest, his heart a steady drumbeat beneath my breast. He reached for my face, kissing me over and over, rapturously smiling and studying my face in between kisses.

Before long, our kisses settled, and we snuggled close and fell asleep.

Chapter 12

Every Spinning Atom

The twittering of synthesized birds and the unfamiliar sound of Beck lightly snoring beneath me woke me. I was still lying across his broad chest, and his arms still held me close.

What on earth did I do?

I pulled back to look up at his face, and the movement woke him. He opened his eyes and smiled at me, and my whole body flooded with warmth and joy. I wanted to do it all over again. All day, every day.

"Good morning," he said sleepily.

"Hi," I breathed, arching my back and pressing closer to him, bringing my leg up onto him without even thinking.

He didn't take his eyes off me until he kissed me, gently grasping my face with his hand. "Somebody's frisky this morning." He pulled me on top of his body, kissing me, running his hands down my back, his arousal already hard against me.

His deep voice rumbled against me. "Do you want to..."

"Yes, a lot," I breathed emphatically into his kiss.

He flipped me onto my back beneath him in a fast, feral movement, and I shrieked with laughter.

It was at least an hour later by the time I kissed him goodbye at the door, and another thirty minutes before I got myself together enough to face the day, even though I skipped straightening my hair. My stomach growled, but I had an errand to run first.

I knocked on the open door of the med bay before walking in. "Hey Zola, how are you this morning?"

"I'm great, Gemma, how are you?" Zola asked, popping a bookmark between the pages of her romance novel. "What can I do for you?"

A blush warmed my cheeks. "I came to see if you have anything…" I paused, but Zola cut me off.

"I'ma stop you right there," she said, slipping past me to shut the door. She opened a drawer of medications. "There's no need to be embarrassed." She pulled a bottle out and handed it to me. "Here."

"But you don't even know—" I started, looking down at the nondescript bottle.

"Gemma," she said, talking low and kindly, "you're not my first customer for contraception today."

My mouth dropped. I didn't know whether to be impressed that he wanted to take responsibility, or horrified that he'd told someone. "He told you?"

"Certainly not! He's too much of a gentleman. But let's face it. Who else would he be knockin' boots with on this ship? You two have been drawing closer for weeks, and it must've been pretty damn good for *both* of your auras to still be looking like all that." She waved her hand around my head.

I blushed and studied my hands, as if I could see what she was talking about. But even all the practice at magic I'd been doing hadn't improved my nonexistent auric vision.

"Looking like what? What do you see?" The last thing I needed was for rumors to fly on this ship, no matter how I felt about Beck.

"Don't worry, I'm the only one on board who can see auras to this extent, but Hannah's got a sixth sense. So I don't know if you're ready for your sister or anyone else to know about whatever's happening with Beck. But let's just say you're both still…energetically connected." She lit a smoke bundle and blew it into a smolder. "May I?"

I nodded. Being with Beck had been so passionate, transcendent even. "Energetically connected, huh?"

She stopped bathing me in smoke to look at me, amused. "Girl, your energy was all over that big man this morning, and he's still all over you. I think I see a sacral etheric cord taking shape."

I didn't understand the words, but she said it with the playful intonation of a girl teasing her friend about a boy.

"Honestly, it's been forming for a while. I first noticed it after the spacewalk. Together you're raising each other's vibration, and that's a good thing, but you still only want your own energy in your aura."

She finished cleansing me and tapped the bottle in my hand. "Here. Take one of these after each encounter to prevent pregnancy."

"Thank you." I turned to go, but thought better of it. "You won't tell anyone, will you?"

"Of course not! Look, there's a water fountain in the front."

I stopped on the way out to take a pill, and I stowed the bottle back in my room before anyone saw me with it.

Walking into the kitchen for breakfast, I heard Beck before I saw him. Hannah and Eyre were filling their plates, and Beck was setting out orange juice and coffee with Summer. Whatever Summer had said had Beck cracking up with his mouth open wide in that approachable, life-of-the-party way he had. He was wearing a black V-neck T-shirt and jeans, and his wet hair was pulled up. He looked up at me as I walked in, and I could've sworn an invisible string tightened from my belly to his. Is that what Zola was talking about?

Was it too soon to get him naked again?

"Look out," he called out, "safety engineer on deck!"

No one in the room reacted to his habitual morning greeting to me, and relief sank through my bones.

"Hey Gem, we've got scrambled eggs and bacon this morning," Hannah called.

"That sounds amazing. I'm starving." I scooped eggs onto my plate, and Beck appeared beside me.

"Your OJ, madam," he said, his eyes sparkling more than usual. I felt rather than saw a change in his demeanor. To anyone else, I hoped he looked the same, but his magnetism drew me in. Electricity nipped my hand when he handed me the cup and our fingers brushed.

"I like what you've done with your hair," Summer said to me.

Hannah came up and played with one of my curls. "She's finally taking some steps away from the straight iron."

I smirked at my sister before turning to Beck. "I've got a shift in the kitchen this morning. Can you get that measurement on the brinwire tubing for me and see if we have anything to run a new line?"

He nodded, chewing and not looking up at me. "Didn't we see some in that box of old mech parts?"

"Yes! Thank you. I knew I'd seen some somewhere, but I couldn't remember where."

To her credit, Zola was a phenomenal actor, and Beck was following my lead to keep whatever was happening between us, between us. And thank God. I didn't understand what Beck and I had yet, and besides, it was too new and precious to share. When other peoples' opinions got involved with my love life, it never ended well. And every time I thought of him, I didn't want it to end.

Because of my kitchen shift, I only saw him during mealtimes when the others were around. But about an hour after dinner, on my way out of the kitchen, I got a text from him: *Can't stop thinking about you. If you want me, I'm at your Beck and call. ;)*

I snorted and tagged his text with a laughing emoji. He thought he was so funny.

I waited until I was back in my room to reply: *Still up?*

I took a minute to refresh myself in the bathroom. His response was waiting for me when I got out.

Yes ma'am. Just got out the shower.

Wicked, shower-related shenanigans with Beck? I texted him back: *Be right there.*

I poked my head out of my room and looked both ways. I didn't know why I was sneaking around. I'd left Hannah in the kitchen, and no one else was on my hallway. Besides. It was a big ship, and hardly anyone wandered around this late. I slipped down the service stairs.

He opened the door at my knock, hair wet, white T-shirt and blue plaid pajama bottoms, and stood back to let me pass. "Hi."

He was smiling the smile he reserved for me, the one that made pure desire shiver through all my sacred places. Despite last night—and this morning—my stomach fluttered, and I didn't know how to act. Would we pick up where we left off this morning? Or did having time to think change his mind?

He closed the door and took me into his arms, kissed the top of my head. "I missed you today," he said, his deep voice and sweet presence calming me.

I wrapped my arms around his waist and sighed. "I missed you too." He was warm and smelled like soap. Again, that intense belonging washed over me from just being near him.

"Hey," he said, pulling away to look at me. "I'm sorry if I was weird today, around everybody else. I didn't know if you were okay with everybody knowing we're a thing, annnd...I wasn't sure if we were a thing. I mean, if we're a thing, I want to shout it from the rooftops. I hope we're a thing," he said quickly. "I really want to be a thing."

I beamed, mesmerized by his eyes and his arms around me. "I really want to be a thing too."

His face lit up with delight as he leaned down to kiss me sweetly. "And where are my manners? Come on in." He led me, arm around my shoulder, to the sofa. His room was smaller than mine, painted gray and stuffed with furniture, rows of bookshelves overflowing with books and records, and a stack of guitar cases in the corner.

We snuggled up on the couch, not far from another hammock hanging from his ceiling. "Do you have a hammock everywhere?"

"I don't have one in my bedroom," he said, raising and lowering his eyebrows at me.

"Maybe you should."

"Well if my Gemma wants a hammock in the bedroom, I'll put a hammock in the bedroom, if you know what I'm sayin'." He chuckled, nuzzling my neck.

"I'm *your* Gemma?" I teased.

His eyes went wide. "I didn't mean— I'm sorry. I meant I want to be *your* Beck, but I didn't mean to be presumptuous or, gods! To suggest ownership or—"

I pulled his head closer to me. "Would you kiss me already?"

"Yes, ma'am," he murmured, leaning down to bless my lips with a sweet, long kiss, his hand slipping along my jaw. He *hmmmed* and pulled me closer, deepening his kisses, then dropping them in a line down my neck.

He was too good to be true. I'd been looking for the deal breaker, the undesirable traits that I worried would break through and be insurmountable. But I hadn't found them yet. I wasn't sure they existed. It was inconceivable that I'd wasted time with any other man when this one was here.

"Where did you come from?" How could he have existed all this time in my hometown, and I hadn't known?

He smiled big. "Same as you, Gem. We're all stardust down to every spinning atom." He placed a warm kiss on my forehead, right over where my old witchy books placed the third eye. Warmth, security, and contentment flooded me.

"Every beautiful cell of your body was forged in the heart of stars," he murmured, tracing my eyebrows with his fingertips, "and it took billions of years for the finest of them all to come together and make you."

"You talk sweeter than sugar cane." I smiled into those mischievous, twinkling green eyes. "But if you think flattery will get me into your bed—" I kissed him. "You're right."

He smiled. "In that case, did I tell you how fine your ass looked in those leggings today?" His hand slid up my thigh, squeezing my backside as he kissed the base of my neck.

"Mmm, no, why don't you tell me about it?" I tangled my hand into his hair to bring his kisses closer.

He pulled me to straddle him and stood up with me in his arms. "It looked so fine that I wanted to bite it," he teased. I giggled and sampled the delicious, warm skin of his neck as he brought me up a few steps and into his darkened bedroom. He squeezed my bottom and put me down. "So fucking fine."

I slipped my hands under his shirt to caress his gratuitous muscles and pulled it off over his head. His hands tucked under the hem of my tank top, his palms warm across my stomach, my breasts, pulling it off, trailing his fingertips down my sides, tucking them into the waistband of my leggings and my panties, pulling them off as I undid my bra and threw it aside.

He led me to his bed and lay down over me, capturing my mouth in passionate kisses. "My Gemma," he murmured.

"My Beck," I sighed, wrapping my legs around him. I reached down to grasp him, desperate to get him inside me, but in one smooth motion, he burrowed his hands beneath me and crushed me gently to him, rolling us over so I was on top.

I lay down the length of him, kissing him, enjoying his hands caressing my skin, exploring the canvas of his body. He was big and solid as a mountain beneath me, and I was desperate to climb him. He cupped my face, kissing me with gentle ferocity. He moaned as I grabbed him with both hands, sank down on the hard length of him, taking him in all the way to the hilt. He gently ground his hips up against me, moving so deeply inside me, our moans intertwining.

He sat up, bringing us face to face, eye to eye, soul to soul, and he kissed me devoutly, like I was the air he breathed. We moved against each other like the motion of the tides, my breasts sticking to his chest, my hands gripping and caressing his broad shoulders, the back of his neck. I ground against him, slower, harder, pulling him deeper, my mouth latched to his, his kisses swallowing my soft moans and cries. I felt him deep in the places I'd never been touched, physically, magically, spiritually, his every kiss a benediction, his every sigh and throaty moan a prayer.

I don't know how long we feasted in our holy union, worshiping at the altar of consummation, living, savoring, blooming. I could live the rest of my life this blissed-out, sacredly joined, magic melding, surrounded by his thick, muscled arms, sticking to his skin, enveloped in his scent, the roaring of his blood and heartbeat, drowning in his kisses.

Our magic mingled, coursing through my body, an interplay that stoked pleasure higher here, drew it out longer there. His body and magic brought me to the peak over and over, sent me spiraling in climax after climax, always leaving me wanting more in the best possible way.

But even witches' bodies have a limit to pleasure. The strongest one yet approached, twisting like springs low in my body. His thrusts became harder, deeper, faster, and I ground against him harder, sucking his kisses deeper. My body became electrified like fireworks, my climax bursting like a dam, shuddering through me. His release came right after, and I squeezed the still-spasming muscles inside my body around where he still penetrated me, squeezing my arms and legs around him to ride his final thrusts.

We stayed joined, wrapped up in each other, sweating chests pressed together for a long time afterwards, kissing, existing. When he lay back, I went with him, still in his arms.

"Gemma," he panted, his voice muffled against my throat, his hand tangled in my hair at the base of my head. He kissed my lips and pressed his forehead to mine. "I'm all yours if you want me." He kissed me again. "If you want me, I'm all in."

"I want you, Beck," I said, greedily sucking kisses into my mouth. "I'm all in." I felt the truth of my words down to the core of my soul.

Chapter 13

Closer to a Reckoning

We spent the next week and a half sneaking around the ship, acting around the others like we weren't naked together every chance we got. I healed the beard burn on my face after every make-out session. He offered to shave it off, but it was far too sexy to let him get rid of it.

At lunch today, Hannah pressured me hard to join the girls for movie night, but I'd barely been able to get my hands on my big, sexy man over the past two days, between our kitchen and garden duties with the others. So I claimed a headache and begged off, and Beck met me in my room.

Stars around us—it was so good.

After making love, we lay in bed, talking about the fix he and Summer had come up with for entry onto Gaia. He'd laid it all out, but I still had questions.

"So this spell," I said as he absentmindedly dropped kisses onto my fingers, "you'll be in the engine room, and she'll be on the bridge, and you think you can connect well enough to manage the deceleration for entry? What happens if our filter clogs again?"

"Mmm, I love it when you talk astro-engineering to me, baby," he crooned, kissing my nose.

"Are you making fun of me, sir?" I teased, threading my fingers through his.

"Not at all. I love that I can share my love of astro-engineering *and* magic with you."

I smiled, but my heart twisted. Why did he have to add "magic" at the end of that sentence? Since he'd been working with me, I'd had no problems holding onto my magic, keeping it in line, even at emotional moments. But that didn't mean I'd changed my mind about meeting Madam Indigo.

He settled his head on top of mine, sighing contentedly. "If the feed assembly was clogged, you're right, I think it'd prevent us from achieving the deceleration we need. So we'll just have to be sure to clean it when we exit the Bifrost, or at latest, when we reach the solar system."

"The fix is still theoretical, though, right? Shouldn't we test—"

A knock at my door. My whole body tensed, but Beck snuggled deeper in.

"They'll probably go away in a minute."

A louder knock, and Hannah shouted, "Gemma! I know you're in there, and I don't care if you're sleeping!"

I untangled my limbs from his and slipped on my robe. "What if something's wrong?"

He sat up, his lower half covered by the blankets, but his torso beautifully bare. "I think they'd page us if they needed something important."

Hannah continued to bang on the door.

"I'll just go check and get rid of her." My robe tied tight, I stepped to the door and opened it partway, trying my best to both look groggy and *not* look naked under my robe. Hannah stood there in her pajamas with a big bowl of popcorn.

"Hey you! I know you said you had a headache and wanted to go to sleep, but I'm worried about you. You've been saying that a lot lately, and I don't want you isolating yourself in here. Please come to movie night?"

"Really, Hannah, I'm fine. Go have fun with your friends."

"But I want them to be *your* friends too," she insisted. "You know what? No. I'm not taking no for an answer." Hannah pushed past me into my suite.

My heart pounding, I rushed after her, trying to walk on her left side so she'd look toward me and not Beck. "Hannah, this really isn't a good time. I was about to go to bed, and I—"

"Gemma, you can't spend your whole life holed up in your room!" She turned to me, gesticulating with her popcorn-bowl-free hand. Behind her, Beck sat relaxed in the bed, bare-chested, in full view, grinning. Why didn't I make him hide in the bathroom?

"I swear, this is just like high school, all over again," she continued. "It would mean so much to me if you'd just come. Please? Just one night?"

She started to turn, but I grabbed her arm to stop her. "If I promise to come tomorrow night, will you leave?"

"What's wrong with you, psycho? Are you hiding something?" She whirled around, facing my bed.

"Hey Hannah." Beck waved from my bed, mischief all over his face.

"Oh my God!" Hannah threw her free hand over her eyes and turned back around to face me. Her hand moved down to her mouth, and she laughed. "Oh my God!" she squealed. "Oh my God! Are you two—really?" She turned back around to look at Beck, who sat there lounging and laughing.

I crossed my arms over my chest, my face burning hot as Hannah practically danced from foot to foot.

"Oh my God! I can't!" She exclaimed. "This is the best— Oh my God! I'm gone! I'm going! Never mind! Carry on!" She rushed out the door, slamming it shut. Her shouts for the others mingled with her retreating footsteps.

Beck fell over laughing, but I sat on the side of my bed, dread solidifying in my stomach. "Cat's out of the bag."

"It was gonna happen sooner or later." He looked at me, and his laughter abruptly stopped. "What's wrong? Are you—did you not want to—are you embarrassed?"

"A little."

His face fell. "Of me?"

"No!" I exclaimed, hugging and kissing him. "I could never be embarrassed of you. I just—" I didn't know how to explain. "Her finding out about us brings her closer to finding out I still have my magic, and that I've been lying to her all this time."

He sat up next to me and pulled my robe down over my shoulder, kissing me there. "She's gonna have to find out eventually, right?"

I didn't answer. I'd been living a lovely dream with him, here in the middle of interstellar nowhere. But every day was bringing me closer and closer to a reckoning. I would have to tell Beck about Madam Indigo, and my resolve to keep lying to Hannah was making me feel worse and worse now that I was near her every day.

"Gem, do you want to talk about why you've kept your magic secret from her?"

His words were gentle, but I shucked off my robe and curled up against him, tucking my face into his neck. "No," I said quietly.

He squeezed me and kissed the top of my head. "Well I feel blessed to be with a witch as amazing as you."

Anguish squeezed my chest at the word *witch*. If he could've seen my scrunched-up face, he wouldn't have kept talking.

"I've dated women without magic, but I knew I'd never settle down with one." His fingers trailed absentminded circles along my skin, turning me on and gripping my heart with the potential energy of great sorrow.

"Especially now that I know how your magic feels with mine, while we're working, or playing..." He squeezed me tight. "I'm so proud of what you can do, and I wish you were proud of you too."

I would tell him about Madam Indigo. Before we landed. Before this bubble we were in, burst. He deserved the chance to make a decision about me after he knew all the facts.

"Beck, you don't want to be with me just because I'm a witch, right?" I asked quietly.

"Of course not." He sounded hurt, and I bit my lip in worry. He cupped my face and kissed my head again. "I love your beautiful brain. Seriously, you're the smartest person I know. Brilliant." He slid the hand down my arm and squeezed it. "I love your kind heart. I love how we work together, and laugh together. And that's not even mentioning how beautiful you are, and how extraordinarily sexy you are."

I loved all the times he used the word "love." He pulled my leg up beside his hip, and I giggled into his kisses. Magic was a problem for future Gemma. In-the-moment Gemma was starry-eyed and turned all the way on as Beck kissed me deeper, more seriously. I ran my hand up his chest.

He hmmmed. "What do you think about taking a bubble bath with me?"

"I think only the best things about that plan."

Chapter 14

Eyes Wide Open

After I explained to Beck that Hannah knowing about us meant that now *everyone* knew about us, he talked me into going to breakfast together this morning, hand in hand, to own it. Sure enough, all four women whooped and hollered the moment we entered the kitchen.

"Good morning," Beck said casually, as if nothing had changed.

Eyre turned her whole body around, her mouth open in an O. "Good morning! What have *you* two been up to?"

The women devolved into squealing laughter, falling together for the support.

"Alright, okay. That's enough." I smiled, but my face burned as I poured myself orange juice.

Beck wrapped his arms around me from behind. "See?" He kissed my cheek. "Like ripping off a bandage. Pretty soon they'll find something else to gossip about."

He started fixing us each a plate, but my face still felt hot and red. Zola was the most mature of us all, so I looked at her for help. But she giggled around her coffee cup. "I knew," she said. "But I promised not to say anything."

"Mama Zo!" Eyre stretched her arms forward and bowed to Zola, "Your secret-keeping skills are unmatched. I would've told all y'all the second I knew."

"Like I did!" Hannah guffawed.

"Poor Gemma, your face!" Summer said, leaning forward to put her hand on my arm. "I hope you know we're all so happy for y'all. We don't mean to tease you, but also, we're extremely hard up for gossip on this long-ass trip."

"It's true." Eyre laughed, turning around to include Beck in the conversation. "I painted my toenails blue, and it was all we could talk about for two days. You *have* to give us this."

They meant well, but I wanted to crawl under a rock. Beck, meanwhile, was scooping eggs onto our plates, grinning and enjoying the whole thing.

"And I just want to say," Hannah said, coming around to give me a big hug, "a big ol' I told you so!" The women fell to laughing again while Hannah continued. "Seriously, how long has this been going on?"

Beck popped a piece of bacon in his mouth with a smile. "Not quite two weeks."

"Two weeks?" Hannah exclaimed, eyes and mouth wide. "How were the three of us so oblivious?" A timer went off in Hannah's pocket. "Oops. Time for me to get back on the bridge." She scooped up a mug and skipped out the doors singing, "I'm so happy for y'all!"

"I'm out too," Eyre said. "Gotta make sure we're on track for the Bifrost and contact the Heimdall Station with our ETA."

"Let's leave the kitchen to the lovebirds," Zola said. "Nobody forget we have a spell refreshing tonight!" She pointed at each of us in turn as she walked out with Summer and Eyre, her long, flowered robe rippling around her legs.

"We'll be there!" Beck called out, sitting on a stool beside me at the kitchen island. When they were gone, he kissed my temple. "See, that wasn't so bad, was it?"

I blew out hard. "I guess not. At least we don't have to sneak around anymore."

"Although that *was* kinda fun." He squeezed me tight before attending to his eggs.

"What time is the spell refreshing, do you know?"

"I think Zola said seven?"

I followed his gaze to the closed door.

"Are you sure you don't want to participate?" he asked quietly.

He'd suggested last night that the spell refreshing would be a good time to come forward about my magic, if I wanted to, since adding another witch to the spell would increase its potency. But he'd also assured me that the five of them would be adequate.

"I'm sure." No way was I ready to face that.

He nodded. "Have you given more thought about what you'll do when we get to Gaia? I know you're not going back to Noble Industries, but do you think you'll want to stay around Nouvelle Orleans, or travel somewhere else to work?"

He asked it casually, but the real question beneath his words was *since we're officially a couple now, doesn't that mean figuring out the world together?*

He'd already decided that his life would keep him near the university to finish his degree and stay on to teach. The only plan I had was to get to New Salem where Madam Indigo was, get some kind of job, maybe waiting tables, and pay for her services. After that? No idea. I'd have to come home for Noah and Zola's wedding, and it'd be a big help to live on the ship while I worked up enough money to live on my own. But how could I make any of these plans without telling him the truth?

"Because I think I mentioned that my parents bought a big tract of land," he continued, "and a bunch of us—Noah and Zola, Hannah and Summer, me, even Eyre's parents, last I heard—we're all buying a piece of it."

Oh, that's right. Hannah asked me if I wanted in on that land months ago, and I'd barely paid any attention to her.

"We're making our own expanded subdivision," he said, "with our families close by. We'll all be staying on the ship while we build our houses. And I'm just saying—my house will be plenty big enough for two..." His hands slipped across my belly as he kissed my neck. "And more down the road, if we want."

His sweet, ardent kisses were the gravity pull of a deep cavern full of everything I'd ever wanted, a trust fall into more contentment than I deserved. I trusted *him*, but how would he ever trust or forgive me after I got rid of my magic?

"That's...a lot to think about," I said quietly, biting my lip to keep my gathering tears from falling.

He took his arms away. "Aww Gemma, I'm sorry. I'm moving too fast, huh?"

"Maybe a little."

"I know you have a lot to deal with when you get to Gaia. Please don't let me stress you out. We can go however slow you want to." He pressed a warm kiss to my forehead. "All I want is to be with you."

"Thanks." I hugged him so I could hide my face while I corralled all my guilt back inside my body.

At seven o'clock, Beck and I went up to the Star Deck, and Zola met us all at the elevator with a smoking bundle of herbs.

"Everyone has to be here, and everyone has to be clear," she said, taking her time to cleanse us each individually. "Even you, Gemma."

The comfy rug and floor pillow area were put away for the night. Someone, probably Eyre, had sketched a sigil in chalk on the hardwood floors that looked like three butterflies intertwined. I sat to the side where I wouldn't interfere, and the members of the coven each took their place at a rounded outer edge of the sigil.

Eyre slid a hammer around the lip of a bronze singing bowl and set it down in the center, and Hannah began the ceremony by speaking in that odd language the others had spoken in before.

"*Nisefe lish, leastre wosu.*"

The others chanted the words in response, and they held their hands out toward one another. To my astonishment, beams of light connected like flashlight beams from one person's hand to the next until they were all connected by a circle of light. They smiled and laughed with each other, their faces glowing in the light of their own making.

The magic inside of me was awed. It didn't push its way out; instead, it stood like a street urchin outside the window of a warm home, looking in on a life they could never have. Was this what my life would've looked like, too, if I'd stayed? If my magic hadn't wrecked my parents' hovercar, I probably wouldn't even have gone to school for astro-engineering.

Wouldn't have accepted the position at Noble. I might've stayed home with Hannah and our parents, and maybe Hannah and I would've figured out the secrets of the witching world together. Or would our parents never have allowed that to happen?

Maybe I would've met Beck sooner. Maybe I would've been his dream witch instead of the haunted woman he somehow cared about who was ready to ditch her magic at the first opportunity. My heart squeezed looking at him now. He seemed like someone I'd already missed out on, even as he turned to me and smiled.

After the ceremony, we feasted on a cheesecake that Hannah made for the occasion, and we fell into different groups, chatting. Hannah slipped her arm through mine and pulled me toward the elevator.

"Do you have time for a sisterly chat before your man pulls you away for the evening?"

"Of course, silly. What do you want to talk about?" I followed her into the elevator, and she pressed the mezzanine level.

"Let's go chat on the diving platform," she said. "What are your plans when we get to Gaia? I've been talking to Summer, even before we knew about you and Beck. We'd love for you to stay on the ship with us while you figure out your next steps."

"Thank you." My intense time with Beck had pushed a lot of those questions out of my mind, but that lovely bubble burst the moment Hannah found out about us.

"Of course, sweetheart. You know we'd do anything to help you. It'll be so much fun to have us all together, under one roof again! And now with you and Beck!" She didn't finish that thought, but her excited tone said it all.

The elevator opened on the mezzanine, and we made our way up the platform to the cozy spot where Beck and I had lain and looked at the stars. No way was that three weeks ago.

"Noah's been renting an apartment, but he's moving onto the ship when we get there." She lay down on her back, and I lay down beside her. "Did Beck tell you about his parents' land?"

"Yeah, he mentioned it." *And it scared the shit out of me.* I'd thought about it all day, about sharing a life with Beck, on land, outside this ship. It was everything I wanted, and everything I couldn't have.

"We're building a witching community there, not just our little coven, but all of our extended families. Have you decided where you're going to apply to work? I hear AstridCo's building a facility in the area."

"I guess I could put my application in." AstridCo was a great choice, but now I was afraid to apply. What if that got me on Evander Noble's radar, and he sent the police for me? And having this break from the sterile laboratories and artificiality of a big city had me longing for something simpler. Porch swings and family dinners I didn't deserve.

Beck with his wonderful heart would still want me around after I had my magic taken away, but he'd resent me in time. He'd said himself that things wouldn't work out if I didn't have my magic. Well, he didn't say it quite like that, to be fair, but that's what he meant.

But staying around to watch him be with someone else? That was out of the question.

Not to mention I'd been low-key avoiding my siblings for years. Could I even live near Noah and Hannah with the weight of what my magic did to our parents hanging around my neck? Could I ever find the courage to tell them?

Hannah grinned. "Maybe you and Beck could live together on his parcel of land," she said, elbowing me. "Turns out he was your type after all, huh?"

"You were right." I smiled, but I was about to cry. "Beautiful and brilliant, also sweet and loving. He's almost too good to be true." He was too good to be true, for me, at least.

She turned to me. "So do you think he's the one?"

I studied the stars overhead. "I hope so, Hannah."

She scooched closer to me and rested her head on my shoulder, and we lay in silence for a few moments.

Far below, a door opened. Footsteps and low voices echoed through the room.

"I'm just saying," Eyre's voice floated up. "I absolutely love her, and I love how happy you are with her. I don't think I've *ever* seen you so happy in a relationship, honestly. I'm just worried about you getting hurt."

Hannah and I exchanged frowns. That would've been a good time to sit up and admit we were there, but instead of being responsible, normal people, we stared at each other.

Beck's voice answered, assured. "Gemma would never hurt me."

His misplaced loyalty was a knife in my heart.

"I don't think she'd do anything on purpose, but you remember the last time you tried to date a woman who wasn't a witch. You were miserable."

I closed my eyes and held my breath, willing him not to out me. Hannah scooped up my hand and squeezed it, no doubt thinking my anguish was for not being a witch.

Beck said something I couldn't make out before Eyre spoke again.

"I get that, I really do. But you, yourself, asked me to remind you the next time you tried dating a non-witch. So I'm just reminding you, as requested. You know how you always rush in. And as wonderful as she is, this could end badly. You're her brother's best friend, we're all about to live together on a big tract of land. It could get messy and miserable for you both later. I'm looking out for her too, you know."

"I appreciate you." His footsteps moved farther away. "But I promise, I'm going in with my eyes wide open, not just my heart. I know she's the one..."

His voice trailed off, and a tear slipped down my face, my neck, down into my hair. Hannah squeezed me, but I took no comfort. He thought everything was okay, but I was a monster.

Only pieces of Eyre's words reached my ears. "What about...girl...not giving up on her?"

"Not at all! I'm tellin' you..." Beck's voice trailed off as the door opened and closed. Then they were gone.

Hannah and I frowned at each other while I tried to work out what that last part meant. Somehow being complicit with her made the eavesdropping feel like less of a transgression, but I saw my stewed-in-guilt feeling reflected on her face.

Hannah gave a sheepish grimace and sat up. "I guess we shoulda told them we were here."

My tears fell harder, and she embraced me.

"Sweetheart, don't cry! It was all good! Beck said he thinks you're the one! Eyre likes you! And that's his oldest friend, so you know her opinion's important."

"But she's right! He'll just be unhappy with me. I can't ever be the witch he wants." Even worse, I was about to kill the witch he loved and bring back a weak simulacrum.

Hannah's mouth opened as if a new thought had occurred to her. "Oh honey, are you sad that you lost your magic?"

Her gentle words were a gut punch, consoling me for my lie to her.

She rubbed my back. "You've never wanted to talk about it, so I guess I assumed you were coming to terms with it in your own way. But now you're extra sad because you're with Beck, and you think he only wants to be with a witch. That's it, isn't it?"

"Something like that," I mumbled. This was my opportunity. I could tell Hannah everything. The truth about our parents, the truth about my magic. I could let go of my guilt but double her sorrow. No. I wouldn't do it.

"Zola and Noah make it work," she insisted. "Zola likes being the only witch in the relationship. She says it makes him easier to impress."

She smiled hopefully at me. I knew she was looking for a laugh, but I didn't have one to give. "I'm glad it works for them. But what if it doesn't work for us?"

"Like Eyre said, I don't think I've ever seen Beck so happy—which is saying a lot 'cause he's generally such a happy guy—and he knows you don't have magic. Don't you worry, Gem. It'll work. Y'all will make it work."

Chapter 15

Speechless

My doubts and guilt hadn't kept me from falling straight back into Beck's bed, and all it took was a hug and a long kiss at the door. Less than five minutes later, we were out of our clothes, and after the stars knew how long of kissing and touching, I was surrounded by the bliss of him moving inside me as he breathed in my ear over and over, "Gemma, you're amazing, so fucking amazing."

And now he kissed me sweetly, his hands roaming my skin as if just touching me brought him joy and comfort. "You make me so happy, Gemma," he said, filling my heart with buoyant joy. I slid my fingers through his beard, pulling his kisses closer.

"You're everything I've ever wanted." He dropped kisses on my brow, my eyelids, my cheeks. He searched my eyes, biting his lip. "I have a confession to make."

A flame of fear licked my heart, and all my guilt and worry flooded back in. Technically, I had a confession to make, too. "What do you mean?"

He took a deep breath and let it out. "Do you remember what I said in the forest that day we had a picnic? About finding a beautiful, dark-haired witch to settle down with, and you asked me if I'd divined her?"

I stiffened. Scenarios, each more horrible than the last, raced through my mind. He was seeing someone else. He was engaged. He was secretly married. He was secretly married, and he wanted me to be another wife. No, no. I was the monster here. Not him.

"Yeah," I said cautiously, "and you said no, that that was just your type."

"And while that's very, very true," he said, kissing my forehead, "it was only part of the truth."

He breathed heavily again, bit his lip. Whatever he was about to impart was huge, and my heart was still pounding from making love.

"When I was seventeen, I started having dreams about this woman. This beautiful, dark-haired witch."

A pang of jealousy, and I cocked my head.

"For years, I dreamed about her. Brown eyes, dark, curly hair." He wrapped one of my curls around his finger. "Seriously, she was the most beautiful woman I'd ever seen. Not every night, but pretty often. Sometimes we were just sitting together, talking or laughing, or doing magic." A shy smile, cheeks reddening. "Sometimes I was talking to our child in her pregnant belly. Sometimes we were making love, other times, we were lying just like this."

The hairs on the nape of my neck stood to attention, my heart hammering like it might break. "And then I met Zola, and Noah and Hannah. I was at their house one day a couple years ago, and there was a framed photo on the mantel I'd never seen there before."

Don't say it. Please say it.

"When I saw it...it took the breath right out of me. It was her." He looked down and back up, narrowed his eyes. "It was you."

"Me?" I whispered, frozen in his arms. All the warmth and coziness had been sucked from my limbs, even as my heart surged with joy. It was both the most romantic and most terrifying thing I'd ever heard.

He bit his lip and tucked my hair behind my ear. "It was you, Gemma, beyond any doubt. I had the dream the night before I saw your picture, but never since, like it'd done its job. That's why I was so nervous when we met, and why I probably acted weird as fuck around you. I've spent the past eleven years knowing you were going to be the one, and I didn't want to fuck it up."

I took a breath and opened my mouth, but I was speechless. The day I boarded the ship, that moment our eyes first met. He'd looked at me as if he recognized me. I didn't understand it then, but I did now.

He drew his eyebrows together. "Am I freaking you out?"

"Yeah, a little." Finally, I'd given him some honesty.

"In a good way or a bad way?"

By the look on his face, his whole world depended on my answer. But I snuggled against his chest, unable to meet his eyes. "A good way," I said in a small voice, not at all sure I was telling the truth. But it seemed to be enough for him.

"I'm sorry I've been tryin' to move so fast. I'll do better. Just know I'm not going anywhere. I've always been yours, will always be yours."

He sighed contentedly and snuggled me closer to his chest, lips buried against my hair. Before long, his breath rose and fell evenly, but it was a long time before I could sleep.

It was hard to lay still in his arms while pieces of my heart calved away. I was about to hurt him so badly that he'd take those words back. Because I hadn't changed my mind about my magic, and my decision was only going to hurt him worse the later he found out.

I had to start pulling away. It would destroy me, but better me than him.

Chapter 16

Made Up My Mind

Beck's confession haunted my dreams all night, and all morning I'd been trying to figure out how to distance myself so I didn't make a bigger mess than I already had.

But it was a terrible day for it. We were approaching the Bifrost, the traversable wormhole that would bring us to just outside Gaia's solar system. Well, "just outside" in interstellar proportions. Everyone was on edge. None of us had been through anything like this before. And even though it was safe by all reports, a dilapidated ship was no one's dream vessel for the crossing.

In the engine room, Beck prepped a shield intensifier spell that would help protect us in the Bifrost while I made the adjustments in the system to accept it. Even with the Bifrost looming, all I could think about was being Beck's literal dream witch, his meant-to-be. Who was about to break his heart.

He was in the best mood, practically glowing, singing everywhere he went. He had to be afraid of the wormhole, too, but what he felt for me seemed like his armor. He was making jokes, kissing me every time he passed me. It was hard to be in the same room, knowing what a fraud I was.

He had *me*, but he didn't have *her*, that witch he'd dreamed about, set his whole future on. I couldn't undo the damage I'd already done, but I had to stop making it worse.

The engine room door opened and shut, and Summer called out, "Hey guys, you're not makin' out or anything, huh? Can I come in and do the spell?"

"We just finished," Beck teased. "Nah, I'm kiddin'. Come on in. Let's get this thing done."

As I stood to the side and held the grimoire for them to read the spell from, Summer and Beck stood outside the extra salt circle he laid around the shield generator this morning. The spell itself took five minutes, and as they finished, the salt circle glowed once, twice, and went dark.

"Think it took?" Summer asked, eyeing the salt circle like she expected it to have done more.

"Yeah, I think it did." He released her hands and stepped back, watching the shield generator for a moment more. "It felt right, looks right. All I need to do now is strengthen the electrical system to take the drain. We'll only have emergency lighting overnight during the wormhole, but the spell'll help the systems exchange more freely."

"Good," she said. "You've got it, right? I've got some more to do on the bridge with Eyre to prep for the passage."

"All good." He gave her a thumb's up. "I'll head up and do it now."

Summer did a little dance on her way past me, squeezing my arm for a moment. "I can't believe we're almost there!"

I winced. I'd stay in this liminal space forever, if I could. On this ship, loving Beck, and never having to face what waited for me on Gaia

Beck tossed his head toward the electrical panel catwalk. "C'mon and help me out with the spell."

I paused, my finger on the page in the grimoire. "No, no, no. This is too important."

"We'll do it together," he pleaded, wrapping his arms around me. "I know you can do this."

I shook my head. "I agreed to help you set it up, and that's all. Let's call Eyre, or Hannah, or Zola. Anybody but me." I pulled free and pushed the grimoire into his hands, but he pushed it right back.

"Now come on, don't be shy," he teased. "It only needs one witch, but it'll be stronger with the two of us. I'm here to help you. What could go wrong?"

I grimaced. "Why did you have to say that?"

"I'm sorry. I'm just tryin' to help you be more comfortable with your magic. You haven't done much in a couple of days, and I don't want you to get back in the bad habit of bottling it up. You need to use it."

I took a deep breath, unable to argue with that. Maybe I could do this. Maybe if I believed in myself the way that Beck believed in me, I could do this small spell with him.

I nodded. "I'll try."

He kissed me. "And look, you're wearing your necklace I gave you. It'll be good luck."

Up on the electrical catwalk, he and I had already placed the candles and drawn the sigil on the floor. Now he blew on the candles to light them while I poured salt over the outlines of the sigil, careful not to mar the design.

We sat cross-legged on either side of the little spell, and he took my hands. "Reach inside for your magic," he instructed, "and think about the intention of the spell."

I took a deep breath. Within, my magic stirred immediately, like dust motes in a shaft of sunlight. Beck's magic slipped into my hands like a natural, arousing high, and my magic surged forward to meet it. A white glow bloomed from our joined hands.

"Recite the words with me. *Rewae chern dlaew.*"

I joined in on his second repetition and shifted my hands with him like he taught me. My magic buzzed through my palms, and white light beamed from our hands toward the sigil, reflecting off the columned facets of the clear quartz at the center of the circle. My intentions, my magic, discovered the purpose of the spell. Smooth transitions of lightning erupted in my imagination, zipping back and forth between two systems, which each lit up at the approach, dimmed at the leaving, sharing the power.

But as I recited the last repetition with him, doubt crept in. If I didn't do this right...what if something went wrong with the electricity? What if I did it right, but I still hurt someone? Something was wrong with me, not just my magic. Why was I doing magic at all? How did I let him talk me into this?

The glow from my hands fizzled out when the line was completed. We sat in silence, watching the candles' flames for the check he'd built into the spell to ensure it'd taken. The flames on the candles lowered, then one by one, they flared and lowered again around in a circle, one candle to the next.

Relief rushed through me. "Oh thank God." But before the circuit was complete, one of the candles snuffed out.

At the zapping of a power surge, Beck sprang into action. Emergency lights came on. Sirens blared. The ship lurched to the side, throwing me against the metal railing. Panic gripped me as a series of other sirens wailed, and the lights in the room flashed red. Metal clunked somewhere behind me, and my body began to rise.

Beck jammed his ankle under the railing, reaching across to the panel, desperately flipping switches. I grabbed onto the railing to keep from floating away as he reset the parameters on the panel and quickly shouted the spell three times.

After a terrifying few seconds that felt like minutes, the artificial gravity kicked back in, and everything returned to normal. Except for the impending doom rattling my heart in my chest.

I settled back to the ground, gripping the railing, my magic spooled up and ready to act, tears streaming down my face. The machines around us hummed beautifully, and the circle of candles raised and lowered around in their circle, circuit complete.

He caught sight of me on the floor and rushed over. "Are you alright?"

Eyre's voice came over the intercom. "Is everything okay down there? We just had a power outage and lost gravity."

He pulled me to my feet and replied to her. "We're all good now, just a problem with my spell I didn't expect. Got it fixed now!"

That was almost the end of us all, and it would've been all my fault. My defective magic.

He came back and peered down into my eyes, speaking gently. "Hey, it's okay, no one got hurt, we fixed it. I'm more worried about you than artificial gravity."

I shook my head. I couldn't let him make excuses for me. "It's not okay. I messed up the spell. I could have hurt everyone on the ship."

"We don't know it was you—"

"Of course it was me!" I cried. "Who else would screw up a backup spell so bad that it affected other systems?" Beck tried to pull me into his arms, but I pulled away. I didn't deserve his comfort. I had to tell him.

His shoulders drooped. "Gemma, you know as well as I do that those systems are wired in tandem. An interruption to the centrifugal motion of the water drums affects the artificial gravity." He threw his arm out to encompass the whole room. "Everything's interconnected, and these spells aren't easy to do. They take practice."

But I knew in my heart that my hesitation put everyone at risk. I shook my head. "I know it's me, because when I do magic, bad things happen."

"You healed my face and nothing bad happened. You saved my life on the spacewalk, and we were all fine. Listen, did I ever tell you that I've always had this fear that I'd die in space? But you saved me in the spacewalk. With your magic. Your not bad, very good magic saved my life."

My blood ran cold, and I took a step back. "Wait, what? You divined that you're gonna die in space, and you let me do these spells?" I pushed past him down the steps. I had to get away from him. Being around me put him in too much danger.

His footsteps followed after me. "No, it wasn't a divination. Those are more...precise? This was just a fear. But you didn't let it happen." He stepped in front of me, pointed at his tattoo. "You did that. You saved me from the abyss."

"We're still *in* the abyss, Beck!" I nearly shouted. "We're about to go through a fucking wormhole on this decrepit ship! And you're letting me do spells?"

"But the spell wasn't that bad. I fixed it. You should've seen *my* first spells. They were a disaster."

Tears streamed down my face, and I shook my head again. "But this isn't one of my first spells. I've been pushing my magic down for a long time now, but I didn't always. You want to know why I lied to Hannah, to everybody about my magic? Because it's shit. My magic is cursed, Beck. I'm cursed."

Beck took a breath as if he would interrupt me but bit his lip instead.

"When I was a kid, and my magic came in, when I realized I could do things other kids couldn't, I couldn't wait to show my parents.

I practiced for weeks. I thought they'd be thrilled, finally proud of something I did. But my magic was shit. It was so unpredictable. Of course it wouldn't work in front of them." I sputtered an incredulous laugh. "Did you know they put me in therapy for months for telling stories? It wouldn't show up for the therapist either. I had to confess I'd been making the whole thing up just so they wouldn't make me go anymore.

"I tried to ignore my magic after that. But it was too tempting. And I thought I could get better. I hid what I could do from everyone, even Hannah for a while, until she caught me. I worked hard at my magic, like I do everything.

"But it didn't matter. The boy I liked in eighth grade invited me to the dance but then invited Sarita Jones a week later to replace me, without even telling me? I tried to make his suit too small so he couldn't wear it to the dance that night, but instead I gave him a full-body itching rash for a week.

"When I found out Lara and Dashana talked about me behind my back, I did a spell to make them—just for a day—get tongue-tied every time they spoke. But I gave them speech impediments that they had to go to therapy for. I was petty, Beck. I was vindictive. And messing up the spells never made me stop trying to do them.

"And then—" I sobbed harder and choked it back. "And then when I was sixteen, we came home from school one day. My parents were leaving for a play, but they'd waited in the foyer for us. They'd found my hidden box with all my magic things. I'd never seen them so angry. I tried to take my things back," I cried. The storm that night had been heavy and wild, with loud gusts of wind sheeting the rain in every direction.

"But they told me they knew what was best. They took my box and threw it in the trash compactor. My crystals, cards, everything. They told me they were sending me back to therapy for my delusions and my lying.

"After they left, I ran up to my room." I hiccupped a sob. "I threw myself across my bed. My magic was at a boiling point. I know it was ready to act. And I screamed, 'I hope you never come back!'"

I wrapped both of my arms around myself, sobbing. I couldn't bear to see whatever horror I knew would be on his face now that he knew the truth about me. "They never made it to the theater," I choked out. "They died, and I caused it."

"Gemma," Beck started, his voice heartachingly gentle.

"No!" I pulled away from his reaching arm and walked towards the door. "Stay away from me. I'm only going to hurt you."

He hurried after me. With his long legs, he got in front of me again and put his hands out. "Please, Gemma," he begged, his own voice ragged. "Please don't walk away from me. Please stay and talk to me."

"No," I cried. "I'm a monster, and you deserve to know the truth about me."

"You're not a monster. I'm so sad you've carried this guilt all this time. Please, just come talk to me," he pleaded.

Here he was with his ridiculous good heart trying to make me feel better, like I knew he would. But I couldn't fall into the loving trap that was his arms. He needed to hear it all.

"I've carried this guilt because it's mine to carry. I made Noah and Hannah orphans. Because of me, Mom and Dad weren't there to see Noah become a doctor. They won't be there when Hannah graduates, or when Noah gets married. I lied and told them I lost my magic, because I never wanted to use it again. I didn't have the guts to turn myself in, so I took myself away the first chance I got. Astronautical safety engineering isn't my passion. It's my *penance*. I couldn't save my parents, but I had to try and make things safe for other people."

"Gemma, what you just described, you weren't at all responsible for their deaths. Witchcraft requires planning. Like when you tried to shrink that guy's suit, did you just point your finger at him and proclaim it?"

I shook my head. I'd gathered ingredients for weeks to put it together.

"When you tried to tongue-tie those girls, did you just yell it at them?"

I shook my head again. It'd taken me all night to figure out the wording for that spell, and all of math class to figure out the sigils. I'd still fucked it up.

He laid his hands on my shoulders, leaned over to look into my face. "I think you hurt *yourself* with those words, not your parents. Who've you been blaming all these years? Not chance, not the circumstances of the crash. You didn't mention either of those. You said you caused it directly.

You've punished yourself, rearranged your whole life to atone for saying those words, haven't you?"

"Of course I've considered it could've been an accident. But the timing of it...it wasn't random. My magic *caused* their accident. You can't convince me it didn't."

"I think you should talk to Hannah and Noah. Because I've heard all about your parents' crash—the drunk driver, the rainy night, the broken stoplight—but neither of them ever once said they thought it was *anything* other than chance."

The old horror rushed through me. "I can't talk to them," I balked. "I can't admit what I've done. They'd never believe me."

He cocked his head at me. "So you want to be guilty."

I tried to speak, but only a few frustrated sounds came out. "No, of course not. That's not what I meant."

"Did you ever think that them not believing you might be a good thing? It might be what you need to break the lie you've been telling yourself. No wonder you've hated your magic so much."

This was the moment. I had to break his heart to protect him. "I'm having my magic taken away."

He stiffened and took away his hands. "Wait, what? What do you mean 'have it taken away'?"

He'd taken his hands away the moment I'd said it. He didn't want me without my magic. A horrible pressure took over my chest, and I suppressed a sob. A lie was on my tongue to make it hurt less, but when I looked into his eyes, I knew I couldn't, wouldn't lie to him. Not anymore.

"I found a woman on Gaia. She says she can take my magic away, and I've already paid her half. I owe her the other half when I get there."

His mouth dropped open as he folded his arms, clear pain etched on his face. "No, Gemma, you're not really gonna do that? Are you?"

"I am." I wiped away the tears streaking down my face, but more came.

"Please don't," he breathed. "Your magic comes out of your bone marrow." He grabbed my hand and kissed the tender skin of my inner wrist, which only made me cry harder. "It's integrally a part of you. Even people who've had bone marrow transplants have kept their magic.

Trying to take it out—I don't even think it's possible. What if you're seriously hurt?"

I pulled my hand away. "It's not a medical procedure, it's magic. I'll be fine. Probably."

"*Now* you're okay with magic over science?" He breathed out, visibly deflating. "Please don't do this, Gemma. You're amazing. You're not a monster. Your magic is good, just like your heart. It heals. It healed me." Tears slipped down his face. "Please just think about it?" he pleaded. "We can face anything together."

I shook my head, crying. "No. I've made up my mind. I can't live with my magic, and I can't ask you to give away that future you wanted, marrying that dream witch and living happily ever after."

His eyes widened. "Wait, what are you saying?"

"I'm so sorry, Beck." I curled up into myself over crossed arms, wanted to melt through the grated floor where I could never hurt anyone again. "I never meant to hurt you. I never meant to involve you with my stupid life. You said it yourself, it never works out when you date women without magic. That'll be me. Better to end it now before we're all living together in your magical, utopian witching community."

"You wanna know why it didn't work out with those women? Because they weren't you. Please don't leave me, Gemma." He gulped, tears escaping from his eyes. "Shouldn't I get a say in this? I'd rather, a thousand times over, be with you, even without your magic, than to be without you."

I put my hand on his cheek, and he covered it with his own. I could barely speak for crying. "I know that, Beck. You and your stupid, beautiful, loving heart. I can't let you ruin your happiness just because you think we're fated to be together. I know you'd choose something that wasn't good for you just because you care about me so much. But I can't let you do that."

"So that's it?" he asked quietly, tears down his face. "Is this really what you want?"

"No. But it's what I have to do." I pulled my hand away from his face, my resolve hardening.

He looked down, breathed out hard, and turned to leave the room. After he opened the door, he turned back to me, locking his eyes on mine. "Gemma, I—"

Whatever he was about to say was drowned out by Summer's booming voice over the intercom. "Bifrost's in sight, and y'all better get up here and see this thing. It's fucking terrifying, but it's also the coolest shit I have ever seen."

He broke eye contact with me and left the room.

Chapter 17

Wishcraft

The electrical system switched over to support the shields, and the lights went out, leaving me alone in the eerie blue backup lights of the engine room. I took the stairs, sobbing all the way up to the bridge, my hands trembling, my anxiety spiraling. My magic caused my parents' crash. How was that so hard for him to understand? It could cause his death in space, no problem. What if he can't tell the difference between a fear and a divination?

I couldn't stop seeing the tears on his face. I hated myself for hurting him. But if anything happened to him because of me... Living with the guilt of my parents' death was devastating. Adding Beck's death to the marks against my soul was more than I could bear to think about. He was hurting now, but he'd get over me. He'd find someone else. That thought was a knife to my heart, but it was for Beck's highest good.

I wiped my face before walking onto the bridge, but tears slipped continuously down my cheeks. The numb shock my body felt over what I'd just done must've been the only reason I wasn't wailing and sobbing. Everyone stood in front of the main windows with their backs to me, Beck on the far left. I crept up beside Zola on the opposite side.

"Holy shit." Summer's voice was barely above a whisper. The wormhole loomed larger and larger, cowing us all into silence.

The Bifrost was a star-speckled sphere on the space horizon, and the lights of the surrounding stars bent around it like a psychedelic hallucination. As our ship approached the mouth, the sphere grew larger and closer, like a great, black planet whose atmosphere we were about to enter. Clouds of gases emerged, whirling in its throat, and beyond lay our starry destination. Even though it was far across the galaxy, the Heimdall station that guarded the other end seemed right in front of us. After a moment, we were inside the throat, miraculously traversing a shortcut through space and time.

Everyone stared open-mouthed out the window, but I watched Beck watch the Bifrost, his eyes alight with equal parts fascination and abject fear. If I were a better woman, I'd have him in my arms right now. He'd tell me everything he knew about it, his whole body animated by his great passion. But his face was impassive, tear streaks glistening on his cheeks above his beard. Did he need my hand to hold just when I'd taken it away from him? Fresh tears streaked down my face.

He glanced at me, his dear features transformed with grief, then he looked down and rubbed his chest. "I think that's about all I need to see of that," he said gruffly, clearing his throat. "I'm going down to check the spells and...maybe say my prayers." He turned and left the bridge.

"Fuck, seriously," Eyre said.

With that exchange, the Bifrost's spell on us all was broken, and Eyre and Summer went to their stations on the dark bridge to navigate us through.

The Bifrost was terrifying. My Beck was terrified. And sad. And alone. I did this to him. I gulped back a sob and rushed from the room.

"Gemma, wait!" Hannah called. "What's wrong?"

I kept going, right out onto the Star Deck. But I stopped halfway across. Where was I gonna go? I belonged down in the engine room with Beck, except I didn't. I belonged back with my sister, except I didn't. Outside the windows the throat of the wormhole was swallowing the ship whole. I wanted it to swallow me whole.

Footsteps. I turned my back to them, trying to hide my face.

"Gemma, what's wrong?" Zola asked.

Hannah came around to face me. "Honey, why are you crying? Are you worried about the Bifrost? Do you want us to get Beck?"

I shook my head and cried harder. She pulled me into her arms with a soft cry.

"Gemma, love. What's wrong?" Zola hugged me from behind so I was sandwiched in between my two sisters. "What happened?"

But I was crying too hard to even tell them. Thank God I'd worked that spell with Beck, or my magic would be erupting out of me. Now, I was just empty.

"Come sit down with us. Tell us what's wrong." Hannah pulled me to the cozy rug area, and they sat on either side of me. "Did something happen with Beck?" she asked gently.

I shook my head, a lie already on my tongue. If I started talking about him, everything would come out. But maybe it needed to. I nodded. "I pushed him away. I—" I sucked in a sobbing breath. "I broke up with him."

Hannah pulled back, fixing her big blue eyes on me. "No! Why? You two are perfect for each other."

Zola pushed a tissue box into my hands, and I wiped my face. I owed Hannah the truth. So much more than the truth. Zola too.

"Because I'm a monster. I've been lying to you. For years."

Hannah frowned, moving my hair out of my face. "What are you talking about?"

"Do you want me to go?" Zola asked. "Am I intruding?"

"No, you need to hear this too." I grabbed Hannah's arm and laid my hands on the long scar from her bike accident. "Actually, let me show you."

I focused on the scar on her skin, the scarring beneath it, and healed the bump in her bone where the simple fracture had been. Hannah gasped. Her magic rose up to meet mine, just as curious as ten-year-old Hannah was the night she showed up in my room and caught me doing magic, holding her teddy bear by one of its feet and asking, "Whatcha doin' Gemma?" with her big blue eyes wide.

There beside me on the Star Deck, Hannah's magic stepped in like a good little soldier. I gave it tasks—mend these cells, bind these proteins—and it dutifully accomplished them, reporting back for another assignment. A wholly different feeling from healing Beck. After only a few minutes, my Hannah's arm was whole, and I took my hands away.

Zola grabbed Hannah's arm, turning to catch it in the dim emergency lights. "Your scar is completely gone. Gemma, that's amazing. Is it healed all the way through?"

I nodded, biting my lip. Studying my sister's face and waiting for her to hate me.

"I don't understand," Hannah said, her voice awed as she ran her finger over where her scar used to be. "I thought your magic left after Mom and Dad died."

"I never lost it. I'm so sorry I lied. I just tried to stop using it."

Her mouth was open, her brows lowered as she stretched and tested out her arm. "Why?" she asked softly.

My eyes filled again with tears. "Because—" She looked at me with such trust. I couldn't run from this anymore. "My magic caused the accident." I didn't have to tell her which accident. "My magic is cursed, and I've been too scared that I'd hurt you or Noah or somebody else if I used it."

Her eyes welled up. "How could you think you were responsible? The guy who hit them was drunk, the light at Veterans and Clearview was out, and—" A tear streamed down her face. "You remember how it was raining that night."

I pushed past the lump in my throat. "I know, but I was so angry at them. They never thought I could do anything right, and magic was the first thing that was mine, you know? But what you don't know is what I said," I sobbed. "In my room. I screamed that I wished they wouldn't come home at all."

She nodded, tears stealing down her face. "I know. I heard you."

I took a breath, searched her face. "What?"

"Yeah. And when they didn't come home, gods, I felt so bad for you. That things ended that way between you. But I never once *blamed* you." She tucked a stray curl behind my ear. "You know magic doesn't work that way, right?"

"That's what Beck said, but—"

"You confided in Beck, but you didn't tell me?" Realization crossed her features. "Is that what y'all argued about?"

My face crumpled. "He thinks we're fated to be together. He wants to marry a witch, and that can't be me. I'm—" I put my head down, unwilling to look at either of them as I confessed my final sin. "There's a woman on Gaia. I'm paying her to take my magic away."

"Gemma, no! Why would you do that?" Hannah gripped my hands and tried to get me to look at her.

Zola huffed. "Only one witch I know of would ever attempt such a thing. Please tell me you're not meeting with 'Madam Indigo.'" She said her name with more contempt than I'd ever heard from Zola about anything.

"You've heard of her?"

"Heard of her? For starters, her real name is Brenda McPhee. That 'Madam Indigo' bullcrap is what she calls herself to sound impressive and mysterious. She's an untalented hack who got kicked out of three different witching communities for her practices.

"Gemma, she's not always successful taking magic away, you know, and it's supposed to be painful, and irreversible when it *does* work. She's messing around in your bone marrow. Do you know how many disorders could result? Leukemias, myelofibrosis, aplastic anemia..." She counted them on her long fingers, her ring flashing in the dim light. "You don't need me to go on, do you?"

Hannah started in. "You're way too smart to be so dumb. Your magic's part of you. It'd be unnatural to take it away, and oh my gods, the way you can heal people? Like wow?" She ran her finger over where her scar used to be.

But I was too good at throwing fences up in front of myself to let them remove any now. Give me a clear field, and I'd still find a hundred barriers in my way, even if I had to make them myself.

"But if it wasn't for me, Mom and Dad would be alive, Hannah. Don't you understand? At its best, I don't deserve it, and at its worst, it's dangerous. It's what busted that window out the first day in flight. It wrecked that spell today. If I get some kind of disorder from having it removed, it's what I deserve."

Hannah used her sleeve to wipe my tears. "Gemma, you didn't cause Mom and Dad's death. You haven't done anything wrong."

I'd never imagined that anything would be alright again if I'd unburdened my guilt. I'd imagined telling Hannah and Noah in a hundred different ways, each ending more horribly than the last. So to be faced with her compassionate disbelief? I was completely at a loss for words.

Zola took my hands in hers, her gaze solemn. "Gemma, when I tell you that I have nearly thirty years' experience with witchcraft, it's because even before my own magic came in, I learned about it through my family. And in my professional witch's opinion, I call bullcrap. You couldn't have had any effect on what happened to your parents. Not only are there no stains on your aura, but Hannah told me about the magic you used to do. And yes, I know all about poor what's-his-name's full body rash, which, incidentally, it sounds like he had coming."

Hannah nodded. "It takes an extraordinarily dark soul a lot of time and effort—and usually wicked, otherworldly help—to directly harm someone. Misfortunes, sure. Broken toes, absolutely. Possession, for sure, if you're sick as fuck and have a willing poltergeist."

I looked up at her, horrified.

"See?" Zola continued. "The look on your face right now tells me where your heart is. A simple statement, spoken in anger, those are just angry words. The worst you could have done was hurt their feelings."

"Yeah, Gem," Hannah said. "The only power a wish has is that it echoes back onto the wishmaker. The whole 'I'm rubber, you're glue' concept. Beck's mom calls it *wishcraft*. Anything you wish on somebody else is gonna bounce right off of them and come back to you, but not because it's magic. Because it's human nature." She frowned and hugged me tight. "Oh baby, I'm so sorry you've carried this for so long. You should've told us!"

I hugged her back, hard. My thoughts were still jumbled, but a lightness sailed through my limbs like the sun peeking momentarily out of dark clouds.

"Speaking of Beck," Zola said, "explain to us again why you broke up with him? Because you thought you were dangerous?"

"He was trying to help me with my magic, keep it from bursting out like it did in San Francisco."

"What happened in San Francisco?"

"Hannah, don't divert her." Zola turned her eyes on me. "Tell us about you and Beck."

"But this whole time he's had this thing about dying in space."

Both women spoke at once. "What?"

"It's just a feeling," I reassured them. "Not something he divined. But how could he let me do magic? On a spaceship? I'm like—" I sputtered. "Magical dynamite. But he has this crazy idea that I'm the girl he's dreamed about for years, who he's fated to be with. I can't let him—"

"Hold up." Zola put her hand on my arm. "*You're* the dream girl?"

"That's what he thinks, but I—"

"No, no, don't glaze over this," she insisted. "Beck told you that *you* are *the* dream girl?"

"Yeah." I gestured at Hannah, to remind her of what she told me. "He said he realized it when he saw my picture at the house."

"Ohhhh," Hannah said. "That selfie I asked you to send a couple of years ago? I figured he just thought you were hot." Her eyes practically turned into hearts. "Gemma, you're his *dream girl*! You know he has a gift for divination, right?"

I nodded weakly as Zola jumped in.

"I remember him being quite taken with it, but he never said why. Well, what did Beck say about you wanting to have your magic taken away?"

"He didn't want me to, but he said he'd rather be with me, without my magic, than not be with me at all. I know he means it now, but he would've come to resent me." Why was I talking about having my magic taken away as some hypothetical? "I know he would."

Both women shook their heads vehemently, and Hannah actually laughed at me. "Girl, do you know Beck at all?"

"Tall, handsome guy? Scruffy beard?" Zola prompted. "He's been pining after you practically his whole life, before he even knew who you were. *Pin-ing*. And if you could see the etheric cord you two share, you would know that man is yours until the stars fall."

"Ooh," Hannah cooed, her eyes bright. "They have an etheric cord?"

"Yes," Zola said emphatically. "A beautiful, golden sacral one."

"What does that mean?"

"That's a soulmate bond," my sister explained. "You have to go make things right with him. You'll never find a love like that again."

"Go make up with him so you can enter the new solar system with your heart open. The fresh start will do you good," Zola said.

"And please no more talk about having your magic taken away, deal?" Hannah asked.

"I'll think about it," I said, surprised to find that I meant it.

I left Hannah and Zola and went straight down to the engine room. Beck wasn't there, but his coffee mug sat on the side table, on top of his journal by the hammock, and it was still warm.

I went to his room and knocked, but he didn't answer. He'd given me a key, but I didn't feel right about going in.

With the comms out, I went through the ship to all his favorite haunts, calling for him. He wasn't in the gym, and he didn't answer when I called for him in the forest or on my second trip to the engine room, thinking I'd missed him in the stairwell.

He was either avoiding me, or I just kept missing him, which knowing him, was more likely. I knocked on his door one last time and went in when he didn't answer. He wasn't there, so I laid across his bed. At least I'd be there when he got back.

The night had been long and cruel. I kept reaching for Beck, finding the bed empty. The wormhole's roaring had haunted my dreams. All night I wanted him. To tell him I was sorry. To see if he was okay. To see if he was afraid.

I woke up to darkness. His clock said it was morning, but there was no twittering birdsong, no faux sunlight streaming through the transom over his door. Something was wrong on the ship.

I crept out of his empty room. The hallways were quiet and ominous, like dawn on a stormy day. My footsteps lit only by the emergency lights along the floors, I went looking for him again.

The engine room was dark, quiet, and empty. Only my echo returned Beck's name to me. Five candles had drowned out in their own wax, and worry prickled up my spine. He'd never let them go out. I fixed them and went on with my search.

Everything by the hammock was untouched from last night, cold coffee in his mug, its handle still pointing toward the top right corner of the journal.

Summer's voice on the intercom broke through my sadness.

"Beck, could you please call in? I need an update on the electricity, please. Some auxiliary systems are back up, but the drive's not giving me the readings I was expecting, and why are the lights still out?"

I went through the console for the information and called her back. "I can't find him, but you're right. The electrical system isn't recalibrating like it's supposed to. I'm not sure if the systems'll shift over, and I'm not sure what to do about it. I'm worried something went wrong with the spell."

"Okay, can you get with Beck and see if you can fix it?"

"Yeah, I'll keep looking for him. Y'all haven't seen him?"

"No," she answered. "No one's seen him since he was on the bridge with us last night, and I don't see him on the CCs. It isn't like him to sleep in, but maybe he had a rough night?"

"I'll find him."

I started on B2, going through every storage room, calling his name. No Beck.

I called up to the bridge, my unease increasing. It was never this hard to find him.

"Have y'all found Beck yet? He's nowhere on B2."

"No," Zola answered back, "and I don't like it. He has to be on the ship somewhere, right? Hannah, will you go get the 1st floor keys and check the other rooms on Beck's floor? Eyre, you take the Star Deck and mezzanine. Gemma, you take B1. I'll take lobby level."

Cold fear seared through me, and I couldn't place it. I remembered what he said to me the day we met. *What could happen to me on the ship?*

I hurried upstairs to B1, stuck my head in the gym and called his name, but he wasn't there. I rushed through all the rooms of the med bay, and no sign of him. I went through the brig and security office. Nothing.

I dashed into the unnatural night in the forest, let my eyes adjust to the fauxglow moon high above the trees. "Beck!" I called out. Nothing but the sounds of startled birds, the breeze through the trees, and the gurgling of the lagoon.

I searched through the garden shed, jogged around the back of the lagoon. Thought of the day that we played hide and seek among the trees, when we'd almost kissed. My magic was queuing up inside me again, rising with a cold dread I couldn't name.

Jogging through the trees, I saw him lying there in the darkness. "Beck! Oh my God there you are! We've been so worried about you. Didn't you hear us calling you?"

But he didn't move or answer me. He was lying on his back, eyes closed. Asleep? Oby was on his chest. He turned and meowed at me loudly, jumping up and rubbing his body through my legs.

"Beck," I said, kneeling beside him, placing my hands on his arm and shoulder. "Beck, wake up. Since when are you such a heavy sleeper?"

I pushed and prodded at him, but nothing woke him up. Flashing back to the spacewalk, I pressed my ear to his chest. He was breathing unencumbered, and his heart was steady and slow.

"Beck, please wake up! I'm sorry."

No response. Adrenaline and magic flooded my body. I laid my palms against his chest and poured my magic into him, seeking for something to fix, but there was nothing to be done. And his magic didn't rise to meet mine.

Tears streaming down my face, I ran to the intercom near the door and threw out an all call. "He's in the forest! Zola, he's nonresponsive!" I sobbed. "Zola, hurry!"

I ran back to him, smoothing the hair from his face, kissing his brow. "Beck, Beck, please come back to me. I'm so sorry I hurt you." My hands on his face and heart, I reached out again to his magic with mine—nothing.

I laid my head on his chest. "I'm so sorry," I sobbed. "I should never have pushed you away." I sat up and looked at his face, his beautiful face that I loved so much.

I loved him, and he was gone.

"I love you, Beck," I sobbed. "I love you. Please come back to me."

The forest door opened, and many sets of feet ran in my direction.

Zola fell to her knees beside Beck, pressing her fingers to his neck. "Beck! Beck honey, wake up!" She gently pulled open each eyelid, then carefully swept his body, running her hands in a claw-like manner down his body, around his head.

Hannah and Eyre ran up, out of breath, the former opening Zola's medkit beside her. Zola grabbed her stethoscope, listened to him.

"I don't understand," she said. "There's no apparent injury. No bleeding, airway clear, temperature *feels* normal. He's not sleeping, but he's—" She pulled out a small light, checking his eyes again. "He's just not *here*. Go get the stretcher. Let's get him into the med bay."

Hannah and Eyre ran off together, and I grabbed his hand, kissing it, crying.

"Did you try your magic?" Zola asked.

"Yes. I can't find anything wrong with him."

"He'll be okay," she said firmly. She sat back and tilted her head, studying the edges of him. She frowned and tears slipped down her face.

"What are you seeing?"

"Maybe nothing," she said, wiping her face. "His aura's dim. Not normal."

Hannah and Eyre came up with the stretcher, and we loaded him carefully onto it. Zola pushed him out of the forest.

The med bay doors opened at our approach, and Zola brought him into the back, pushing his stretcher under the AI nurse and locking it there. She initiated the AI nurse and connected him to a heart monitor. "Step back ladies. Let Nurse Clara do her thing," she murmured.

I stepped back beside Eyre, could see Hannah through the window talking to Summer tearfully over the intercom.

"Zo, can you see his aura?" Eyre asked, wiping her face.

Zola bit her lip and shook her head as she went around to the consoles. "It's there, but it's dim. I don't know what that means. I've never seen that before."

I joined her at the consoles. A full MRI scan of Beck's body came to life on the screen. I didn't understand any of what I was seeing, except that his heart rate was normal, like he was sleeping. His blood pressure was low normal. Oxygen level, normal.

Zola tapped on the monitor, expanding the MRI of his brain. "He looks completely normal, except he's not. I don't understand enough about his brain scan. She's going through common scenarios. It may take her a while." Her eyes darted around the screen, making sense of data I couldn't hope to understand. "Not consistent with a coma. No trauma. No injury. No swelling." She looked at me and Eyre. "Y'all can go back to him. Clara's done."

Neither of us had to be told twice. I took one hand, and Eyre took the other. We waited quietly by him while Clara compiled and compared data. I was almost too numb for tears. I kissed his knuckles and smoothed hair from his face. No way was this real life.

Hannah came in. "Eyre, I'm so sorry, but Summer needs you on the bridge. Now that we're through the Bifrost, she wants to make sure we're on the right track with no deviations."

"Yeah, okay." Eyre's dark eyes met mine. "Let me know if anything changes?"

"Of course," I nodded, swallowing hard.

Eyre left, and Zola followed her out. Hannah came around and put her arm around me.

"We're gonna figure this out, Gemma. He has to be okay." I fell into her arms crying, still not letting go of Beck's hand. "You two are too good together. We'll figure it out."

Summer's voice came over the intercom. "Gemma, I'm so sorry to ask, but can you meet me in the engine room? We have to get this electrical problem under control. We only have a few more hours until we land, and we don't have what we need to decelerate for entry. The entire ship's in jeopardy."

Chapter 18

A Magical Problem

I pressed a kiss to his forehead and let Hannah lead me out of the room, downstairs, and into the engine room. Hannah was right. I was being so, so stupid, just as stupid as when I let Beck walk away. There was a chance, however small, that he was still okay, and that's what I had to cling to. He wasn't just the man I loved, because I knew now that I loved him, more than anything. But he was also the man everyone loved.

He needed me, and I wouldn't abandon him to whatever this was any more than I would've left him to drift in space, before I knew what he'd mean to me. He may not want me back, but I had to try. And if I had to use my magic, I'd be the best damn witch the world had ever seen.

Summer met us in the engine room. We hurried through the dark room, guided by the blue runs of emergency lights on the floors, past the flickering expanses of candles in the spells that were still working, still protecting the ship.

Once we were up by the electrical grid, I asked, "Do you think we can get the lights working in the ship again? The electrical panel's not my forte."

"Yeah." She studied the panels with a frown. "A bunch of the breakers are flipped. That must be what was causing all the problems. I mean, it doesn't make a lot of sense, but I'm no electrician."

"Neither am I," I said, paging through the ship's systems on a console. "Beck's so much better with this than me."

Summer went along the panel flipping switches. A short buzz accompanied by a small flash, and she yelped.

"What the hell was that?" she balked, shaking out her hands.

"What?" My attention was still pulled into the shield readings. The energy density seemed really high to me.

"This shouldn't be able to shock me. It's all coated in Abidi composite insulation. And I just switched these wires. Why are they back the way they were before?" Frustration coated Summer's voice, edged with panic.

One tap would shatter the delicate shell holding me together, but I tried to bolster her. "I believe in you, Summer. Just take a breath."

"I *know* that's not how I left it," she fussed. "Gemma, did y'all mess with the wiring?"

"No, not since the spacewalk." I pulled my gaze away from the console. "What's wrong?"

"It doesn't make any sense. There's no reason—"

A sharper, louder buzz, accompanied by a brighter flash. Summer yelped. A tiny flame leapt to life in the electrical equipment. Before I could grab an extinguisher, Summer pinched the fire out with her fingers.

"Can you hand me that tritonic driver over there?" She pointed to the tool chest where several tools sat on top.

I took two steps toward it, and the tritonic driver flew off the tool chest, barreling at my face. I threw my arms up on reflex, batting it aside, and the handle smacked Summer on the side of the head.

"Ouch!" She gripped her head and turned to me, her mouth and eyes wide. "Did you just throw that at me?"

"No! Why would I do that?"

A wrench flew out of the toolbox. It whirled over me and barreled at Summer. She ducked, and it hit the electrical panel.

Summer growled and slammed a panel shut. "When did y'all start keeping a poltergeist down here?"

My heart fell to my feet. "A what? Nothing like that's happened the whole time I've been here," I insisted.

"It might be afraid of Beck. I bet it never does it when he's around. Misogynistic piece of shit ghost!" she shouted. She flipped a switch and turned the apparatus's handle to push it back in. "That oughta—"

The apparatus she'd just pushed in shot out again. It smacked her dead center in the chest, throwing her backwards off the catwalk. She landed with a clatter below.

Hannah and I shrieked her name and sprinted down the steps.

The electrical panel rained sparks through the dim room against a backdrop of red lights flashing. Summer groaned and turned from her side to her back. She looked up at the electrical panel and screamed, her face twisted in terror. Amid the falling sparks, Hannah ran in at a slide on her knees and threw herself between Summer and whatever was scaring her.

"*Trislof noeb*!" she shouted. A bright light shot like a comet from her outstretched hand, and in its penumbra, a figure's silhouette retreated toward the ceiling.

Summer sat up shakily, and Hannah wrapped her in her arms, kissing her head. "Baby, are you okay?"

She nodded and clung to Hannah.

All my magic felt moved to the outer layers of my skin like armor, prickling all over. "What was that?"

"Some kind of spirit," Hannah answered. "You're sure you're okay?"

"I think so. I almost had everything ready," she said, straining to speak and curling into a ball.

Hannah craned her neck up at the ceiling. "I think it's gone now. Crap—not just sparks!"

She ran back up the steps, grabbed the extinguisher by the toolbox, and sprayed down the whole panel. "The whole thing's melted together," she lamented.

"The whole panel?" I asked.

"Yeah," she said, coming back down the stairs.

Summer started to cry. "No more daytime. It's all night from here til Gaia. It'd take that long to rebuild it."

"Where are you hurt?" I asked.

"I think I just got the wind knocked out of me," she winced, her voice tight, "but my back really hurts."

"Ok. Don't move." I laid my hands down on her stomach, and she looked up at Hannah confused.

"It's okay, love," Hannah said. "Gemma still has her magic. She's apparently an advanced healer." She tilted her head and glared at me in mock irritation.

After I fixed her injuries, Summer went back up to the bridge. Hannah and I reported the poltergeist to Zola. Her expression grew more and more confused as we talked.

"And you and Beck never saw anything like that before down there?"

"No, nothing."

The two-way video rang, and Zola flipped it on. "First things first. Let me tell you what Clara came up with." She pointed at her screen where Beck's imaging was pulled up. "She says that his MRI shows activation in several areas on the left side of his brain associated with kinesthetic imagery. But the visual cortex is *deactivated*."

I exchanged a confused glance with Hannah. "What does that mean?"

Zola's face fell. "I have no idea, and neither does Clara. We know he's not in a coma. We know he's not asleep and dreaming. I can't understand why his aura is so dim, but I'm thinking we have a magical problem, not a medical one. Because as soon as I got him in here, I noticed something else unusual about his aura."

"What is it?"

"Well, your aura's an extension of your soul. It's kind of the luminous edges that surround your human body, protecting you from other entities, picking up information for your senses. But his is dim, and it's also—" She walked around to Beck's head, looked around the edges of him. "It's sort of pinched off, here." She rested her hand on the top of his head. "And there's an etheric cord that just...goes off into the distance. I can't see what it's connected to, but I'm guessing it's connected to the other part of Beck's spirit."

"So part of his spirit has left his body?" Hannah asked.

"That's my current theory," Zola said.

As she spoke, a whirlwind of miscellaneous items—pens, herb bundles, medicine bottles, bandages—suddenly whipped up in the room, then showered down on us, and I covered Beck's head with my body.

But Zola watched the disturbance carefully. I tracked her eyes back to Beck's head.

"Zola, is the poltergeist...Beck?"

She opened her mouth, but Summer came back over the video.

"Ladies, the antimatter drive went offline, and I can't get it back up. I don't know what that intangible fuck in the engine room did, but the pressure's dropping, the shields are weakening, and the heat exchanger system's failing. Worse than that—" She flicked a switch on the console. "We got nothing. I'd say we're dead in the water, but we're hurtling through space."

My stomach sank. Out in this frictionless vacuum, a body in motion would stay in motion on the same path, forever, until it hit something. The near-constant state of panic I'd entered since I found Beck on the forest floor ratcheted up a notch.

Eyre put my icy fear into words. "We're entering our new solar system in just a few hours. If we don't do something, we're gonna overshoot it or crash land on Gaia."

Discussions broke out around me. We couldn't fix all the problems with the ship without Beck, especially the electrical ones. He wasn't only my number one priority because I loved him, he was key to our survival.

"Okay look," I shouted, "listen! The pressurization system can reach twenty percent before we're critical, same with the shields. If we're desperate, we have oxygen masks in the storage room. But we need Beck if we're gonna land safely. Eyre, how long do we have until we're shot out of the sky on Gaia?"

She tapped at her console. "Five hours."

I turned to Zola. "You're the chief séance officer, right? Or was that just a joke? Do you think this entity is really Beck? Can you talk to him and find out what happened to him, and how we can help him?"

She nodded. "I absolutely can."

Chapter 19

Chief Séance Officer

Ten minutes later, the five of us sat around the table where Hannah, Zola, and I had tea. Was it only two months ago? Summer lit three white candles, and their smoke writhed up to entangle in the lemongrass incense that already scented the room.

The others joined hands, Zola and Hannah grabbing onto mine.

"Spirit of the ship," Zola began, "present and explain yourself. Why are you throwing things, sabotaging our ship, and generally being a pest?"

Nothing happened. Was Zola too rude to it?

The temperature dropped even farther than the endemic interstellar chill, and the hair on my arms stood up as. My exhale fogged in the candlelight.

Mist gathered over the flickering flames, growing thicker and thicker until a man's silhouette shimmered inside. All the hairs on my body stood at full attention, but I leaned toward it on instinct.

"What is your name?" Zola asked imperiously.

A voice bubbled out of the air as if emanating from deep within the ocean and breaking the surface to escape.

Help. The spirit's pained voice cut to my soul and slipped down my spine like ice.

But Zola continued, her face placid. "Why do you disturb the peace of this place?"

I don't want to go. I need...help.

"What help can we give you?" Zola asked, her brows furrowing.

A frigid wind came out of nowhere, pouring from another plane onto this one like a door cracked open in a blizzard. The very air above the table trembled and writhed, and the voice continued.

Gemma...my journal.

"Beck?" I shouted.

An icy wind tore through the room, guttering the candles and overturning an empty stool. All the noise and candles went out.

"Beck!" I called again, but there was no answer. Only silence.

A flame flickered to life, and the haunted faces of the witches around the table reappeared.

Zola relit the rest of the candles. "So. The intangible fuck is Beck. Do you know what he was talking about? Does he keep a journal?"

The engine room. "Yeah, I think he does."

I ran down the central stairs to the bottom of the ship, pushed through the engine room door, and I didn't stop until I was moving his cold coffee mug to pick up his journal.

Guilt twinged in my chest over invading his privacy. "Sorry," I murmured, flipping through the pages, trying to figure out what he wanted me to see without prying into all his secrets.

The book naturally fell open to a folded-over piece of copy paper stuck between the pages, a print-out on astral projection. On the journal page it was stuck into, dates were listed in Beck's neat, all-caps writing, with check marks and X's beside them, and some commentary. The first date was a couple of months before liftoff. I scanned down the list until I came to the first checkmark.

10/4. I did it! I astral projected for almost a whole minute. Fucking terrifying. I saw my body, freaked out, slammed back into it. Feels like a hurricane hit me.

Then several more X's but more and more checkmarks.

11/16. I'm getting bolder. Went to City Park. This one nasty demon thing cursed me out, but the other entities I passed either can't see me, or I don't merit their attention. Fine by me—they're scary AF. I don't love being in the spirit world so much, but I come back to my body refreshed and calmer than I left it. But idk why I was worried about getting stuck. Going back is a breeze.

The last several entries were since we'd been in space.

12/11. I met HER. I knew she was coming, and I still almost lit the ship on fire when I saw her. She's amazing. So fucking perfect. So much MORE than I ever dreamed. Note to self: do not fuck this up.

My hand over my mouth, tears streaming, I read on.

12/13. Too terrified to AP in space, but damn I'd love to not be freaked out for a while. But what if I get out of the ship on accident and get lost in space?

12/15. I did it and took a quick trip around B2. I think I scared Eyre in the hallway. My bad.

12/16. Can't sleep. Space travel sucks. But at least I get to spend all day with Gemma tomorrow. That beautiful woman is keeping me sane. She's my future. No doubt. She's my everything. Wish I could tell her.

1/14. Didn't AP. Not sure I ever will again. Real life is too perfect. Slept my first peaceful night since take-off. With G. ♡ I'm so in love.

The most recent entry was last night.

2/2. Gemma doesn't want to be with me. I can't explain this pain or how much I love her. We're in the Bifrost. Ship seems good, but now abject fear is escalating with the grief. I'm too wrecked to stay in my body right now. I'm going to the forest to AP. Hoping that calms me down enough that I can go talk to Gemma. I can't lose her, not when I've just found her.

A sob escaped my lips, and I closed his journal before my tears could sully the pages. But he gave me the answer. I kissed its cover before putting the book back and ran all the way to the med bay.

"He astral projected!" I shouted, rushing into the room and breaking up whatever conversation was happening. "He astrally projected. He's been practicing for months. He must've gotten stuck. How do we get him back?"

Zola's eyebrows knitted. "But if he's been practicing it, why wasn't he able to go back into his body?"

"I don't know. He had a list of dates in the journal. Maybe it had something to do with interference from the Bifrost? He did it in space before without mentioning any problems."

Eyre got up. "Zo, don't you have a spell for someone to go into the spirit world and bring someone back?"

I snapped my head to Zola. "Can we go in and bring him back? I'll go."

"It would have to be that spell. None of us can astral project, unless anybody else has been keeping magical secrets." She eyed us each in turn, but we all claimed innocence.

"Okay, but first let me run this through Clara and see if there's any precedent, or if astral projection is consistent with his brain patterns. I want him back, too, but it'd be crazy to send someone into the spirit world if we don't have to."

"I'll go," I said again. "Where's this spell?"

Zola pointed to a bookshelf on the far wall. "It's in the white book, there on the top shelf."

While Zola perused her tablet, I grabbed the book and opened it to the spell. Hannah came to read over my shoulder.

"This is the right spell, yeah? Do we have all of these ingredients?" I asked.

Hannah frowned. "I think so...shit. Everything but a diamond."

Eyre came around my other side. "I don't know how we'll make up for that. It's not like replacing eggs with applesauce in a cake."

"I have one," I blurted, looking at Hannah. "Mom's ring."

"Oh thank God you still have it."

Eyre paused with her finger on the spell. "Gemma, it may not survive the spell."

"I don't care," I said, all thoughts of Madam Indigo gone from my head. Hannah nodded in solidarity.

Zola laid her tablet on the table. "Here's something. About a hundred years ago, scientist witches did a study. They did an MRI on a person's brain while they had an out of body experience, and it's consistent with Beck's imaging." She scanned the article. "Okay. Okay, now I'm on board."

Thirty minutes later, we'd moved our base of operations to the Star Deck, the only space large enough to perform the spell. There, Hannah and Zola had a potion cooking in the cauldron from my birthday celebration.

"So if we're really doing this—" Hannah began.

"We're doing this," I said. I was on my hands and knees on the wooden floor, helping Eyre chalk sketch a massive triquetra—a circle woven inside the three points of an endless Celtic knot—for the spell. Beck lay on a pallet of blankets inside the triangular space at the center with Oby curled up beside his head.

I paused in my work and leaned over Beck, smoothed his brow with the un-chalky back of my hand. "I'm coming for you," I whispered, hoping he could hear me.

"A full coven of witches would make the spell more potent," Hannah said, "which, considering one of us is going after him into the spirit world, would be a good thing."

I wiped my tears. "How many is that? We don't have enough?"

"Five is the minimum, but Beck's our fifth," Hannah explained.

"I'll do it," I said. "I'll take Beck's place."

Eyre frowned. "Wait, I thought you lost your magic."

Guilt twinged through my chest, but Hannah answered before I could open my mouth.

"She had reasons for keeping it a secret," she said, "but I think it's okay to tell you now. She's a powerful witch, and Beck's been working with her on practicing her magic."

Eyre's jaw dropped.

"I'm sorry for not being honest. I'm not highly trained, but I'm highly motivated."

"Yeah okay. That explains a lot." She was silent for a moment, long enough for me to recall her conversation with Beck. What must she think of me?

"But you know," she continued with a small smile, "you'd have to be initiated into the coven to make the magic stronger."

My face flushed, but I pursued the idea anyway. "I'm not trying to invite myself in or anything, but I'll do everything in my power to get

Beck back in his body. Anything and everything, even if he doesn't want me back."

"Again, how so smart and yet so dumb?" Hannah slid something off her cutting board into the cauldron. "Surely you know the size of Beck's heart by now. We always vote on new initiates, but I think we'll all agree. Especially Beck, so we'll count his vote as a 'yea.' We'll talk to Zola when she gets back with the lilacs, and I know Summer'll be okay with it."

"I'll feel better with the full coven, and Zola will too. This spell is high-level magic," Eyre explained. "It calls for a double-ended tether."

"What does that mean?" I asked. "What's a double-ended tether?"

Before either of them could answer my question, Zola came back, rolling a cart with the final spell ingredients, and Eyre jumped up from her spot on the floor. "Did you bring me that big bag of salt?"

I repeated my question. "Hannah, what's a double-ended tether?"

Zola looked up from handing Hannah the lilacs. "The spell calls for a double-ended tether?"

Hannah nodded, but I nearly shouted. "What is a double-ended tether?"

Zola pressed her lips together. "A tether is a person. Someone you have a spiritual connection with—an etheric cord—who can act as your anchor in the living world and bring you back. Often it's a family member, but not always. Etheric cords are common, but those needed to act as a tether in a spell are more rare." Her eyes slid to Hannah. "What's the arrangement of the tether?"

Eyre paused and leaned over the book. "From the spellcaster to the spirit walker, and from the spirit walker to the trapped spirit."

"We all love Beck. And Eyre, I know he's like your brother. But none of the rest of us could be *your* tether," Zola said. "Only one possible arrangement could work."

Hannah's mouth set in a determined line. "Me to Gemma, and Gemma to Beck. That's the only way."

Zola nodded in agreement. "But listen. Being someone's tether, having a tether, isn't something to take lightly. You have to trust each other implicitly, or don't do it at all. Any one of you tugs the wrong way, not in concert with the others, and either Gemma—or Hannah and Gemma—goes barreling into the spirit world, and we can't get any of them back, or Gemma comes out too soon, and Beck's trapped. He could even pull you both in with him. You'll literally have each other's souls and lives in your hands."

I trusted both of them with my life, my soul. Even if Beck would never forgive me.

But I turned to Hannah. "Nannapie, I don't want to ask this of you."

"Good thing you don't have to ask me. I volunteer. I trust you, Gem, and I trust Beck too."

"I'll keep you safe, Hannah, I promise. And so will he."

"I know, and I'll keep y'all safe too." She winked at me. "Let's go get your honey back. What else do we need to do? We're running out of time."

Eyre glanced at her watch. "We only have three and a half hours left to prevent ourselves from crashing on Gaia, and even less time to save Beck. We're ready here, we just have to set the ship on autopilot and get Summer for the initiation and the spell."

Zola smiled at me, showing all her teeth. "An initiation? Does that mean what I think it means?"

I nodded. "If you'll all have me."

Zola crossed the room and hugged me. "We wouldn't have it any other way."

Chapter 20

The Spirit World

Twenty minutes later, I'd been initiated into my first coven—on an emergency basis—in a simple, abbreviated ritual involving smoke cleansing and vows to do no harm. Zola promised a full ceremony after we landed safely on Gaia, if I wanted to, and if Beck agreed. But I was too worried about getting him back, spiritually and romantically, to think about what that might look like, or if it was truly something I wanted.

Nearly ready to begin, we poured thick lines of salt over Eyre's triquetra sketch on the floor. I stepped barefoot over two salt lines to sit in the triangular center beside Beck. Scooping his hand into mine, I kissed it and sent up a prayer that this spell worked.

Hannah sat inside one of the knots, close to me, and she reached across the salt line between us to hold my other hand. Our high priestess filled a vial from the potion and took her place outside the peak of the knot nearest Hannah, and Eyre and Summer placed themselves outside the peaks of the other two knots.

Hannah leaned in and wrapped her arms around my neck. "For luck," she said, squeezing me tight. "I believe in you, Gem. You can do this."

"Gemma," Zola said, "this spell will confine the estranged aspects of Beck's spirit, and your own, inside the spellspace. But also," she warned, "other, lower entities—demons, other spirits—may be temporarily suspended inside the spellspace as well. They might talk to you or try to deter you from your task. Know that they speak neither truth nor wisdom. Their goals are their own, and the only thing you can trust about them is that they want to lead you astray from love, truth, and light. Ignore them. Find Beck's estranged spirit half, and anoint his spirit with this oil."

Zola crouched before me and dabbed her fingertip into the vial. The heavy aroma of lilacs and fresh cut grass came alive in the air as she rubbed the oil in a star pattern on my forehead, right over my third eye. She made the same shape on Beck's forehead, then placed my mother's diamond ring over it. She returned to her position, folding her hands. "Gemma, focus on a happy memory with Beck, when you felt closest to him. Hannah, focus on a happy memory of Gemma, when you felt closest to her."

Hannah smiled at me, a million childhood joys between us: running outside, playing with our dolls, riding bikes.

I closed my eyes, focused on choosing a memory with Beck. I'd had so many close, sweet times with him in the short time we'd known each other. Lying under the stars on the diving platform, hiding and laughing in the forest, forming a deeper connection when we made love, working companionably together in the engine room.

But the memory I focused on was the night we'd officially become "a thing," as he called it. My heart warmed, remembering the deep murmuring of his voice, the bliss of him surrounding me. *I'm all yours if you want me. If you want me, I'm all in.*

The coven chanted softly around me, Hannah's sweet soprano beside me.

Quickly, I fell into a different space altogether. But instead of panicking, I was calm. Hannah's hands were warm around mine, and even though I drifted into the unknown, I had a purpose, and a peace that I was supported and safe in my sister's hands, no matter where in the realms I wandered.

I opened my eyes to the spirit world, the in-between where souls lingered after this life and before the next. It shimmered in a thousand shades of gray and white, shadows and light. The silence hurt my ears. I looked down to see my hands, transparent here, but vaguely prismatic. I had no heartbeat, no rush of blood through my veins. My senses, whatever they were in this form, adjusted, and soon I could hear a silken rush like phantom waves on the gulf.

The bright auras of the women in the coven—Zola, Eyre, and Summer—flared like rainbows around the perimeter of the spellspace, drenched in luminous colors. A radiant golden cord connected from my heart to the flame nearest to me: Hannah, the flame I recognized. My heart warmed at the shimmering golden cord stretching from Hannah to Summer's belly, strong and secure. Another stretched from Zola's off into infinity. Toward Noah.

A golden tether pulled low at my belly, the same one I felt the morning after my first night with Beck. It was stretched thin, and I couldn't see the other end of it, but it glowed golden and bright. As if it would cover any amount of distance, even if pulled to an airy thinness. Lines of an ancient poem flitted across my mind. No matter how far apart we may be, I was connected to him, and I knew that connection couldn't be severed.

I got up and followed my tether to find Beck, but dark, ugly splotches were peppered across the spellspace, pulling at my attention, bubbling beneath the surface of the shadowy ground I walked on. I forced my eyes to track them.

One in particular, larger than the others, squatted off center of the middle of the circle beside the pale aura of Beck's body. Its two stubby horns rippled beneath the veil between worlds as if it were silk woven of black sparkling shadows.

It lunged at me, its long arm like a sea serpent beneath the waves, and I recoiled. The little coiled rainbow soul near Beck's head hissed at it.

Parent killer. Its gravelly voice sifted through the veil like dirty sand. *You have no power here.*

Another horrid voice spoke nearer to me.

You cannot have him. He is growing weak, and we shall have him.

Shut up! I shouted. Dread mired each step across the spellspace, yet still I went on.

Another cackled, a swarm of cicadas to my ears. *Parent killer tells me to still my voice when she treads where she should not!*

Beyond the vile forms shifting under the veil, a pale rainbow caught my attention, tenuous as the sun shining through the spray of a backyard hose. I moved toward it.

Unnatural coward, the first hissed. *You killed your parents with your dark gift. Embrace your soul's corruption. We will come for you next.*

You're lying, I told it. But fear and doubt snaked into my heart, and I suddenly felt mired in the clay of my corporeal body. My vision in the spellspace wavered against the insides of my eyelids. But I forced myself to persist in the spirit world. *The only way to Beck is past my fears*, I told myself. I took a tentative step, and another.

You're weak, another spat. *You cannot tread here. You cannot save him.* This one lunged at me, but it seemed fixed to its position. I took a step. And another. The only way to Beck was past them all.

Gravelly voices scraped together like bones in a graveyard. *Yes, come closer so we can claim you too.*

Zola said they were lies. I armored my heart and went on. I was almost within the grasp of the largest entity, but I forced myself to keep placing one foot in front of the other.

I will drag you into the blazing sulfur and watch your godless soul writhe in its flames!

It scrambled its top half toward me on spindly arms like a spider, lunging at me from beneath the veil. I winced and cried out, but its swipe went through me, neither dividing me, neither disturbing my own bright flame. A pulse of love traveled across my tether from Hannah, into my spirit. Warmth like sunshine beamed through me, and I grew bolder.

The pale rainbow soul was definitely Beck, persisting as an oasis of beauty in that dark, gray space. A net of shifting rainbows connected from him to a point at the center of the spellspace. His body.

The estranged part of Beck's spirit resembled him, but it was transparent and palely prismatic, not much different than my own form in this place. Spirit Beck was transfixed, watching a space off somewhere to my right.

Beck, I said, following his gaze. Golden, humming sunshine poured out of an aperture that not only cut through the veils, it transformed them. How was that not the first thing I'd noticed here? It was like standing next to a star that didn't burn you but rather infused your entire being with light and unconditional love.

It was the opposite of a void. It was an *Abundance*, a bounty of joy and contentment, tranquility and acceptance, and my soul yearned for it. Even the fringes of that light touching me were enough to make me want to dive headlong into its embrace. How had Beck resisted it this long?

Beck's voice, like a pattering of low-pitched wind chimes, broke through my reverie.

Grandpa? Máthair Chríona Niamh—you're here?

I turned from the Abundance to Beck, but I couldn't see what he saw, and my fascination with it distanced.

I rushed to his filtering rainbow spirit and took his hands, surprised to find them solid in mine. *Beck, it's not time for you to go there!*

Still he stared into the Abundance, his eyes alight with raptured fascination. *I'm getting weak. I can't fight it. I have to go.*

No! You have to come back to me! I tried to turn his face toward me, but he wouldn't budge. *I need you,* I told him.

He spoke, still not looking at me. *Your parents are here. They want us to come.*

Reluctantly, I peered into the light, expecting to see my parents standing in judgment, but I saw nothing in the Abundance except the humming sunshine.

Beck's face clouded over. *But not now,* he said.

Then listen to them! You have a life among the living, people who love you. And look, I placed my hand against his belly. *Look what we have together.*

He tipped his head down. The golden cord connecting his belly to mine was strong and thick, golden and ringed with rainbows. Mist swirled in his eyes when he looked at me. *You're all I ever wanted, but I've already lost you.*

No, I said emphatically, placing my hands on either side of his face. *You didn't lose me. I'm so sorry I pushed you away. I chose fear instead of love, but I'll never do that again. I love you, Beck. I love you with all my heart. Please come back to me.*

A beautiful smile transformed his spirit face, and he put his hands gently on my wrists. His irises cleared. *Really?*

Really, I told him. *I love you. And I'll never let you go.*

His spirit shimmered brighter. *I have loved you all my life, Gemma, even before I met you. And I will love you always.*

The dark entities' venomous words rose and congealed. I pulled Beck toward the center of the circle, but he winced at the terrible noise they made.

They can't hurt you, I told him. *Don't listen to their lies.*

He nodded, and we slowly stepped around the demons as they spat their vitriol at us.

She killed her parents!

Push her into the void!

Beck ignored them, but his beautiful face clouded with worry. *I don't know how to go back. I've been trying to find my way back to you, but I can't.*

I ran my fingers across my forehead. The oil persisted in my spirit form like Zola said it would. I made the shape of a star with it on his spirit forehead, and the flames of Summer, Hannah, and Eyre moved toward his body at the center of the spellspace.

Say these words to go back, and go back the way you used to, when you astral projected.

I repeated the words once, and Beck's wavering spirit voice chanted with me.

Omdnna duouo, omdnna duouo...

As the shadows diffused at the turning of the spell, the network of golden cords connecting Beck to his body, pale and tenuous at first, grew stronger, thicker, and more radiant. Spirit Beck winked at me and released my hands. He turned around and executed a melodramatic trust fall into his body.

My cord to Hannah tightened and solidified. How would I go back? What if I got stuck here and—

But the beautiful flame that was my sister gently pulled me, so I closed my eyes and let go. My limbs were heavy and jerky, like waking from sleep paralysis in a prehistoric tar pit. I pried open my gritty eyes to see Hannah—actual, physical Hannah—smiling at me.

"You did it!" she squealed, squeezing me tight.

My physical hand was holding Beck's. He still lay on his back on the floor, but one of his knees was up and moving.

Zola and Summer wafted the smoke of four different bundles of leaves over and around his body, saying prayers or spells over him, I didn't know which. His hand in mine moved experimentally, the other hand moved to his face. I turned my whole body to go to him but stopped. Would he remember what happened in the spirit world?

Chapter 21

Hurtling toward Gaia

Beck sat up gingerly, and my mother's ring fell to the floor with a clink. He rubbed his whole face with his free hand as Zola wafted the smoke behind him.

Should I go to him?

His gaze landed on me, and he leaned forward. "That was real," he said quietly. "That really happened. You came for me." He scrambled to his knees and threw his arms around me, whispering into my hair. "I didn't think I'd ever hold you again."

Choruses of cheers and "get a room!" erupted around us. He kissed me, and his aura felt to me like the Abundance.

"Yes," Summer said, pulling up on our arms. "Get an *engine* room. That spell took almost three hours!"

Eyre rushed forward to help pull us up. "Later on I'm going to kill you for scaring me to death, but right now we're approaching Gaia at four hundred and thirty-three miles per hour, and if you don't get that antimatter drive online in the next ten minutes, we could burn up before causing a global extinction, but more likely we'll be shot out of the sky."

Beck stumbled to the side, and I threw my shoulder under his arm, wrapping my arms around his waist.

"Can you make it?" I asked.

He squeezed me tight. "I can make anything if you're with me."

My heart soared, and the more I moved, the more normal I started to feel. I explained the situation to him as we went down the five levels to

B2. Once in the engine room, Beck tore up to the electrical panel, and I skidded to a stop beside the antimatter drive.

Nothing but clicks and snaps from above. Then Beck's very emotional voice came back. "I hope we live through this so we can talk about what just happened. What's the drive lookin' like now?"

I tapped at the panels, but only the backup power remained, flashing an error message. "All propulsion systems are offline, and the atom smasher isn't responding."

"What about—" He grunted and a loud thunk echoed through the room. "Now?"

The blessed hum of electricity woke the drive. "It's powering up!" I shouted excitedly, the glow of the screen lighting up my face. "The atom smasher too!"

He was at my side again, paging the others on the comms. "Eyre, are you all set for the reentry spell?"

"Wilco!"

"Summer, you got the wheel? Are our shields holding?"

"Got it, shields are perfect."

Summer left our connection open, and a man's voice crackled on her end. "New Houston to *WitchCraft*, you are *not* cleared for entry. Decrease your speed or we will fire! Acknowledge!"

"Affirm, New Houston, Wilco! Do not fire! I say again! Wilco! Do not fire!"

"Oh this shit's gettin' real," Beck lamented, standing at my side by the atom smasher's screen, tapping.

I hadn't gone into the spirit world to get Beck back to lose everything now. "Drive's online, propulsion engaged."

"But our production's not sufficient for deceleration. Shit, we're gonna burn up if we don't do something."

I spun out the cache. "It's not the production. The feed system's strangling again."

A roar like a tornado rumbled outside the ship, and it rocked violently. Beck and I wedged ourselves under the railing.

It was machinery, and I was an advanced healer. Zola's words came back to me. *Your first mistake is separating animate beings and inanimate items in your head...if you're clever, you can do healing work on more than people.*

"Give me your hands!" I shouted, taking his hands and pressing them with mine against the feed system. "Join your magic with mine! Concentrate on clearing it!"

My magic and his both responded, and our hands glowed brightly against the feed system. I clenched my eyes shut and imagined the clean, pristine functioning of antimatter drives in the labs at work, and I focused our magic on the feed system that controlled the release of antimatter to collide with matter, focused all my thoughts and magic on the process. I had no rational idea if it would work, but I believed it would. It had to. It was our last hope. All of our last hope.

Within a few moments, the drive in my mind's eye functioned like new, and the ship stopped rocking. It shimmied into a smooth track, and Summer's whoops poured over the intercom.

"We're inside! Cleared for travel to Nouvelle Orleans!"

I stumbled back from the drive and jumped up into Beck's waiting arms, wrapping my arms and legs around him, celebrating our win with cheers and kisses.

With the bulk of our propulsion needs dipping, the lights flickered on.

"Come on," he said, "let's go see our new home!"

We took the elevator all the way up to the bridge. Everyone else was already there, gathered around the windows to catch our first in-person glimpse of Gaia. Beck and I got there in time to see a vast blue lake disappear past us. A mountain range, an ocean of pristine forests—just like the history books, but real—and blue skies stretching to forever.

Chapter 22

Reunion

Summer settled us down into the woods of Beck's family property, and we all dashed to the massive cargo door that'd last been open when we left Earth two months ago.

Zola peered out the window as Beck manned the controls to open the ship. "I can see Noah!"

"You go first!" Eyre squealed, nudging Zola to the front of the line. "Y'all have waited way too long for some sugar!"

The ancient door struggled to open up from the floor, the growing crack sucking in a billow of the crispest, cleanest air I've ever breathed. The women rushed forward, but my legs wouldn't move.

Not just my brother, dozens of people had come to meet us. I took shallow breaths through a tight throat. I didn't deserve to breathe that precious, free air. My actions on Earth irrevocably tainted my fresh start. No money, no job, Madam Indigo to reckon with...shit, maybe jail time too.

My grip tightened on Beck's hand as I scanned the crowd. Parts of it converged on Summer, Hannah, Zola, and Eyre as they ran. A small group with an older couple who both looked like Beck shaded their eyes against the sun, looking expectantly into the darker mouth of the ship where we stood. But not one police officer waited to cuff me and take me away. Where were they hiding?

Beck's warm, comforting magic slipped tenderly into my hand. "Hey." His soft voice in my ear.

"Beck, I can't move my legs. I can't—"

He kissed my temple and turned me towards him, setting both my palms flat against his chest, and his hands over mine. "You got this, and I got you. Just breathe. We can go meet our future together. We'll be okay."

He pressed his lips to my forehead, and I closed my eyes, counting five of his steady heartbeats on each inhale and exhale. Entwining our magic into one force, I pulled it through my body, using it for the first time in years to calm myself, to heal the tension ache from my jaw and shoulders. Our magic warmed me from the inside, intimate, loving...amorous.

My hips nudged against his, and he chuckled, his hands slipping around my waist.

I kissed him through my smile. "Damn, that turns me on every time."

"Me too, but we'll celebrate privately later. They're calling our names."

With Beck's hand on my shoulder, I went down the cramped drop-steps, and we met Gaia in all her early fall finery. A wholesome chill gave the atmosphere a sweet, exciting bite and made the riotous fall forest—young yet from the terraforming—sway in broad strokes of greens, golds, and reds. This world was almost too beautiful to be real.

Stepping to the soft grass with my eyes still adjusting to the sun, I almost didn't recognize Noah with that full beard. Zola was still in his arms, both of them crying and kissing over and over after nearly a year of being on literally different worlds. Except for my brother, I didn't recognize a soul among the people shouting and cheering in the forest's clearing.

"Mom! Dad!" Beck shouted, pulling me toward them as they rushed forward calling his name. "Come on!" he said, excited as a little kid on Christmas morning.

He let go of my hand to fall into a hug from both parents, the three of them laughing through tears.

"Gemma!" I turned at Noah's voice and his hand on my arm. He wrapped me into the fiercest hug, and I hugged him back, gulping back a sob. Hannah hugged both of us, and we threw our arms around her too. I had my family again.

The crowd's laughter and talking filled my ears, and all I heard was Noah say over and over, "You're here!" Beck, Eyre, and Summer were engulfed by their families. For a moment, I was engulfed too, in the emotion of our new homecoming, the joy of the people embracing their loved ones again, and in receiving my siblings' love, something I hadn't thought myself to be worthy of ever again.

"Thank the gods y'all are here!" Noah shouted, squeezing Zola again. Behind him, Beck caught my eye through the crowd. He grinned mischievously, put his finger to his lips for my silence, and ran up behind Noah. Grabbing him around the middle, he lifted his best friend up in a bear hug, both of them whooping with laughter. Hannah and I still clung to each other, cackling at their reunion.

Beck's parents approached us, ushering forward a couple with two kids. The man called Beck's name, and he turned from his conversation with Noah to dive into an embrace with the man holding a little girl, who looked a lot like him, and the woman holding a baby.

Watching Beck reunite with his family, talk to his niece, and cry with joy over his baby nephew, it all filled my eyes with happy tears. My magic made that possible, in part. If my magic could do that, could fix Hannah's arm, help bring Beck back from the spirit world, help our ship land us safely on Gaia, maybe I could learn to live with it. Maybe...appreciate it?

Beck turned to me with a baby in his arms. "Gemma! Come meet my family!" I wiped my face and went up to them. "Everybody, this is my partner, Gemma. Gemma, this is my mom, Ellie, my dad, Emmett..." Beck's roll call went on, and I hugged whoever appeared before me. How would I remember all these names?

"...and my niece, who isn't quite sure about her Uncle Beck 'cause she doesn't remember him." He laid his hand on the little girl's back, who clung to her dad but smiled shyly at Beck. "And this beautiful boy right here is my nephew, Henry. Just look at him, Gem."

"Hi, beautiful," I crooned, rubbing the soft fuzz of his warm little head. The only thing sexier than Beck was Beck holding and talking seriously to a baby.

"You're the most beautiful boy on the planet." Henry pulled at Beck's beard and giggled, babbling back at him. "Yes you are." Beck put his arm around me, pulling me close and kissing my head. "Y'all can thank Gemma for me making it here alive. She saved my life more times than I can count on the trip here," he said. Henry started to fuss. "Oh no!" he babytalked to him, kissing him again before handing him back to his mom.

"Gem!" Noah broke into the group. "Before I forget, call your boss back."

Adrenaline seared through my limbs, but Noah's smile didn't falter. "What?"

"Evander Noble?" He laughed. "Remember him? Rich guy? Family owns the company you work for? He wants you to call him right away so he can get your start date for remote work. Said it's really important for him to know when you're starting back."

Beck's arm stole around me, washing his calm through me. His guarded face looked as confused as I felt. So...maybe I won't be tried for accidental attempted murder? "When did he call?"

"Last week," Noah answered, already turning his attention back to Zola.

But I was stuck in fight-or-flight again, chewing on the inside of my lip.

"—yeah, Mom, we're absolutely coming to dinner," Beck was saying beside me. "But we have to take care of something first." He steered me away from the crowds. "Gem, that doesn't sound like a message from a man who wants to press charges. Maybe it's okay?"

I twisted my hands together. "I don't know. I'm scared. Why would he just say *that*?"

"Only one way to find out. Why don't you go call him back, so it's not hanging over your head?"

I twisted my hands. "Will you come with me? To call him? I know I should just be an adult and handle it myself, but—"

He cupped my face and kissed me. "Gem, you're my partner. We face the world together. Always. Of course I'll come."

On the bridge of *The Witchcraft*, the planets-and-stars animations of StarTalk twirled on the screen, mocking my churning stomach.

Beck sat opposite me where Evander wouldn't see him, holding my hand across the table. "Whatever he says, it'll be okay. We'll handle it together."

"Okay." I took a deep breath and squeezed his hand. "Okay."

The screen resolved into my boss's face. I sat up straighter and swallowed hard.

"—emma? Hey, it's —vander. Can you hear m—?" Evander's face filled the screen, his brown eyes and dark hair coming into focus. Behind him, his office windows were boarded over. Shit, that was my fault.

Beck rubbed his beard, his gaze drifting to the other StarTalk screen across the room where he could see my boss's video. My ex-boss? Who tried to kiss me two months ago.

"Hi Evander. Yes, I can hear you." Barely, over the pounding of my heart. Maybe my doom would fall fast.

"Hey Gemma! You get to Gaia with your sister okay?"

His smile was completely disarming, the lilt of his British accent charming as always.

"Um, yeah, we had some close calls, but we made it in one piece. We landed not an hour ago."

He opened his mouth to speak, but I couldn't take the small talk. "Evander, I'm so, so sorry. And I don't know how to explain what happened, but—"

"No, Gemma, I'm the one who's sorry. I thought we'd been flirting for a while, and I don't know." He scratched the back of his head. "I thought you *wanted* to kiss me, but I still shouldn't have—"

"No, you were right. I did." I squeezed Beck's hand. "At the time."

"But I'm your boss, and I shouldn't have crossed that boundary. Especially because I suspected you were a witch with suppressed magic."

A cold paralysis sank into my chest. Beck's eyebrows shot up. "A—a what?" I stammered, my face heating up. "I don't know what you're—"

Evander laughed. "It takes one to know one, Gemma." He snapped his fingers, and his dark hair turned flaming white. Another snap, electric blue. A third snap, and it was back to normal. "I'm really sorry I cornered you and scared you."

I breathed out slowly, all my limbs easing into relieved jelly. I put a quivering hand over half my face, peering at him with one eye. "I'm sorry I threw you across your office and broke all the windows. I absolutely didn't mean to. I thought for sure you'd have the police waiting to arrest me."

Evander laughed. "No, not at all. I wasn't hurt, and we're abandoning this building anyway. But hold on." He leaned closer to the screen. "Did you say a minute ago that you *did* want to kiss me? Because I won't be coming to Gaia until next year, but—"

"I *did*. Past tense." I smiled at Beck's caress on my hand. "But I met the love of my life on my sister's ship."

Evander's eyebrows went up, and he smiled. "That's great. I'm very happy for you both." He ran a hand through his hair and swallowed hard. "Well, I won't keep you. Will you let me know when you're ready to take on some remote work? Now that I know you're a witch, I can diversify your workload. I wish I'd known sooner. I really could've used your help on my Argonaut project."

"I don't think I have the clearance for that. Isn't that top secret?"

"Only because magic's involved." Evander smiled. "But yeah, I truly value your work with us, Gemma, and your job is waiting for you. And hey, if you know of any artificers willing to do some contract work, especially if they have a degree in astro-engineering, I could use them."

Beck nodded a maybe face, and I smiled. "Thanks, Evander. I just might know where to find one."

By the time Beck and I made it back out of the ship, the party in the forest had largely broken up and moved off towards a house in the distance that I hadn't seen before. Tents lit with white string lights sheltered crowds of people from the falling dark, but Beck pulled me in the opposite direction, towards the line of trees along the clearing.

Birds sang here and squirrels raced up trees. I ran my fingers down the fresh bark of the nearest tree and closed my eyes against the soft breeze on my face. It was almost perfect.

Beck's arms encircled my waist, and I leaned back against his chest, settling my arms over his.

"Isn't it beautiful?"

"Yes, you are," he murmured in my ear. I turned around to wrap my arms around his neck, and he kissed me with his whole heart.

"You went into the spirit world for me," he said, pushing a curl away from my face.

"I'd go anywhere for you," I said. "I love you." My heart surged at the smile he gave me back.

"I love you, too. Does that mean what I think it means? You're not gonna get your magic taken away?"

I smiled. The clouds obscuring my future had cleared like the smoke trail of an extinguished candle, but he was fun to tease.

"That depends." I tipped my face up to his. "Are you still looking for a smart, beautiful, dark-haired witch to settle down with?"

"Nah," he said, his face close to mine. "I'm not looking. I already found her."

"Yeah, you have." I smiled. "And I'm never letting you go."

He leaned down and kissed me, pulling me up into his arms, my legs around his waist. His lips were warm, sweet, and reverent, filled with longing and belonging. *Now* this planet was perfect.

"Beck and Gemma, huh?" Noah walked with Zola toward us, their arms around each other.

Beck set me down and cleared his throat, grinning at his best friend. "Dr. Abadie."

Noah raised an eyebrow in a failed expression of formality and gestured between us with his free hand. "So a funny thing happened on the way to Gaia, huh? What exactly are your intentions towards my little sister, Dr. Breaux?"

Beck laughed, pressing his forehead against mine and cupping my face. "I'm gonna marry her, if she'll have me."

I pecked his lips. "She will."

"And I'll spend the rest of my life making her happy. Does that work for you, Dr. Abadie?"

Noah laughed. "Can't argue with that."

Chapter 23

Epilogue: Eighteen Months Later

The spring day was perfect. Robins and thrushes sang in the birch grove ahead, and one more turn would bring me and Noah on the path of rose petals that Beck's niece, Charlotte, had thrown in my honor. My brother released my arm for a moment to adjust the star-strewn embroidered veil that cascaded down my shoulders, and the cellos began to play.

"Come on," I teased, tucking my hand into his crooked elbow and pulling on him. Each step in my long sheath gown with the trailing overskirt of stars brought me closer to my meant-to-be. We turned left, and my gaze skipped past our family and friends who had gathered for us in their finery. Because truly, only one man mattered to me today.

Beck stood beside the arbor he'd built for our wedding, and warmth hummed through me like the Abundance. How was he even more obscenely beautiful today than the day I met him? Dressed in a suit woven in the deep, dark blue of the night sky, he stood with clasped hands, watching me as if I was the only person in the whole forest.

The cellos played Maasai Malone's "Dream Girl," and I smiled all the way to my groom.

"Treat her right." Noah winked at Beck. "Or I'll walk next door to let you have it."

Beck grinned back. "Yes sir, Dr. Abadie."

Noah kissed my cheek and stepped back. Hannah came forward, her purple maid of honor skirts swishing, and took my bouquet of roses, sweet peas, and hydrangeas from me before taking her place beside a very pregnant Zola. And I turned and slipped my hands into Beck's.

"Welcome, friends and family," Summer said, "to the joyous occasion we've been..."

But Beck's eyes met mine, and the warmth bubbling up from my heart and into my smile washed out everything she said. I squeezed Beck's hands, knowing with full certainty that I had found my soulmate.

"Do you, Gemma Louise Abadie, take this man, Beck Carter Breaux, to be your lawful husband, your partner in life and love?"

"I do," I said, meaning it with every spinning atom in my body.

"And do you, Beck Carter Breaux, take this woman, Gemma Louise Abadie, to be your lawful wife, your partner in life and love?"

"I do, with all my heart and soul," he said, the love beaming from his face making my spirit soar.

"'A cord of three strands is not easily broken,'" Summer began, "and so Gemma and Beck have chosen to bind their wedding vows with three ribbons, each color representing wishes for their marriage, and each presented by someone important in their lives." Summer motioned to Beck's parents to come forward.

Beck and I clasped our hands together, left to left, and right to right.

"Ellie and Emmett Breaux bring forward the blue cord, symbolizing devotion."

Beck's parents, who had already proven that I'd won the in-law lottery, came forward with three braided silk ribbons in different shades of blue. As Summer spoke, they loosely wound the braid around our hands as many times as it would go, then gave us each a hug and kiss before they returned to their seats.

Ellie and Emmett welcomed me into their family without reservation, and in them I'd gotten a second chance at being a daughter. Ellie went all Mama Bear on Madam Indigo—whose practices were apparently outside witching law—and within forty-eight hours, all the money I'd paid the woman was transferred back to me. Madam Indigo's unwilling refund went toward the home that Emmet, an architect, worked with us to design. It even included a stargazing tower in the forest, my surprise wedding present to the amazing man standing before me.

"Hannah Abadie brings forward the yellow cord, symbolizing joy."

My sister handed my bouquet to Eyre and stepped forward to wrap a woven trio of yellow silk ribbons around our hands, her engagement ring from Summer flashing in the late-afternoon light.

"And Zola and Noah Abadie bring forward the green cord, symbolizing fertility."

Then Noah and Zola stepped in, her bridesmaid gown accentuating her pregnant belly as they both wound a cord around our clasped hands in a trio of greens.

After they finished, Zola smiled and rubbed her belly as Noah kissed her cheek, drawing whoops and ooohs from our guests, including raucous rabble-rousing from some of Beck's childhood friends. Beck grinned, raising his eyebrows lasciviously at me. A familiar thrill skipped through me.

"Settle down, folks." Summer waited for the laughter to die down before she began again. "Gemma and Beck, in your hands is the heart and the life of the one you love. Let your hands always seek to bring each other comfort, build a lifelong, joyful partnership, and lessen each other's burdens. In your hands is also a choice, a daily opportunity to choose understanding over judgment, laughter over anger, and love over fear."

With that, Summer tied the silken ribbons together beneath our clasped hands. "And now, please recite to each other the vows you've written." She nodded at Beck.

He squeezed my hands and looked into my eyes, smiling. "I guess everybody here knows how I dreamed about you, how I knew you were my meant-to-be, years before we met. On our wedding day, it's important to me that you know *you're* the woman I fell in love with, not the dream girl. I feel so in harmony with you, more than with anyone else, ever. You make me laugh, you challenge me in all the best ways with your brilliant mind. I aspire to be as brave as you, and as selfless. Into space or into the spirit world, it means everything to know you'll always come for me. You saved me from the abyss." He glanced at his arm and returned his gaze to me.

We both smiled through happy tears as he continued. "I will be faithful and dedicated to you, past when the last stars fall. I'll work hard every day to build a happy life with you, for each other, for our family."

He smiled bigger. "Wow I love the sound of that: 'our family.' I want to grow very, very old with you. And I promise: no more astral projection." Quiet laughter rippled through the congregation. "Because I don't want to miss a minute of my life with you. I love you with everything, Gemma, and I dedicate my life to being your partner in all things."

My heart was so full that I stepped up and kissed him, even though it wasn't time for that yet in the ceremony. He kissed me back, beaming, and I stepped back to recite my vows to him with a happy-tear-streaked face.

"When I first met you, I was in such a dark place, trying to banish my magic and run away from my past. I thought, 'wow he's the most beautiful man I've ever met, if only he would one day smile at me.'" I laughed. "Then you *did* smile at me, that day we bonded over fixing the antimatter drive filter. You smiled at me, and everything in my life started to bloom. Like after a long winter. You treated me with such respect, such kind honesty. You took care of me when I didn't know how badly I needed it. You make me laugh, you make me glow from the inside out with my love for you. You accept me for who I am, and every day you choose loving kindness, to me and everyone around you. I will always come for you," I said, going off script for a moment, "and I promise to be faithful and dedicate my hands, my heart, my magic in service to our life together. I love you, Beck."

Summer wiped tears from her cheeks. "And now Gemma and Beck will tie their cords, which will be hung up and honored in their new home."

I called my magic forward easily. It was eager to join with Beck's magic that was already stealing sweetly into my hands. When our hands began to glow, we unclasped one hand at a time, rejoining them, and worked together to tie a knot in our handfasting cords, allowing them to fall into the decorative box Summer held at the ready.

"May we have the rings, please?" Summer asked, and Hannah and Beck's brother Jude came forward. Summer nodded at me to begin.

I took Beck's ring from Hannah and turned back to my groom. Holding his left hand in mine, I slipped a silver band onto his ring finger. "I offer this ring to you as a symbol of my undying love and devotion."

Beck took my ring from Jude and took my hand. "I offer this ring to you as a symbol of my undying love and devotion," he said, slipping a delicate ring onto my finger. He pulled my hand up to press a warm kiss to it, and the fine gold stars on my pink fingernails sparkled in the dappled sunlight.

"It is my great, great honor and joy to now pronounce you husband and wife. You may kiss the bride!"

Beck reached for me, beaming. "It's about damn time."

I laughed, rushing into the arms of my future with pure joy in my heart, and he kissed me.

Dirty, muddy feet, grass on the kitchen floor, wildflowers in a jar by the sink. Messy little chocolate faces huddled up in blankets by a campfire, their bellies full of smores, listening to Beck tell them about the stars.

Thanks for Reading!

★ ★ ★ ★ ★

I hope you enjoyed *Until the Stars Fall*. Please consider leaving a review on Goodreads or your preferred retailer to help others find my book!

For the latest information about more in the Interstellar Witches series, other books, and more, find me online:

writerhollyrose.com
Instagram: @writerhollyrose

coming soon from
HOLLY ROSE

If Our Worlds Collide

Interstellar Witches
Book 2

Prologue

Valor

Minerva *Aurellia Grace.* I ran my fingertips along the carved letters and met the reproving eyes of the statue who wept, draped over the tombstone. Clearly, she disapproved of me, too.

My lips brushed the brown paper bag concealing a bottle of whiskey and connected with the cold, hard glass within. Tipping it back sent a rush of alcohol burning down my throat, and I coughed, first from its bite and then from the polluted air on this dying planet Earth.

The scant crowd of mourners—fewer than twelve, not one of them mourning—were gone now. The moment the drones started shoveling dirt over the casket, they'd left, averting their eyes from my morning libation and scurrying to their hovercars to avoid the scorching spring sunrise. Vultures, the lot of them. Only come to see my mother off so they'd be less conspicuous when her attorney holds court with the will tomorrow.

I stepped back, stumbling over a dead tree root and catching myself against the trunk. She'd chastise me from the beyond if she could see me right now, drunk at 6:30 in the morning at her funeral. I huffed out a laugh. As if she believed in life after death, or anything beyond her five senses. Case in point, her judgmental mourning statue was conspicuously wingless—the only non-angelic stone being in Hillridge Cemetery.

Love is weakness. There's no magic and no miracles in this life, son, and the sooner you accept it, the better off you'll be.

I'd never get her voice out of my head. And the worst part was, she was wrong. Another swig of whiskey. She was wrong, and I hadn't realized it in time to rub it in her face.

And I hadn't realized it in time to keep the only woman I'd ever love. *Portia.*

The past four days were littered with Mom's unraveling lies, and I tripped over them at every turn. Some were small, personal lies. My favorite childhood nanny didn't quit because she hated me. Mom fired her after overhearing me tell the woman I wanted *her* to be my mother.

Others were big, life-changing lies. We weren't in witness protection because my father was a criminal who'd escaped prison and was after us. Mom simply hated him, for some reason, and she kept him out of our lives by any means. She was also rich and well-connected enough to avoid felony charges from intercepting all communications sent to me for my entire life. These last two bombshells were indelicately handed to me by an ex-FBI agent who came clean three days ago.

So I made Mom come clean too. Her real name was etched on her gravestone, and she couldn't hide anymore. I wouldn't hide, either: Bennett Julian Clay died along with his mother, Harriet. Killing Bennett Clay—the only name Portia knew—was another way to punish myself for how I made her leave.

The hollow ache in my chest knew I'd never see her again. Not as thoroughly as she'd disappeared. No matter how many messages I'd tried to send her. She'd erupted into my life like a surprise garden, surrounding me with colors and love and joy and belonging like I'd never known.

I closed my eyes against the aching loss of her, replaying that morning in my head like it'd been yesterday and not five months ago. She'd ensorcelled me in the enchanting warmth of her love, yet somehow I was shocked when she told me she was a witch. That magic was real. And I lost her for my own ignorant weakness and fear. Not even lost—I shouted at her. I told her to leave because I was afraid of her. And then I ran.

I'd love to blame my mother for that, too, but it was all me. And I'd never forgive myself.

So I'd be Valor Julian Grace again, the name I was born to. Fat lot of good it'd do me. I had this bottle—another sip seared down my throat. I had a shitload of money. An empty, worthless mansion I inherited on a burning planet that the human race was abandoning for dead.

But I didn't have *anybody*. Mom made sure of that. Why bother leaving and heading to Gaia, humanity's new planet? I may as well stay here and die, too.

Hot, old anger burned deep in my chest, and I threw my bag of whiskey at her headstone. It shattered, ripping the bag and spilling gold liquid over the turned earth.

"I'm sorry for your...loss?"

Listing to the side, I surveyed the stranger with the polite British voice who'd approached me from behind. He stood beside me. About my height and age—mid to late twenties, I judged—he held a bouquet of white lilies. Mom hated British people, for God only knew what reason.

That made me want to trust him more.

I nodded at him. "Thanks."

He placed the flowers on the alcohol-sodden dirt before the tombstone and stepped back beside me, hands in the pockets of his fine, black suit. "Kind of a sad end for Glenfiddich Whisky."

I huffed a drunken laugh. "Did you know her?"

He breathed in sharply. "Not well. Only when I was very young, and not for long."

Lucky bastard. "You didn't miss out on much, unless you like emotional abuse and gaslighting."

"No more than the next man."

I turned to him. "So why are you here?"

His dark eyes slid to me. "Because you're Valor Grace."

Apprehension prickled my skin, and I ungracefully moved a little away, cursing my alcohol-muddled reflexes. "How do you know that name?"

"Because my father sent me to find you," he continued, dark eyes kind, a small smile. "I have information about your family."

I laughed. "Nice try. I don't have any family. If you're looking for money—"

"No, no. I have plenty enough of that." He frowned as if disappointed. "Tell you what. Let me buy you coffee, and I'll explain everything. I think you'll want to be sober for this, and I promise, Valor, I will never lie to you."

"Yeah…" I eyed him doubtfully. "I don't think so. I don't even know you."

"Where are my manners?" He pulled his hand from his pocket and reached it towards me. "Evander Noble, at your service."

That name rang a muted bell in my whisky-laden head. But I was too intent on the other bottle stashed at my apartment to think hard about it. "And why do I care?"

"Because, Valor." He leaned forward and grasped my shoulders with an excited smile. "I'm your brother."

Evander—my brother? apparently?—added sugar to his coffee and stirred, his restless eyes darting from me to his mug, lips twitching as if he had a million things to say to me.

The bitter, black coffee jolted my system, nauseating me as much as the iconic mascot of the Witch's Brew Cafe on the mug and shop window—a misogynistic caricature of a buxom blonde woman stirring a magical cauldron of coffee with a wink. Portia had hated it, too, but she insisted they had the best coffee in town. The last cup of it she kissed was still sitting on my nightstand, right where she left it.

"So you're my brother," I stated. He smiled and nodded back. "Evander Noble, heir to the throne of Noble Industries. You're trying to tell me that millionaire Caius Noble is my father, and Noble Industries *still* turned me down for a job last month?"

Evander's laugh made me smile, in spite of myself. He looked at me like he was a kid at Christmas, and I was the big ticket gift under the tree. "Don't hold it against them. They didn't know any more than I did. I found out the day after your mother—our mother—died." He pulled a rolled-up piece of paper from inside his suit. "Here's a copy of your *original* birth certificate. Our grandfather was the head of the FBI for over nearly twenty years, with alleged ties to organized crime. And he apparently did anything his daughter asked of him. Including illegally removing your birth father—our Dad—from your official birth certificate."

I unrolled the paper, nearly the same as the one I had at home. But this one was stamped an original and had *Caius Sterling Noble* instead of *Unknown* where the father's name went. My nose stung with springing tears. "Why would she do that? I mean, I'm sold that she would, but...why?"

"Our parents divorced when I was two, and I only learned the truth myself two days ago. Minerva hated Dad, and she certainly couldn't get rid of *me* fast enough." He frowned but shook his head to clear it away, as if covering a gaping wound with a tiny bandage. He pulled out a tablet and handed it to me, photographs of world-famous Caius Noble holding a very familiar baby—me. "She sent me away with Dad, but she kept you. She had her father's people enforce complete silence and ostracization, but it expired at her death."

I rubbed my scruffy beard, swiping the screen to see a wedding photo of my mother and Caius. A photo of Mom in the hospital holding another baby—Evander, I guess—with Caius at her side. Even there she didn't look happy. But he did.

The FBI agent who told me I didn't have to hide anymore said there was more to tell, but that she wasn't the right person to do it. I never imagined it would be something this big.

Tears flowed freely down my face, and when I looked up, Evander wasn't trying to hide his either.

I swallowed hard. "I don't understand."

Evander rubbed his face with both hands and leaned forward on his elbows towards me. "Little brother, I hoped you'd have known something about all this, almost as much as I hope this isn't a surprise." He leaned to the side. "All clear, John?"

The barista looked around the shop, bored eyes passing over the three other patrons. "Yeah. All clear."

"Our mother hated our father...and me. Because..." Evander took a deep breath. "Because we're witches." He waved his hand, and his coffee mug floated into the air, spun around, and set down again.

I stared at him, my chest an angry storm. "Are you fucking kidding me?"

Chapter 1: Five and a Half Years Later

Portia

Ten miles to Bland, Virginia—that sounded about right. For miles now, there'd been nothing but the burnt-up crisps of trees and some new growth under the denser canopies, now that what passed for spring on this doomed planet was underway. Not another traveler, not a station, not shit-all. I took a deep breath and looked in the rearview mirror. At least my sweet Juliet was still asleep, her long lashes fluttering against her smooth, four-year-old cheeks.

The air cushion beneath my hovervan, Bassiano, stuttered over the heat-buckled interstate just past the sign, jarring my body and setting my jaw on edge. That last job may've provided the final bit of cash for our ride offworld, but it sure as hell kept me till the last damn minute.

I checked my watch. A little over twelve hours till lift-off in New York City. It'd be tight, but we should get to the *Andromeda 12* with an hour or so to spare, if I drove all night. The road evened out as far as I could see, so I depressed the accelerator to make some time.

I rubbed the sun-bleached dashboard fondly. This trip would be a trial for brand new shocks, and poor Bassiano's were about ready for the junkyard, even with the spells I'd paid that Nashville artificier to keep him running smoothly. Damn near everything on this hovervan was ready for the junkyard, but Bassiano was my home, and after my daughter, my one true love.

I'd put off taking us away from Earth for as long as I could, partly to save up enough money for our passage, partly because it was hard to leave the only planet you'd ever known, and partly because Juli hated spaceships.

Maybe I should've left with my sister, Eyre, and her coven. Working with her on that ship's forest a few years ago, letting Juli get to know her and her coven, it had all been...kinda nice. Lord knows my daughter had been asking for "Uncle Beck" almost since we left. I glanced into my rearview mirror at the mini-forest of plants Juli and I had growing in racks along the walls. Besides this van, the ship's forest had been the first place where I'd had a garden that was almost like my own.

So why didn't I take her up on her offer?

I blew hair out of my face. Who the fuck knows.

Maybe I didn't want to be a burden. Maybe I couldn't get past my childhood crush on Beck, who was still hung up on looking for the woman he kept dreaming about, that he was convinced he'd meet soon. Still. I should've tried calling to see if they made it safely to Gaia. I shouldn't have disappeared on Eyre, either. I was a shit big sister. Always had been, always would be. But twenty-six years into this life was too late to start being better.

Besides—everything I did, I did for Juli. It'd been her and me for her whole life, and that's how I liked it.

The hovervan dipped hard in a rough patch of road hiding in a late-afternoon heat mirage. The crystals and mini-wind chimes hanging from my rearview mirror jangled against each other against the discordant backdrop of metal scraping and sparking against asphalt.

"Godsdammit," I muttered under my breath, pulling to the side of the road—as if anyone would be coming through, but better safe than sorry. I cut the engine and slipped my boots on, glancing back at my sweetheart—still napping peacefully. Pushing the door open, I swung my feet out onto the pavement and got out to scan the hovervan's side. But my attention skipped to the road behind where small pieces of metal wreckage trailed, glinting in the searing sunset.

"Godsdammit," I called out, waving my hand over my head to make a spell umbrella against the evening sear. Echoes of my curse laughed back at me from the darkening hills.

My angry footsteps slapped against the concrete. "I should've gotten a complete check-up." I magicked on a potholder mitt and leaned over to pick up a dented, cylindrical piece of metal shit that'd fallen off. "What the fuck is this, Bassiano?" I gathered three other pieces, none of which I could make sense of, and sat them in the back of the van.

Slumping back in the driver's seat, I slipped off my boots and shut and locked the doors. Pressing my thumb into the ignition, I murmured, "I hope that was all optional equipment, Bass, otherwise you and I are gonna have words."

He started up again right away. "Yessss. You are so lucky I love you." Pulling back onto the road, I cautiously sped up. A thunking-slash-grinding noise crunched against my ears, but Juli only sighed in her sleep. I drove thirty feet, and Bassiano went silent.

"Oh shit," I whispered, applying the brakes—we weren't slowing down. "Shit-shit-shit!" We hit a big rift in the road and lurched sideways toward the line of trees. I pulled the emergency brake, and we spun in circles. Juli woke up screaming. I threw out a force field that wrapped around us and the van, and just in time. Bassiano rebounded against the trees and shot back toward the road. Airbags pummeled my face and body. Then everything was still.

Blood on the airbags. My ears rang over my daughter's crying.

"Juli!" I shouted, undoing my seat belt with shaking hands, frantically pushing the air bags away as I scrambled from my seat. The scents of blood and dirt mingled in the air. Juliet kicked and cried in her booster seat.

"Baby!" I reached her and unbuckled her seat, and she fell into my arms crying *Mama*. "Are you okay?" I pulled back to examine her beautiful face, her dark brown eyes, her long, mussed-up curls. She nodded through tears as I checked out her arms and legs. Not a scratch on her. "Does anything hurt, baby?"

"No," she cried. "Mama, you're bleeding."

I pressed my hand to the pain above my forehead and came away with blood. The whole left side of my body felt like it'd gone a few rounds with a prize fighter, but none of that mattered. My sweet girl was okay.

"I'm okay, baby. I'm okay. We're okay." I squeezed her to me and sat on the floor of the van, kissing her sweet head and rocking her until her tears let up.

She was okay. Frightened, but okay. And that's all that mattered.

"Mama," she sniffed, "what happened?"

"Bassiano had an accident." I kissed her head over and over, thanking all the gods that she was okay. All around us, cracked pots, loose dirt, and the sprawling, uncovered roots of plants had spilled all over the back of the van. Our poor green babies.

"Where's Mimi?" Juli wiggled out of my lap and looked around the floor for her white stuffed cat. "Mama, this is a *mess*! Mimi!" she called. "There you are!" She scooped her beloved toy up from a pile of dirt and brushed her off.

"Such a mess," I agreed.

Calling my magic out, I reset the airbags and tested all my limbs—sore but nothing broken, thank Hera. The cut on my forehead wasn't deep, just bleeding a lot, as were a few other cuts on my face. "Bassiano," I mewled, leaning my hand against the sidewall. "I thought we had an understanding."

My magic didn't excel at healing, but between it and my first aid kit, I stopped the bleeding, at least. My gaze fell on the dash clock—4:30 p.m.

Of fucking course it was. I lobbed my bloody gauze and bandage wrappers into the trash. That number had been following me for almost six years. It was Juliet's birthday and the time she was born. Nearly ten months before that, it was the time showing on my phone when Bennett called, minutes after I left him: a last chance I didn't take.

Well, a different number was my last chance today. I grabbed my phone and dialed #777. Maybe the three lucky numbers of roadside assistance would turn this nightmare around.

Three hours later, it was full dark. Juli was fed and curled up with her favorite cartoon. I'd set all my plant babies to rights with magic, using old junk jewelry to mend the pots, Kintsugi-style, and I'd cleaned up everything else that'd gone flying when we crashed.

I popped the last bite of a peanut butter sandwich made with the heel of my last loaf of bread into my mouth and laid on a pallet beside my girl to look at the stars through the sunroof. In ten hours, the *Andromeda 12* would take off for Gaia without us. Just about the time the tow truck would reach us here in the middle of nowhere.

Tears tracked down my face, and I wiped them away before Juli noticed. The *Andromeda 12* was taking a lot with it. Three-quarters of my life savings. Our own little cabin. A spot for Bassiano to park in style. The honor of being the last public transport off the east coast.

I'd waited too long. I couldn't let Juli get stuck here. How would I live with myself if my child was one of the last three-hundred Earthers worldwide going down with this sinking ship?

"Are we gonna make the ship, Mama?" Juli looked up at me with her wrinkle-browed frown. She was the spitting image of her father, and even more so when she made that face with her big brown eyes that were so much like his.

I kissed her forehead and forced good cheer into my voice. "We might! And if not, we'll catch an even better ship. Don't you worry. We're going to Gaia."

She sighed and shifted against her pillow, yawning. "I can't wait to see the forests."

"Me too, sweet girl."

When she nodded off, I kissed her precious, warm head, adjusted the amethyst necklace around her neck—the one Bennett gave me all those years ago that she somehow sniffed out from my jewelry box and decided was hers—and grabbed my notebook. There had to be someone I knew left somewhere on Earth. I'd traveled around the United States for twelve years and had met a ton of people, and I'd gotten smart enough three years in to start a list of the best of them.

I curled up in the driver's seat on the opposite side of the hover from where Juli was sleeping. I scratched off Eyre, Beck, and Zola. So stupid not to go with them. I scratched off Mom and her new family, and Dad and his new family. They'd been gone for years.

I could call Bennett.

Fuck no, I couldn't call Bennett. He'd never responded to the letter I sent, which meant he either got it and was pissed, or didn't get it and *would* be pissed that he had a daughter he didn't know about. What if he tried to take Juli and leave me behind?

No, he could never be an option. I went back to my list, grabbed my phone, and started checking the remaining names in my notebook in the WISH app to see, as the logo promised, "Who Is Still Here."

A half-hour later, I'd found twelve people on WISH I knew, and they were nearly all leaving on public transport in the next few days—on the west coast, the gulf coast, and from Europe. Nowhere I could get to. Only four were on the east coast, so I started dialing.

Jexxa's phone was disconnected.

Benji's voicemail said he was on his way to Gaia.

I left Josh a message, but I didn't have high hopes for him. He was a diehard Earther, so if he knew about transport off Earth, he certainly wouldn't be able to help me catch a ride.

"Celie, you're my only hope." I took a deep breath, dialed her number, and waited.

Three rings, and no answer.

Thinking about my time in Charlotte, North Carolina put a Bennett-shaped knot in my stomach, much like the Bennett-shaped scar carved indelibly onto my heart.

Five rings.

"—ello?"

Relief flooded my body. "Celie? It's Portia. Is that you?"

"Portia?"

"Portia Bell, the green witch? We met...like five years ago at the summer solstice?" Old pain twisted in my gut. The scent of the bonfires. The scent of his skin—

"Portia! Of course I remember you! I'm just surprised to hear from you! That's crazy, I was just talking to my sister, Blythe, about you the other day. Are you on Earth or Gaia?"

The perennial question. "I'm on Earth." I sighed. "Stuck, on Earth. Maybe forever." She listened as I explained my situation, empathetically punctuating with *oh's* and *oh no's!* "Do you have any leads on a ride offworld? It's gotta be cheap. I'm not expecting to get a refund from the *Andromeda 12* for a few months, if ever."

"You know? I just might. We're leaving late tomorrow with the company we work for, Noble Industries? I think we can fit you, and it's free if you're willing to work. But I have to be honest. The Argo's kind of a weird, um…" She laughed. "It's a really weird ship, Portia. Let me give you the details so you can decide if this is really what you want."

"So Celie, it's not just me. It would be for me and my daughter."

A pause on the other end, and then a happy squeal. "Portia! You have a daughter? Oh my gosh, that's wonderful news! When did this happen? What's her name?"

I smiled, peeking on my sleeping sweetheart. "Her name's Juliet, and she's four—well, she'll be five in a couple months."

"I can't wait to meet her. So it's just you and Juliet?"

"That's right." I scrunched my eyes, waiting for the usual *Where's her daddy?* question that everyone asked, pre-biting my tongue not to rage about people needing to mind their own business.

"I think we have room for you, and my boss is such a big softie that I can't imagine he'd say no. But I still have to check with him really quick. Can I call you back at this number?"

"Can you text me? I'm running low on electricity."

"Of course. But listen, you should really let me tell you about the ship, because—"

"Celie, I really don't care. I can't let my child get stuck here." And the only way to make a decision was to make it fast and commit to it. It's the only way I'd taken care of us on my own this long. Decisiveness, strength of conviction, and no small amount of magic. "I honestly don't want details. If he says yes, we'll be there. But oh—is there room for my hovervan, too?" Most ships had room for vehicles, but there was always a chance.

"Yes, plenty of room. The last shuttle leaves tomorrow at noon out of Charlotte. Shouldn't take me long to talk to my boss. I'll text you in a few minutes with details."

"Thank you, Celie!"

I hung up and laid my phone on its charger while I put the directions to Charlotte on my nav. Two-and-a-half hours away from here. It would be a little tight, but we could definitely make it if roadside came when promised. And that was a big if, these days.

But I had to think positively. I puttered around Bassiano for a few minutes, washing our three dirty dishes, checking Juli's bag and mine for boarding. I'd probably have access to Bassiano, but not until after launch, so we needed at least a couple days' worth of clothes and toiletries. I lit a candle and knelt before my little statue of Flora, the goddess of green and blooming things, and prayed for help and protection.

My phone chimed.

I took a deep breath and read Celie's message.

Couldn't find Dr. Noble, but I found his brother. He said yes, absolutely, he'd never turn down a mother and child. We're leaving from Dock 430...

Relief flooded me despite the foreboding dock number. Thank the gods for this brother. Whoever he was, I would have to refrain from hugging him and sobbing with gratitude when I thanked him in person. Bless him and everyone he loves.

All things considered, and besides the body aches and blooming headache, things were coming up roses for me and Juli. Wrapping Bassiano in a magical stealth mode and security system cocoon, I snuggled next to my sweet Juliet for our last sleep on Earth.

I buckled our seatbelts and popped Juli's headphones on to help distract her through the shuttle launch. I wished I had something to distract me from this Noble Industries release form they handed me when we boarded. I should've heard Celie out. It wouldn't have changed my mind, but at least I would've been prepared for whatever the fuck this meant. I started reading again from the top.

...agree to travel underground on Argo, formerly known as Trans-Neptunian Object (TNO) (145453) 2005 RR43, through interstellar space to humanity's new planet, Gaia...

I grabbed the arm of a passing shuttle attendant. "Hi!" I said brightly into his surprised face. "I should probably know this, but remind me what a Trans-Neptunian Object is again?"

The attendant and nearby passengers started laughing like I was onstage at open mic night. My face burned. Juli looked up curiously all around us then went back to her picture book.

"You're very funny, miss," he said, scooting out of my grasp and settling into a seat on the other side of the cabin.

I glanced out the window just in time to see Earth disappear. So the Argo wasn't in orbit? I typed the "formerly known as" string of numbers and letters into my phone—a dwarf planet in the Kuiper Belt.

The Kuiper Belt? I reread the forms. It definitely said the Argo is the *vessel*. But...everything in the Kuiper belt was rock covered with ice. You couldn't travel on a planet unless you counted the infinite, orbital swirl of planets pulled behind a sun's gravity through the galaxy.

The rest of the form was the standard "if you die on the travel accommodations we're providing it ain't our fault" of all space travel. I scanned down the rest of the form and signed it. Nothing I could do about it now.

The passengers around us were all ages, some kids, but none Juli's age. A few other witches, it seemed. Not that there was a surefire way to tell, but that family in the corner with crystal necklaces and the mom clutching a medal of Abeona, Roman goddess of travel protection—they were a safe bet. The shuttle was posh, at least. Noble Industries was a lucrative geotech company with locations all over the world. Hell, they helped terraform Gaia. So I could probably trust whatever they'd concocted. But I'd sure like to know who was running this bullshit and how likely the "dying on their watch" part of it was.

Acknowledgements

I couldn't have written this book without the love and support of my husband, Brett, and my sons Luke and Jack—y'all are my universe. Forever grateful to my sweet Mama, Schoener Ann, who's always told me "you should be writing!" Look, Mama, me do it! Thanks to: my brilliant sister and true BFF, Schoener M., whose love was the foundation of Gemma and Hannah's relationship and whose expertise helped Gemma save Beck after the space walk; my dad, Carl, whose love, humor, and generosity have enriched my life in so many ways; and my beloved Uncle Joseph, who shares my love of scifi and old spaceships, makes the best popcorn and fresh cut fries, and bought me more Barbies than I could ever count. I love you all so much.

Thank you to Hop and Barbara who made this self-publishing venture possible. I absolutely won the in-law lottery, and I love you both endlessly.

Thank you to Sarah for your unending cheerleading, handholding, and breakfast-and-crystal-buying adventures. I'm so grateful for your friendship, insightful beta reads, and amazing memes about escaping to the beach for naps. We will yet win the lottery and buy our private island. I love you!

Thank you to Julie, without whose encouragement and support I never would have written, finished, or queried this book—I love you! Thank you to Martina for your love, support, and helping me keep sight of my bread crumbs—I love you! Thank you, Barrett, for taking my dream seriously and giving me the best career advice of my life—I honestly needed that push. Thank you, Theresa, for seeing something special in this book and taking me in.

To Hex Quills, my family: Thank you for your support, encouragement, and love in helping me set out on this self-publishing venture. I'm ready for a permanent HQHQ so I can squeeze each one of you and see you irl whenever I want! Your love, support, and friendship means the literal universe to me, and how are you each so damn talented? Special thanks to my beta readers and critique partners who respond with open arms no matter how many manuscripts I want to throw at them: Marina, for your support and brilliance, especially that Zoom meeting where you helped me figure out, like, everything to fix this book in revisions; Kahlan, for your perpetual sunshine, advice, cheerleading, and the essential UtSF meme; Darcy, for your insightful suggestions, unending support, and excitement for my writing; Kalla, for your amazing feedback, support, and kind awesomeness; Shay, for your undying support for this book (there are CATS ON A SPACESHIP!) and for finding the book's title. Thanks to Skyla for your support and for inviting me into the best freaking writing group on the planet; Olivia for your support and amazing publishing advice; and all the HQties who beta read, positivity passed, and in general give me so much love and support literally every day. I don't know what I'd do without you: Abby, Alex, Brit, Cassie, Crystal, Helena, Juliet, Kara, Kat, Lindsey, Livy, Mackenzie, Maria, Morgan, Phoebe, Rachel, Sam, and Wajudah.

To my dear Owls: I'm eternally grateful for your support and encouragement. May all owls fly free and high.

And thank you, dear reader, for taking this interstellar trip with me. I hope you enjoyed the ride!

About the Author

Holly Rose lives in Louisiana with her husband, two sons, and two cats, Loki and Olivia Newton John. She eats too much cheese fries, loves stargazing, and writes books about people falling in love.

www.ingramcontent.com/pod-product-compliance
Lightning Source LLC
Chambersburg PA
CBHW021153310726
48971CB00002B/608